CAN OF WORMS
BY
PAUL TREMBLING

Copyright © P. Trembling 2025

The right of Paul Trembling to be identified as the author of this work has been asserted by her/him in accordance with the Copyright, Designs and Patents Act 1988. All rights reserved. No part of this publication may be reproduced or transmitted in any form or by any means, electronic or mechanical, including photocopy, recording, or any information storage and retrieval system, without permission in writing from the publisher.

Print ISBN: 978-1-915981-12-7

Published by Resolute Books www.resolutebooks.co.uk

First Edition 2011

This Edition 2025

This novel is a work of fiction. All names, characters and incidents portrayed in it are entirely the product of the author's imagination. Any resemblance to actual persons, living or dead or to actual events is entirely coincidental.

This book is dedicated to Dad.
With thanks for the hours you spent reading to me, and for the love of stories that you gave me. This is the result of that investment!

Author's Note

This book is largely set in a fictional English town, in a fictional English county, situated somewhere between London and the Midlands. It is the early 2000's: mobile phones are not very smart, cars still have to display tax discs, people rent videos to watch on their VCRs. The police have computers but have not yet worked out how to use (or afford!) digital cameras.

Practices, procedures and equipment as portrayed are broadly accurate and reflect those of many British police forces at that time. In some cases details have been altered.

What readers thought of Can Of Worms – first edition reviews from Amazon.

Can of Worms was a really excellent read, enhanced by a form of realism in both the CSI details and in the reactions of the characters. Not only that, the main character was someone I could empathise with and who wasn't a superwoman but an ordinary woman who ended up in an extraordinary situation. The events were believable, too, and while the overall effect was of gritty reality, it never became gratuitously gruesome.

V. Tuffnell (Author, 'The Bet', 'Strangers and Pilgrims')

This is a cracking British crime thriller, with a believable female lead in Marcie, the SOCO who can't seem to resist getting involved, despite being thwarted at every turn. I thoroughly enjoyed this. Good solid investigative details against a clever plot that culminates in a thrilling finale.

'Bookworm'

Paul Trembling has been a scene of crime investigator and his experience gives this book real authenticity. It's not your usual detective novel. The protagonist ignores good advice and digs into matters that should not concern her. I found the plot convincing and the final chapters nail-biting. The ending, too, was satisfying and realistic. It's a very good read.

G. van der Rol (Author, the Ptorix Empire series).

Unexpected and Satisfying

Can of Worms is a page-turner that I could not put down once began. Danger, action, surprising turns and an unexpected ending make this book a keeper. The heroine, Marcie, is far more real and satisfying than the James Bonds who usually populate suspense novels. There is a little bit of the Hobbit to Marcie – not the person we would choose to engage the forces of evil nor the one we would expect to vanquish them. But the choice of Marcie was inspired. And on the way I learned what a Scenes of Crime Officer (SOCO) does. You gotta read this one.

Philip Skotte (Author, '20 things to do after you die')

Finally a realistic novel!

As an operational CSI myself it was really nice to read a realistic book about police investigations, I can actually see some of the characters in my office!

The book is incredibly gripping, I was given it for Xmas and had read it by Boxing Day, it keeps building and building and the end is really exciting. Good solid plot throughout, excellent character development, a thoroughly riveting read!

O. Mott (Senior CSI).

Gripping fast-paced crime drama

A compelling crime drama with action and dogged determination. I can't recommend this highly enough and I also found it an invaluable education into forensic techniques – an area of personal interest.

Elinor Carlisle

PROLOGUE

Someone once told Ben Drummond that he was 'too bloody cantankerous to die'. It wasn't meant as a compliment but Ben, being Ben, took it that way. Ironic, really, since it was his sheer cussedness, his awkward, obstructive, cantankerous nature that would kill him. That and a nine millimetre bullet.

Standing at the far end of the cavernous duty garage, Ben felt even more belligerent than usual. He'd been stuck here doing cars all day, and Ben hated doing cars. Some Scenes Of Crime Officers – SOCOs – liked cars. There was a lot of shiny metal and glass to take fingerprints, there were often cigarette ends in the ashtray, or bottles under the seats. There was a good chance of bringing something back if you went and did some cars.

Ben didn't give a shit about bringing anything back – not for a crappy little stolen car job. Twenty-five years he'd been in the job, and he shouldn't be spending his time on piddling small stuff. In Ben's not very humble opinion, anything less than an aggravated burglary was a waste of his time and experience. But Slippery Mick had come over all officious that morning, and started on about sharing jobs out equally. So Ben was here doing cars, while kids with ten minutes in the job were on burglaries and assaults. Stuck in a damp, cold, badly lit garage, bugger all good for any sort of proper forensic exam anyway, on a damp, cold, badly lit day at the arse-end of October, looking at his sixth car of the shift. And this one wasn't going to lift his mood either, because it was a burnt out wreck. Waste of time, the dimwit PC who had the case shouldn't even have requested scenes of crime.

Unless, perhaps, this was something a bit special? Involved in something serious perhaps – kidnapping, armed robbery? Please, at least a GBH! With a flicker of interest, Ben looked through his paperwork, dug out the incident log, and swore. Just a bloody Taken Without Owners Consent. A bunch of kids had TWOC'd it for a joy ride and torched it for fun. The owner hadn't even reported it until it had already been put out by the Fire Brigade.

Well, he wasn't going to waste any time on this one. Not even worth getting his kit out for.

Ben dumped his file on the fire-blackened bonnet and began scribbling on a report form. Ten minutes, he thought, then back to the station for a cuppa and maybe a sausage cob.

Behind him, there were footsteps on the concrete, which he ignored. Probably the garage staff bringing in another car. Well, if they were thinking of asking him to do it before he left, they'd think again bloody damn quick.

'Make – Vauxhall Cavalier.' Ben frequently muttered to himself whilst working. 'Condition – severe fire damage, engine and passenger compartment, all windows out...'

'That's my car.'

Scowling, Ben put his pen down and turned round. The man standing a few yards away was hard to make out. The random failures of the strip lighting had left him in a pool of shadow, back lit by the bright halogens further down.

'What?' Ben growled.

'Are you Police?'

'Scenes of Crime Officer. And this is a forensic examination area. Not open to the public. Garage office is over the other side.'

The man stepped a bit closer, into what light there was. Ben saw a dark beard, chunky dark coat, eyes shadowed by a baseball cap. 'That's my car there.'

'I'm nearly finished with it. Go over to the office, you can sort things out with them.'

'Did you find anything in the car?' The man spoke sharply, demanding an answer.

Ben almost smiled. He loved the chance to be truculent, obstructive, and downright rude if possible.

'Like I told you, this is a forensic examination area. Contact the OIC if you've got any questions. That's the Officer In Charge of the case. Now bugger off!'

The man kept his hands in his pockets, seemingly casual, but there was no doubting the aggression in his voice or in the way he leaned forward as he spoke.

'Tell me what you've found in my car!'

And for a brief moment, Ben was tempted to say, 'Sod all mate.' But that would have gone against a lifetime's habit, and instead he snapped back, 'Can't tell you that. Police business. Now piss off!' And for the first time that day, he felt almost happy. He was staring straight at the man, glaring in joyful fury at him with such intensity that he was barely aware of the hand that came out of the pocket, or what it was holding, or of the muffled thud.

But he felt the massive impact in his chest, the tremendously powerful blow that flung him back against the scorched metal of the car. Flung him back and also spun him round, so that he was grasping at the roof, trying to pull himself up, but he had no strength left, none in his arms, none in his legs, and he couldn't stop himself slipping to the floor. He thought of his radio, but couldn't move to reach it, and already it was very dark, even darker than normal.

And then it was utter black, and Ben Drummond hadn't even had time to realise what had happened.

*

The shot seemed to echo for a long time, the acoustics of metal walls and concrete floor extending its lifetime beyond the normal. The man with the gun stood listening while they faded – not looking at the body, but at the entrance to the garage. He did not expect interruption from the staff, who were watching telly in their portacabin on the other side of the yard. However, just in case, he looked and listened for a while longer, with his pistol hanging casually from one hand.

Finally satisfied that there would be no interruptions, he slipped it back into his pocket, and turned to the body, ignoring its empty gaze. He had certain business to conduct here, business made more difficult by the SOCO's intransigence. Which, in the man's mind, was reason enough to shoot him.

Even in such a situation, with a dead body at his feet, his practicality came to the fore. There was no point in lingering. When he had done as much as could reasonably be done, under the circumstances, he left. The whole thing was something of an irritation, especially as his intervention now seemed unnecessary. But at least he'd made sure if it. It might not have been the best solution, or the ideal outcome, but it had been dealt with quickly, and on the whole, satisfactorily. He took some pleasure in having tied up the loose ends.

In the garage, nothing moved. Even the pool of blood beneath the body had stopped spreading. In the poor lighting it was hardly distinguishable from the oil stains nearby as it slowly congealed on the damp concrete.

CHAPTER 1

A week after Ben's murder, the Scenes of Crime office was still in a state of shock. Alison – big, bouncy, irrepressibly bright on a normal day – seemed crushed and near to tears.

'I still can't believe it,' she said through a tissue. 'I keep expecting him to walk in at any moment.'

'I know, Ali, I know. We all feel the same'. Doug reassured her. 'It's just doesn't seem possible.' Doug was usually the one to bring some calm reason into a situation. With his rimless glasses and neat, grey-shot beard he was the sort of person people instinctively felt they could trust.

Marcie, just back off leave, was finding it hard to adjust to the news. It felt as though she had a weeks' worth of trauma to catch up with. She looked round the office. Nothing had changed – it was still cluttered with too many desks covered with too much paperwork. It still smelled of stale coffee and the occasional whiff of diesel drifting in from the car park outside (they were right above the refuelling point).

But there was something missing. Or rather, someone.

Like Ali, she kept expecting Ben to shamble in at any moment, with a sarcastic comment and a dirty joke. She'd cried too when Doug phoned her at home with the news. Cried some more when she saw it on TV. Not that she'd got on with Ben – not any better than most people, anyhow – but a sudden hole had appeared in her world. A presence that had seemed as solid and enduring as a mountain range was abruptly gone forever.

But one of the biggest shocks was seeing Alison Patrick so distraught, considering that she and Ben had disliked each other intensely.

'What I don't understand,' Marcie wondered out loud 'is why anyone would shoot a SOCO anyway? Have they got any ideas yet?'

'Drugs,' grunted Mac.

'You've heard that?' asked Doug. 'Mick and Jimmy won't say a word about it.'

Mac – Philip MacAlistair, but no one ever called him Phil, even if they knew it was his name – was of the same generation as Ben, and had been in the job about as long. Short and solidly built with a mass of unruly grey hair, he'd been the closest Ben had had to a friend in the department. Marcie thought he seemed less upset than Ali. He shook his head as he answered Doug.

'Not heard, no, but it'll be drugs. Always is.'

'Scary thing is,' put in Sanjay, 'It might have been any of us. Ben hardly ever did cars. Just sheer bad luck. Scary.'

From the silence that fell, Marcie deduced that the same thought had occurred to everyone else, but no one had wanted to put it into words. Sanjay was the quietest one of their team, but when he did say something it was straight to the point. Even if no one else wanted to go there.

'So, where *are* our revered Seniors?' asked Mac. 'We supposed to wait all day for them, or what?'

'They're in conference with CID,' said Doug. 'Message was, everyone was to get their jobs and then sit tight – they want to make some sort of announcement.'

'OK – time for a brew, then. Anyone want a cup?'

The way it worked in their office was that the city was divided up into operational areas and all the SOCO's took one – or two, if they were short-handed. Then you had to search the Force computer system for incidents in those areas that had been referred for Scenes of Crime examination. Which meant that the busier it was, the longer you had to spend on the computer before you could even get started.

It was made worse by the fact that there were never enough computers to go round. Marcie had to wait twenty minutes before she could get on one. And of course – sod's law – it was at that moment that the missing Seniors made their entrance, along with Marcus Hubert-Hulme, Head of Scientific Support (which included Scenes Of Crime).

Marcus was widely known throughout the Force as 'The Prof' – not just because he looked like a professor, white beard, glasses and all, but because he was in fact a Professor of Forensic Science, internationally renowned for his specialist knowledge.

Ben had referred to The Prof as an 'over-educated ivory tower ponce' who 'knew less about real SOCO-ing than a cow knows about flying.' Marcie herself thought that The Prof was a pretty good boss, in that he mostly kept out of the way and let them get on with it.

An expectant hush fell over the room.

'Ahem – ladies and ah – gentlemen.' The Prof was unremittingly formal on all occasions. 'As you know, your Senior Scenes of Crime Officers here at Ash Ridge Police Station – Michael and James – have been heavily involved in the investigation relating to our murdered colleague, Mr Benjamin Drummond. My thanks to them for what has undoubtedly been a personally difficult task, carried out with the usual professionalism and – er – competency.' There was a brief pause. Marcie wondered if they were expected to applaud.

Gathering himself, The Prof resumed. 'Certain facts have now come to light. Not yet to be made public, of course, but it was felt that you the colleagues of the – ah – deceased – should be kept informed.'

'So we don't read about it in the paper, after being kept in the dark for a week.' whispered Doug, sitting on the desk next to Marcie.

'I rely on your discretion, of course, not to talk to the Press. However, the facts I referred to... a full forensic examination of the vehicles Mr Drummond had examined on that day has revealed a bottle of Morphine Elixir, a controlled drug, concealed beneath the seats of a Ford Mondeo estate car.'

Mac nodded in satisfaction, with a 'told you so' expression on his face.

'Traces of this drug were also found on used examination gloves in Mr Drummond's pockets. It is now believed that during his examination of the Mondeo, Mr Drummond had found and recovered some of these drugs, but was unfortunate that the drug dealer came to the garage in order to reclaim them. It appears that the offender, or offenders, took not only the drugs, but also Mr. Drummond's paperwork and exhibits relating to all the vehicles he had examined that day.'

'We cannot say at this stage whether or not Mr Drummond resisted them, or if he was shot to prevent identification. However...'

The Prof removed his glasses, and looked at them for a moment. 'However – we do intend to find out. In our business we see much of the worst of human nature – and its consequences. We are used to seeing victims, and I would hope that, as professionals, we always do our best to bring the offenders to justice. But this time, ladies and gentlemen, this time it has reached out and touched us personally. Mr Drummond – Ben – was one of us. He spent his career achieving justice for others. We will do no less for him.'

Marcie felt herself both moved and comforted. Inspirational speeches weren't The Prof's forte, but it was clear he felt this deeply and spoke from the heart. The quality of the silence that fell suggested that the others had heard the same.

The Prof replaced his glasses. 'Well then – thank you for your time. Your Seniors will keep you informed. It is anticipated that Mr Drummond's funeral will take place as soon as the body is released by the Coroner. It has been agreed that the Force will show its solidarity on that occasion, and it is expected that all of you will wish to attend. Scenes of Crime cover for the city will be arranged from other Divisions, so you will be free to do so. Ah – that is all. Please resume your duties.'

The Prof left with his entourage, and a subdued buzz of conversation broke out. 'Told you!' said Mac, with what Marcie thought was an unseemly degree of satisfaction. 'Drugs! Told you, didn't I?'

'You did, Mac' Doug agreed. 'You did indeed.' He paused, frowning. 'But what I'm wondering is, how come Ben missed this bottle of morphine? Come to think of it, if the offenders came back to get the drugs, how come *they* missed it?'

'They were probably in a hurry,' said Ali, drifting over to join in the conversation. 'They shot Ben, took the stuff he'd recovered, and legged it.'

'Not that much of a hurry,' said Marcie. 'They had time to get all his notes. And if they'd hidden the drugs in the first place, they'd have known where to look for the rest.'

'Perhaps they thought that Ben had got them all?' Sanjay suggested.

Mac was nodding. 'Yeh – but Doug's right. Ben wouldn't miss anything like that. You know what he's like. What he was like. If he'd thought that there were drugs in that car he'd have gone through it like a bloody bulldog! I can't see him missing any morphine.'

Speculation was interrupted by the return of Slippery Mick – so called because it was damn near impossible to get a straight answer out of him. 'Ok, meeting's over!' he announced. 'Let's get out and fight crime! Who's going to Northdale?'

'That's me, Mick,' said Marcie.

'Good. Can you drop in at Callahan's and do a car, since you're in the area? OK?'

Marcie felt a little twist in her stomach. 'Callahan's? As in Callahan Recovery? Where Ben was shot?'

'Of course. Problem?'

'I just thought that they weren't taking cars in there any more. 'Cos of the investigation.'

Mick assumed a particularly shifty look. 'The scene's finished with now. That part of the investigation's over, so they're opening up the garage again. Only – there's a car there that Ben didn't get round to looking at before he was... anyhow, we want it sorted, ASAP. If you don't mind, Marcie. Won't take long, it's a burn-out. Just eyeball it, write up a negative report. No sweat.'

'Didn't I hear that we're dumping Callahan's?' asked Doug. 'Breach of contract – inadequate security?'

Mick was now definitely living up to his nickname. 'Possibly,' he muttered, not meeting anyone's eye. 'It's under discussion. Just don't mention it while you're there, Marcie, OK?' And with that, he slithered back to his office at speed.

'Why do I get the feeling that something warm and smelly has just been dumped on me?' Marcie wondered aloud.

Mac snorted. 'Jimmy and Mick should have sorted it as part of the investigation. Probably got too excited when they found the drugs – anyhow, Mick's panicking a bit now, because if Callahan's get the shove, they're not going to be very cooperative. Which will leave our Senior SOCO's with an embarrassing loose end.'

'Might as well do it anyhow.' Doug said to Marcie. 'Get Slippery Mick out of a hole and he might look on you favourably next time you ask for leave.'

'Yeah, sure – like I've got a choice?'

Examining a burnt out car, even one which someone else should have done, didn't bother Marcie much – as Mick had said, it wouldn't be a big job. Going to Callahan's was never a joy, but if it was likely to be the last time, she could live with it. She just wasn't too comfortable about seeing where Ben had died.

'Go there first,' she thought. 'Get it out of the way.' Logging out of the computer, Marcie gathered up her gear and headed for the station car park.

Northdale had once been one of Faringham's more exclusive areas, and there were still some quite pleasant parts – mostly around the centre, or 'Old Northdale' as the residents insisted on calling it, though without any official sanction. East Northdale, next to the University, had been largely taken over by student accommodation and the associated support services – bars, fast food outlets and video rentals. West Northdale, out near the edge of the city, was a confused mixture of old housing, new tower blocks and light industry.

It was out in this part of the city that Callahan Recovery had its premises, a badly built and poorly maintained warehouse. On the basis of the cheapest bid, Callahan's had acquired the police contract to recover stolen and suspicious vehicles from the city area, and to provide facilities for forensic examinations of the same. They had then set out to maximise their profits by keeping investment to the minimum. The vast shed was unventilated in summer, unheated in winter, and poorly lit in any weather. Other facilities were minimal or non-existent, and the staff were as surly and unhelpful as they could get away with.

Along with every other SOCO in the City Division, Marcie had been complaining bitterly about Callahan Recovery from the beginning. But meetings, consultations and complaints had failed to produce any change. Getting rid of Callahan's was a move that would delight every SOCO. It was a pity that one of them had to be killed to bring it about.

One advantage in waiting for the Seniors was that the rush hour was over, and it was only twenty minutes after leaving Ash Ridge nick that Marcie pulled the SOC van up to the rusty gates. It took another five minutes of blowing the horn before someone ambled out of the office and came over.

'What do you want?' he growled. A beefy young lad in dirty overalls with 'Callahan Recovery' barely discernible across his back.

Marcie opened the window and leaned out. 'Scenes of Crime,' she explained, as if it wasn't written all over the side of the van. 'You've got a car for us.'

'No we haven't. No cars in since your mate got himself shot.'

So now it was Ben's fault? Marcie bit back a sharp retort. 'It's from before that happened. Cavalier. Burnt out.'

'Oh. Thought you'd done that.'

'I'm here to do it now – er – Neil?'

Marcie hoped that she had got the name right. The embroidery was frayed and fading.

'Yeah, Neil. Thing is though – it's out in the yard.' Neil gave her a worried look, as he should. Out in the yard meant exposed to the weather, which meant a much reduced chance of finding any useful fingerprints or DNA. The car should have stayed undercover until a SOCO had signed it off. Marcie doubted if anyone had, which was why Neil was looking anxious.

'Doesn't matter,' she said reassuringly. 'It's burnt out anyway, and the Fire Brigade would have soaked it. Outside won't make a difference.' In this dump, it might even be better, she thought. 'I just need to look at it.'

'Oh – OK, then.' Neil fumbled for his keys, and finally swung the gates open. 'Over there in the corner.' He pointed.

Marcie drove over, got out, and looked at the wreck.

Whoever had torched it had done a good job. Some burnt out cars had no more than a small charred hole in a seat. But this one had been burned by an expert. There was barely a patch of un-scorched paint from the headlights as far back as the boot. All the windows were out, and as she leaned through the frames, Marcie saw that the seats were reduced to a twisted metal framework. She wrinkled her nose at the smell. A burnt out car may not be the worst aroma in the world, but it's strong, distinctive and unpleasant enough.

Inside, the floor was deep in ashes and blobs of melted plastic, still soaked from the Fire Brigade's efforts. Nothing was left of the steering wheel or dashboard.

'That's your mate's blood,' said Neil from behind her.

Marcie jumped and hit her head on the door frame. 'What?' she snapped, glaring at Neil.

Neil grinned at her. 'Mind your head!'

'Yes, *thank you*! What did you say about Ben?'

'He was standing just about where you are when he was shot. Leastways, that's where we found him, on the ground next to the car. That's his blood on the door.'

Marcie turned quickly, and crouched to examine the door that she had been leaning against. It was hard to see against the scorched and now rusting metal, but there were dark reddish-brown stains smeared down the side.

Marcie felt her guts twisting. Why hadn't Mick told her? She wouldn't have thought that even he would fail to mention it.

Fighting for a calm voice, she turned back to Neil. 'Was... was it you who found him?'

'Yeah!' said Neil eagerly. 'Well, me and Pete. See, we were over in the office, and Pete said, 'Time to lock up.' So I went out with the keys, only the SOCO van's still here. So I told Pete, 'SOCO's still here.' Thing is, we'd thought he'd gone long since.'

Marcie nodded. 'That was when?'

Neil shrugged. 'About five o'clock – ish. Anyhow, Pete says, 'Go and tell him to get a move on, we want to lock up'. So I went to the shed, and looked round – couldn't see him. Shouted a bit, but he didn't answer. So I got Pete, and we went looking. And then Pete says, 'Over here, Neil!'. And there he was, laying down next to that Cavalier.'

Involuntarily, Marcie glanced at the floor: she was standing in the same place, relative to the car, that Ben would have fallen. She took a quick step back, with cold chills running down her. 'What did you do then?'

'Well – first off, we thought he was ill. Heart attack, or something. So Pete says, 'Help me get him up!' thinking we'd take him over to the office. So we started to pick him up, then I said 'Shit – he's bleeding!' And Pete said, 'Bloody hell!' and we put him down again. Then he says, 'Go and phone the ambulance.' I ran back over to the office, and when I'd phoned the ambulance, I thought, better phone the police as well. Then I went back, and told Pete, 'Ambulance is on its way.' And Pete said, 'We'd better not move him. But we'll have to make space to get the ambulance in.' So I got on the forklift, and we shifted some cars around. Then a copper arrived, and then the ambulance came, and *they* said, 'He's been shot!' And next I knew, there was coppers and CID everywhere.'

Marcie nodded, thinking. 'Neil – when you moved the cars around – did you move this one as well?'

'Of course we did!' Neil was indignant, as if his word was being doubted. 'Like I said, we had to make room for the ambulance. And this 'un was right next to him.'

'So where did you put it?'

'Well – just here, of course. Out of the way.' Neil paused, then decided to cover his back. 'Like Pete told me.'

'Ah. So – when the police came, this car was already out here? Nowhere near the body?'

'Well – yes. Suppose it was.'

'And did you tell them about it?'

Neil look confused. 'They didn't ask about this car. They asked where he'd been found, and we showed them, and they asked what cars he'd done, and we showed them. But they didn't ask about this one.'

Well, of course they didn't, you pillock, thought Marcie. By the time they got here, it was nowhere near the body – just an old wreck over in the corner of the yard, along with a lot of others.

'Where's Pete now?' she asked, looking for some corroboration.

'Off work. Stress. Hasn't been back since then. I'm here on my own just now.'

'Right. Well – stick around. I've got to talk to someone.' Marcie got out her mobile.

'Mick – it's Marcie. I'm at Callahan's. You know that Cavalier you sent me here for? Well, there's a bit of a story with it…'

Marcie repeated what Neil had told her, and listened to a long silence, as Mick absorbed it. Finally he came back to life.

'OK, Marcie, good work. You can carry on and finish the car. Just as normal.'

'But Mick…'

'Yeah, I know. Strictly speaking, you should have a Senior down there, as it's connected with a murder. But, thing is, this doesn't make any difference. We know why Ben was shot, and it's nothing to do with that car. So in actual fact, it's really just a TWOC, and that's no problem for you, is it Marcie?'

'Well, no, Mick – but…'

'Look, Marcie, just treat it like any other TWOC, OK? Fine then. See you back at the office.'

Mick hung up. 'Thanks.' Marcie said to herself. 'Thanks very much.'

She looked at the Cavalier. 'Just like any other TWOC? I don't think so, Mick.' For a start, she'd get a swab of that blood. Ben's blood. Mick would hit the roof; he'd never allow it to be submitted. If it got matched to Ben, it could screw up Mick's carefully constructed scenario of what had happened. It probably wasn't relevant, as he'd said - but if anything came up later, Marcie didn't want to be the one accused of doing a sloppy job.

She went back to the van, got her kit out, and set to work.

Half an hour later, she'd got a full series of photographs, exterior and interior, and two swabs of the stain on the side – correctly tested first, to confirm it was blood and not a tomato sauce spillage. There were no unburned areas to fingerprint, so she was now looking speculatively at the boot. It was the only (relatively) undamaged area of the car, and she was wondering if anything inside it could have survived. Only one way to find out.

It was locked, of course. She got out a crowbar and poked around a bit, but with no result.

'Hey – Neil.' she called.

Neil had been watching from a distance. 'Yeah?' he asked cautiously.

'Come over here and pop this boot open for me.'

'Well – we don't have a lot of tools here at the moment. Might need to get the fork lift on it.'

'OK. So get the fork lift on it.'

Neil grumbled off, and in due course, came back in the fork lift. After much manoeuvring and swearing, he managed to get the fork blades under the boot lid, and wrenched it open.

'There!' he said with satisfaction. 'So what's in it?'

'Nothing,' said Marcie with disappointment, looking in. 'Spare wheel and a jack. But I had to be sure. Stand back, Neil, I'll need photos.'

She got her camera again, snapped off a few frames, and paused to think it through.. Was there anything more to be done?

'That it then?' asked Neil.

'I'm not finished yet.' she said evenly. 'I'll let you know when.' She went back to the van, pulled on a fresh pair of latex gloves, and picked up the crowbar. Leaning through one of the Cavalier's back windows, she stirred through the sodden black ashes.

Something caught on the crowbar. She pulled it out gently. A few lengths of bent wire emerged from the ashes. Perhaps the framework of a bag of some sort? She scraped at another solid lump which could have been a roll of gaffer tape.

Aware of Neil's impatient stare on her back, Marcie transferred her attention to the front of the car, but here it was nearly all melted plastic from the dashboard. Any other items were permanently entombed in the shapeless grey mass.

For the sake of completeness, and to piss Neil off thoroughly, Marcie went round to the other side. There was some glass left in the driver's window; she eyed it warily, and gave the door an experimental tug.

To her surprise, it creaked open. As it did so, something shifted in the door pocket. Peering in Marcie saw something lighter than the surrounding ashes.

Dropping the crowbar, she felt cautiously down with gloved fingers; brushed through a layer of char and pulled out a thick wad of tissues. Scorched brown on the outside, the inner layers were still white. She sniffed cautiously. The faint chemical smell was familiar. Windscreen wipes? The outer plastic cover had mostly burnt off, but the dampened tissues had survived surprisingly well.

Interesting, but not very exciting. No forensic value. Marcie dropped them back in the door pocket, and as she did so, she saw something else. A small, dark regular shape that had been hidden beneath the wipes. She reached in again and gave the object a tug.

It resisted at first, but then, with a firmer pull, it came free, shedding ash and melted plastic as it did. She lifted it into the watery daylight, cautiously wiped off the residual soot.

A flash card. Marcie felt a thrill of excitement. A digital camera storage card. Which might or might not have anything interesting on it: but it was, as Doug would have said, 'Better than a poke in the eye with a sharp stick.'

She slipped it into an evidence bag, and got out the mobile.

'Technical Forensic Unit, Sam Goodwin.'

The TFU dealt with things like computers, mobile phones, and – she hoped – flash cards. 'Hi, Sam. Marcie from City Division Scenes of Crime. Listen, I've just recovered a compact flash card from a burnt out car. Will you be able to get anything off it?'

There was a pause. 'Perhaps – depends how bad it is. Does the case look melted?'

'No. Just very dirty. It was in a heap of ash, but underneath some wet windscreen wipes, which seem to have protected it from the worst of the fire.'

'OK, might be possible then. If it's just smoke damage, we can clean it up and try to download anything it might have. But if the chips themselves are damaged, forget it. Send it up, we'll have a look.'

'Great – thanks, Sam.'

'No problem. But – one thing, Marcie – could it be the legitimate owners? No point it going to a lot of trouble just to recover the family's happy holiday snaps!'

'Good point. I'll check it out. Thanks again.'

Marcie hung up, and gave Neil a big smile. 'See? Persistence pays.'

'You're finished now?'

'Oh, not just yet. I'd better take some more photos – and then write up the scene report.'

In the end, it was another half hour before Marcie pulled the van out of Callahan's. Neil hastily slammed the gates shut behind her before she could change her mind.

Marcie still hadn't decided what to do about the flash card. Ringing the owner's number had connected her to an answering machine. She'd left a message, but how long would she have to wait till they got back to her? It would be better if the card could be submitted today. Of course, she could go ahead and send it anyhow, but if it did turn out to be legitimate, Sam would be pissed off with her, and he was too useful to antagonise.

She looked at the log again. The registered keeper's address wasn't far away, in Old Northdale – and in fact – yes – she had a burglary to attend just a few streets from there. OK, then, she'd drop by, and see if anyone was in. Then at least she could say she'd done her best.

She thumbed her radio. 'X-ray Mike Two Seven to Control.'

'Go ahead, Two Seven.'

'Show me resumed from Callahan's, please, and travelling to 34 Cyrus Street, for related enquires.'

'Ten four.' The operator didn't sound very excited, but Marcie was feeling quite cheerful. The day was getting interesting.

CHAPTER 2

Cyrus Street was lined with dark, cold trees and red brick Victorian mansions. They had a gothic look to them, with a tendency to break out in odd little towers and elaborate balconies. Cue sinister organ music in the background, thought Marcie.

Number 34 appeared typical, apart from the glaringly new steel fencing that cut off her view of all but the upper storey. The industrial strength gate was a match with the fence, and to complete the set a pair of CCTV cameras stood guard. Clearly, these were people who took their security seriously. Apart from getting their car nicked.

A speaker grille was set into the gate post. Marcie pressed the button. A long pause. She pressed it again, and one of the CCTV cameras swivelled to stare down at her. She gave it what she hoped was a confident smile, rather than a nervous grimace.

'Yes?' said the speaker, curtly.

Not about to waste time on formal greetings, Marcie noted. 'Marcia Kelshaw. Police – Scenes of Crime.' She waved her I.D. card at the camera. 'Are you Mr Maddox?'

'What do you want?' the voice demanded.

'I want to speak to Mr Maddox, in connection with your vehicle that was stolen. The Cavalier.'

There was a pause. Then a peremptory command. 'Wait!'

What for? Marcie wondered. Probably not 'Wait while I get the kettle on and we'll talk about it over a cuppa.'

There was a buzz and the electric gates swung smoothly open gradually revealing a poorly kept gravelled area, an overgrown garden, and the front of the house, almost choked with laurels. A white Transit van and a middle aged Mercedes saloon in silver were parked on the drive.

The front door opened, and a man strode briskly out. Thirty-ish, Marcie thought. Dark hair and beard, padded black coat, hands thrust into the pockets, leaning forward slightly as he walked towards her, glaring aggressively. Marcie had been about to walk forward to meet him, but then changed her mind. Instead, she gave an involuntary glance around. The street was deserted. She fingered her radio for reassurance, and held up her ID again.

'Well? What is it?'

'Are you Mr Maddox? The owner of the Cavalier?'

'Yes! Of course! I was told it was burnt out – a wreck.'

'That's right. It was, but we were able to carry out a forensic examination, and this was recovered. Do you recognise it?' She held up the flash card, in its clear plastic evidence bag.

Maddox looked at it, and for a fraction of a second, an expression flashed across his face. Shock? Horror? Fury? It was gone too quickly for Marcie to identify. But the intent gaze he turned on her was definitely threatening. She took a step back.

'Where did you find this?' He wasn't quite shouting, but it sounded as if he wanted to. He took a step towards her. A long step, that cancelled out her retreat so that he was almost in her face. Marcie moved back again, uncomfortably aware that another step would put her up against the van.

'It was in the driver's side door pocket. We need to know if it was left by the offenders, or if it's yours.'

Maddox's face now showed indecision. He half reached for the bag with his left hand – his right was still deep in his pocket. Since Marcie had it in her left hand, he had to reach across, and Marcie was able to pull it back out of his reach.

He glared at her with such concentrated fury that she felt her legs weaken. 'I – I can't let you have it,' she gasped out. 'Unless it's yours of course, and you can have it if it's yours, if you can identify it, you'll have to sign for it, but we have to be sure you understand, because it could be evidence, of – of a crime – and it has been in a fire so it may be useless, probably is of course, but we want to be sure and of course if you're claiming it as your property that's not a problem….'

She was aware that she was gabbling, that fear had sent her into overdrive, but she was finding it hard to stop. 'Only, if it was left by the offender it might have come from another crime and if so we'll want to try and match it up even if it's completely ruined because it was in a fire, and the car's completely gutted but if it's any use to you, you can have it back if it's yours of course.' Somehow, she managed to regain control and stuttered to a halt. 'I, I just need, need to know if it's yours. That's all.'

For another moment he stared at her, a cold, unrelenting anger in his eyes. If he tries to take it again, thought Marcie, he can have it, and forget getting a signature.

But something in her flood of verbal incontinence had made it through to him. Abruptly, he stepped back.

'It's not mine,' he said, brusquely. 'Never saw it before.' Without another word, he turned sharply and strode back to the house. The gates swung silently shut behind him.

Marcie found herself leaning back on her van, legs quivering. 'Th-thank you,' she whispered. 'Thank you very much.'

Still shaking, Marcie, scrambled back into the van, started the engine, stalled it, started it again and took off down Cyrus Street with a screech of rubber. She felt the CCTV camera's staring at her the whole time.

*

Back at the office, at the end of the shift, Doug was incensed. 'Why didn't you call it in? He could have been done for assault!'

Marcie shook her head wearily. 'He didn't *do* anything, Doug. I couldn't even say he was abusive – didn't swear, didn't shout. It was just the way he looked at me!'

Mac laughed. 'A man looks at you and you go weak in the knees, eh, Marcie?'

Doug glared at him. 'Piss off, Mac. Can't you see she's been scared shitless?'

'I wouldn't say it was that bad.' Marcie put in hastily, overlooking the fact that she *had* been scared shitless. How she'd got through the day she wasn't sure. Fortunately all her other jobs had been routine burglaries. 'It was just – he seemed – dangerous.'

Mac gave a sort of shrug. 'Well, I suppose after what happened, we're all a bit jumpy.' He caught Doug's eye. 'Sorry.'

'It's OK, Mac. Perhaps I did over-react a bit.'

'I'm glad it wasn't me,' said Ali. 'I'd have handed it straight over.'

'But he said it wasn't his,' Doug pointed out.

'He was lying.' They all turned to look at Marcie. 'It was the way he reacted when he saw it. I'm sure he recognised it.'

Mac scratched his chin thoughtfully. 'If that's so, then there could be something dodgy on that card. Something he doesn't want to be connected with. But now he's denied ownership, it could be difficult to tie him in with it.'

'Do you think it could be connected to Ben?' asked Ali. Which was exactly what Marcie had been wondering.

'I don't see how,' said Doug. 'Ben hadn't even got to examine the car.'

'Actually, it seems that he had.' Marcie told them about the blood, and the way the Cavalier had been moved. 'I suppose I'd better run it by Mick, hadn't I?'

'You should tell somebody,' Doug agreed. 'I think Mick's at court, but Jim's around.'

'Better Jim than Mick,' said Ali. Marcie nodded, picked up a copy of her report and headed for the Senior's office.

Whereas Mick was tall, slender, with thinning blonde hair and watery blue eyes, Jim was chunky and dark-eyed, with curly brown hair. Mick was slippery, reserved and up-tight. Jim was open, approachable and laid back. Mick fancied himself as God's gift to women. Jim might have been God's gift to women, if he hadn't been gay. He was on the phone when Marcie knocked on the open door. He smiled, waved her in and moved his feet off the spare chair without breaking his flow.

From the end of the conversation she could hear, Marcie gathered that he was bullshitting an officer about the probable results of an examination. Apparently, he'd made promises that forensic science couldn't deliver and was now blagging his way out of it. Since he was very talented in that department, it didn't take him more than a few minutes. He hung up and looked expectantly at Marcie.

'Jim – can I run something by you?'

She told him the full story, including her suspicions about Maddox – but downplaying her fear, and emphasising his reaction to the flash card. Jim listened without interruption, but quickly lost his usual expression of lazy good humour and began to look more serious than she'd ever seen him before. When she'd finished, he sat for a moment, drumming his fingers on the desk while he thought about it.

'Thanks for coming to me with this, Marcie. Good work, especially finding that flash card. Thing is though, there are some issues here which you may not be aware of.' Jim paused, ran a hand through his hair. 'When it happened – Ben getting shot – it was a bit of a cock-up right from the start. His fault, really. You know how bad he was at following any sort of procedure?'

Marcie nodded. Ben had been notorious for not respecting any rules but his own.

'Well, Ben hadn't called his location in to Control. They had no idea that we had anyone at Callahan's that day. The first report they got – from those dickheads down there – was that someone had collapsed. Control got the idea that there had been some sort of industrial accident, and they sent the nearest spare copper – who turned out to be a young lad still on probation. Shouldn't even have been out on his own, but there was a bit of trouble kicking off in the city centre, and they'd sent most of their resources over there.'

'Anyhow, this lad walked straight into a murder scene, without knowing what it was. He'd been told 'industrial accident' so that's what he assumed. His first thought was to get everyone to safety – including Ben. Callahan's staff had already moved Ben once, and when the ambulance crew arrived the PC had taken him out of the shed and was busy trying to revive him. Already long past that, of course. Hell of a shock for him, when they told him that Ben was dead, and shot dead at that. Even so, it wasn't until CID arrived and someone noticed the SOCO van over in the corner that they started putting two and two together.'

'So by the time me and Mick arrived, the crime scene was totally compromised by Callahan's and the PC. Poor old Ben had been moved at least twice and there was blood everywhere, so it was hard to say exactly where the shooting had taken place. The old bloke – what's his name?'

'Pete?' suggested Marcie.

'Yeah, him – he'd got himself taken off to hospital, suffering from shock. The other one, Neil – none too bright at the best of times, and by now he'd been questioned by the PC, the ambulance crew, CID – he was having trouble remembering his own name, let alone what cars he'd moved where. Even if anyone had thought to ask him. Which is why no one knew about that Cavalier until now.'

'But now you do know,' Marcie pointed out.

'Yes, of course.' Jim leaned forward earnestly. 'And you did exactly the right thing, Marcie. Technically speaking, I suppose Mick should really have come out to the car when you called him. But – as he said – this doesn't actually change much as regards Ben's murder. We've got the drugs connection, we know why Ben was shot. Exactly where was always a bit iffy, like I said, but it's not the main concern now. The investigation is looking at tracing the drugs. And Marcie – this is a big thing, you know?'

'Big in what way?'

'Well, as far as I know it's the first time that a SOCO's been murdered in the course of duty. I'm sure you've seen that it made the national headlines. What you may not know is the amount of interest at high level – *government* level, Marcie! The Home Secretary's been phoning the Chief Constable about it. There's a lot of pressure coming down the line to get this sorted, and quickly. Introducing this Cavalier won't help anyone. It would confuse the investigation and cause a lot of problems, without actually changing anything significant. We don't want to open a can of worms. You see what I mean?'

Marcie nodded. She saw what he meant, alright. She didn't like it, but she got the point. 'And what do you want me to do?'

'Just put in your report. Don't submit the blood. We're ninety percent certain it's Ben's, anyhow. Keep it in the freezer. Send your film up, but we don't need to request prints.'

'What about the flash card. And Maddox?'

Jim shrugged. 'What the hell? Submit the card. It might give us a clue about the TWOC'er. If it's not completely wrecked by the fire. Not much we can do about Maddox, if he's denied knowledge of it. We'll have to let that go. OK, Marcie?'

She nodded, a little dubiously. Jim picked up on it.

'Marcie – you've done everything right. You came across some information, you've reported it, and now it's out of your hands. If the crap hits the fan, you're in the clear.'

'Yes, sure – it's not that though. It's just that I'd hate to think we're missing something. It would be like letting Ben down, somehow.'

Jim smiled reassuringly. 'Trust me, Marcie. It's not connected. No way.'

'OK then. Thanks, Jim.'

'Any time.'

Marcie left feeling happier, but not entirely comfortable with the feeling. Knowing Jim's reputation for expert bullshitting, she wondered if she could trust his reassurances. Not that she had much choice.

In any case, she had to put it out of her mind when she got back to the SOC office and found it empty. The late shift had taken their jobs and had gone out, her shift had gone home. Which meant that she was running late, and on her first day back from leave as well! She hurriedly filled out the paperwork and tossed the flash card into the submissions box. Everything else could wait until tomorrow.

She clattered down the stairs to the car park with coat, bag and keys, whilst simultaneously trying to call the child minder on her mobile. Fortunately, a friendly copper happened along at the right time to hold the door open, just as the child minder picked up.

'Julie, it's Marcie. Sorry, I'm running late again.' She reached her car, dropped her keys, and knelt to scrabble for them whilst carrying on the conversation. 'I'll be about half an hour – maybe a bit longer, traffic's building up. Kids alright? Good. Thanks – see you soon!' She found her keys, dropped her bag, opened the door, dropped her phone, swore, picked everything up in a heap and dumped it inside. As she went round to the driver's side, the phone rang. She swore again, dived into the pile and managed to retrieve it.

'Hello – Marcie Kelshaw.' Trying not to sound out of breath.

'Marcie – it's me. Where are you? I've been trying to get you at home. Thought you'd be there by now.'

Marcie's husband John was accustomed to working long hours himself, but he didn't much like Marcie doing the same. He didn't like Marcie working for Scenes Of Crime. He didn't like Marcie working.

'Hello, love. Been a busy day – I'm on my way now.'

'What about the kids?'

'They're fine, John. I've just spoken to Julie. No problem.'

'The reason I'm ringing is that we've run into a bit of a problem with the SuperScan launch. They've called a crisis meeting – I'm just going there now. I can't say when I'll be home, could go on a bit.'

Pause, while Marcie took a deep breath. 'OK, love. I understand. Do you want me to keep some dinner for you?'

'No – you go ahead and eat with the kids. I expect we'll get something sent in. Got to go. Love you!'

'Love you too.' Marcie tossed the phone back on to the seat and drove off. The traffic was indeed building up, and she had to concentrate hard. Not altogether a bad thing. It kept her from thinking about what she wanted to say to her husband.

Marcie and John had first set up home in a comfortable but unpretentious semi in South Herrick. Julie Cregg had been their next-door neighbour. When John decided that increasing prosperity meant a move out of town to the village of Ashford, Marcie had practically begged her to take Rory and Kady on to her books as a childminder. It added a significant distance to her journey, but she considered it more than worthwhile to have the kids in a familiar environment that she and they felt secure with. John had been bewildered by this. 'There's a perfectly good nursery in Ashford,' he pointed out. But Marcie, none too enthusiastic about the move, had made it a condition of her compliance.

A bus had broken down on the main southbound dual-carriageway through Herrick, making the traffic congestion even worse than she'd feared. By the time she pulled up outside Julie's house, she was scared to look at her watch. Rory and Kady (officially Katy, but at two and a half Rory hadn't been able to get his tongue round it. Now she was two and a half and wouldn't answer to anything *but* 'Kady') were running out of the front door before she could switch the engine off.

'You're very late.' Rory announced judgementally as he reached the car.

'And you're getting far too much like your Dad.' Marcie replied, a little sharper than she'd intended. Actually, people always said how much like her he looked, with his unruly brown hair and the expression of wide-eyed innocence. But he was showing more and more of John's traits as his character developed – imaginative, intelligent, with the ability to shut out the rest of the world almost completely in order to concentrate on whatever had captured his attention.

He also had John's irritation with any intrusions from the real world. 'We're going to miss Ninja Knights!' he complained with a five-year old's passion for the really important things in life, as he clambered onto his booster seat.

'Sorry about that.' Marcie said, half to Rory and half to Julie, who gave her a weary shrug. Kady sat patiently as she was strapped into her chair. Marcie wondered, as she often did, just where the genes had come from for that pale blonde hair – not to mention the calm and gentle disposition. Neither had any obvious connection with her or John.

'I'm hungry, Mummy,' she stated matter-of-factly. Not complaining, just making sure Marcie knew.

'Mummy's been busy!' Rory informed his sister before Marcie could speak. 'She was finding thingy-prints to catch bad people.'

'Fingerprints, Rory.' Marcie corrected. One way in which he did differ from his father was in his wholehearted enthusiasm for her job. He considered that he had the coolest mummy in the world, which did a lot for her self-esteem. 'Yes, darling, I've been busy.' She clipped the final buckle into place, apologised again to Julie, and got back behind the wheel.

'Listen, kids,' she announced with as much cheerful authority as she could muster. 'There's a lot of traffic, so it's going to be a bit longer getting home tonight. Please behave yourself in the back and let Mummy concentrate on her driving, or you'll make us have an accident.' Having thus passed all responsibility to her children, Marcie got her Focus back in the commuter stream heading out of Faringham. Which immediately slowed to a crawl. Despite her efforts to concentrate on driving, she found her thoughts wandering back to the day's events.

Could that Cavalier be connected with Ben? Jim had been very keen to reassure her otherwise – but what made him so certain? If all Ben's paperwork had been stolen, it was only speculation that he hadn't examined it: and he had been standing right next to it when he was shot.

There was a bit of a queue over the South Herrick bridge. 'Rory hit me!' wailed Kady. Calm and gentle she was, but it didn't mean she couldn't stand up for herself.

'Don't hit your sister, Rory,' Marcie admonished.

'She poked me!' Rory complained.

'Didn't poke!' said Kady with righteous indignation.

'Settle down, both of you!' Marcie answered, with what she hoped was loving parental firmness, and not tired parental irritability.

The traffic was moving again. Once over the bridge Marcie turned off into the maze of country lanes that ran up behind River Heights.

Of course, even if Ben had examined the Cavalier, he hadn't found the flash card. If he had, would that have been taken as well? But it was unlikely it would have been found. A straightforward examination of a TWOC'ed and burnt-out car wouldn't merit the level of inspection Marcie had given it. She wouldn't have bothered herself if Neil hadn't told her about the blood.

In fact, Mick had *told* her to give it a negative report. He was going to be pissed with her tomorrow.

They finally pulled into the driveway of Mill Cottage. It was a picturesque little place, all warm red brick and glossy white wood. Not so little, either – it extended a long way back, right to the river which had once powered the mill. John had loved it from first sight. Marcie couldn't deny its attractiveness, but worried about the long-term maintenance of wood frames and old brickwork.

She also questioned the value of a beautiful house that she never had time to admire. Arrival home meant the end of independent thought for a while, as she plunged into the routine of teatime, bath-time, story-time and bedtime. She missed John. It was hard enough with two to share the load. By the time the last request for another bedtime drink had been denied, she felt ready to drop herself. Instead, she put a glass of wine by the bath, and settled down for a long soak.

She woke up in a cold bath, with tyres crunching on the gravel outside. Dragging herself upright, she wrapped a towel round herself and, crossing to the bedroom, peeked out through the curtains. John's BMW had indeed pulled in, but John was still at work. Briefcase open on the bonnet, he was talking earnestly into his mobile while he sorted paperwork.

Marcie stood and watched him for a few moments. It occurred to her that she hardly ever did that anymore.

There was a time, in the early days of their relationship when she couldn't look at him enough. She had wanted to fill her eyes with him, fill her mind with his image. She had wanted to capture every subtle nuance of his lean face, every wry smile, every little furrow in his forehead when he was concentrating on some problem. She'd even stared at his hands sometimes, admiring the strength and sensitivity in his long fingers. When she wasn't looking at him, she was looking at photographs of him.

She tried to recapture that now, looking down on him, to put aside her annoyance to see him as he was now. Not so very different, if she was objective. The sandy hair was perhaps a touch thinner, the face a bit more lined, the tall lanky body a little softer at the middle and more stooped at the shoulders. The real differences were more subtle. He smiled less and frowned more.

Or was that just her own perception, born of frustration?

The door slammed. She pulled on a comfortable old track suit and went down stairs.

Seen close up and in the light, John looked tired and a little grey – skin and hair both, Marcie thought. 'How did the meeting go?' she asked brightly.

'We've got something together,' he answered with a half-smile. 'An action plan... don't worry, it'll come together.'

'Do you want something to eat?'

'No thanks. A glass of wine, perhaps?'

Marcie poured him one, and another half-glass for herself, to be sociable. They sat together in the living room. Her favourite place at the end of the day. It was at the back of the house where the mill machinery had once been. Somehow, it managed to be spacious and cosy both at the same time, with solid comfortable furniture tucked away in the odd angles that history had left in the architecture. A real fire would have been nice, but the 'living flame' gas came close enough. And it was easier to light.

All in all, a good place for relaxing and talking at the end of the day, with *News Twenty Four* on to catch the headlines.

'How was your day?' asked John. He sounded as tired as he looked, but at least he was making the effort to be interested.

'OK – not bad, for a first day back at work, you know.' Marcie answered, thinking it better not to share any details.

'Anything happened about that colleague of yours – the one who got murdered?'

Oh, don't bring that up! Marcie thought – though it was a natural enough question, considering. 'Ben Drummond. Yes, they've found morphine in one of the cars he examined. So it's probably drugs related. Keep that to yourself, though, John – it's not public knowledge yet.'

Probably best not to mention that she'd spent the morning recovering swabs of Ben's blood.

John nodded, and sat thinking for a moment. 'Marcie...' he began.

Oh, no, here we go again, she thought.

'In view of all this,' John continued, 'I really wish you'd think again about your job.'

Marcie gave him her best smile. 'John – I know you're concerned, and I appreciate it – but I was talking to one of our Seniors today, and he told me that this is the only case on record of a SOCO being murdered in the course of duty. I've got more chance being run over by Elvis in a UFO than of being shot!'

He managed a laugh. 'But there's really no need for you to work at all.'

She sighed. So predictable. 'We've been over this before.'

'You would have more time for Rory and Kady.'

Marcie winced. That was below the belt. She suppressed her first inclination, which was to lash out with 'So could you!' Instead she kept her tone even. 'Rory and Kady are doing fine. Julie's a brilliant childminder.'

'Yes, but I really don't think...'

Time to change tack – she most definitely did *not* want a full scale fight tonight.

'John, do you remember what I was doing when we met?'

He laughed properly then. 'You were up to your knees in shit!'

She laughed with him. 'You exaggerate. It was only calf-deep!'

'Norrington Sewage depot. How romantic can you get!' They laughed together then and she felt the tension easing. 'I was trouble shooting their software – those days, we took any work we could get to get the company up and running! Last thing I expected to see was a vision of loveliness wading through the muck!'

'Vision of loveliness?'

He nodded. 'Oh, yes. Especially those big hazel-brown eyes... good figure, as well, even in overalls!"

'Admit it – it was my perfume that really attracted you!' Still laughing, they hugged.

'So what attracted you to me?' John asked, his arm warm around her.

'Oh – well, let's see... good looking, intelligent, better dressed than most people round a sewage farm.'

'No wellies, you mean! But do go on!'

'You were intense, and energetic and enthusiastic – you chatted me up with a detailed account of sewage control software!'

'Over a plastic cup of coffee in the canteen!'

'Not that I understood one word in ten, but I loved the way your eyes sparkled when you got to the really clever bits.'

That was before you got into the management side, and became prosperous, and tired, Marcie thought with an unexpected pang of loss.

'So anything else?'

'Well – what girl could resist the man who gave her a hand up out of the shit!'

They laughed again. John finished his wine, then gave her a quizzical look. 'Was this just a change of subject, or is it going somewhere?'

She sat back, met his gaze. 'My job then wasn't just wading in shit waiting for a tall handsome stranger to rescue me. I went all over the county's water system, doing chemical analysis of the purification process at every stage. It was busy, varied, with a lot of travelling around, mostly working on my own. Quite a responsible job, for my age. I was lucky to get it, and I loved it. Apart from the smell, but you get used to that. John – I gave that up to marry you. And I've never regretted it. But...'

'Yes?'

'I'm *that sort of person*, John. The sort of person who likes a job with some shit in it. A bit of a challenge. And I like this job. Scenes of Crime. Different sort of shit, but a lot of other things are similar. Do you see?'

He looked at her for a long moment, with a half-smile on his face. 'I don't think I do, entirely, but I take your point. Sort of.'

She smiled back, relieved. 'That'll do then.'

'Only – be careful, Marcie. Please.'

'Always.'

He nodded, and they shared a kiss and a hug, somewhat spoilt by his jaw-breaking yawn. 'I'd better get to bed. Early start in the morning!'

'What – after you've worked so late? I thought you might want to sleep in, and maybe take the kids over to Julie's?'

'Sorry, no chance. We've figured out what to do, but it's going to take a lot of pushing and shoving to get it working. We're on a tight schedule, the launch is just a few weeks away!'

For a moment, a flash of the old John showed through the tired business man – the computer whiz-kid who saw problems as challenges and challenges as victories waiting to be claimed. Marcie felt a surge of relief to see that, deep down, he was still the same John Kelshaw who had helped her out of the sewage tank ten years ago.

'Anyhow – shower and bed, for me. 'Night, Marcie.'

'Night, love.' Marcie busied herself with some tidying up, and then caught the news headlines. Ben's murder had already dropped off the top slot, she noticed.

She turned everything off, checked everything was locked up (much more careful about that since she'd been in the job) went up to bed, and slipped in beside John, who was already snoring gently.

Tired though she was, thinking about Callahan's had brought to mind the other events of the day. She went over her examination; had she missed anything? Had she done anything – or failed to do anything – that Mick might pick up on?

Nothing sprang to mind. Drifting now, she thought about Cyrus Street. Number 34. Maddox. She shuddered slightly as she remembered the cold, intense fury of his eyes, as he reached for the flash card and she held it away...

There was something strange about that. He'd reached with his left hand – reaching across his body, because Marcie had held it in *her* left hand – while his right hand was kept firmly in his pocket.

Deep in his pocket.

Marcie was suddenly wide awake again. If Maddox had reached with his right hand, he might easily have grabbed the flash card off her.

'Perhaps he was left handed?' she whispered to herself. John grunted in his sleep.

Perhaps he was, but that wouldn't stop him using his right hand. But he'd kept it in his pocket. As if he was holding on to something. Something he didn't want to let go of, and didn't want to bring out either.

She shook her head. 'Shut up, Marcie. Stop speculating. Go to sleep.'

Eventually, she did.

John

I always had the idea that the longer two people were together, the better they'd understand each other. It must have been two other people, because there's no sign of that happening with me and Marcie.

I realise that she wants to work, and that she wants to do something interesting. But joining the police – Scenes Of Crime – now that's a decision I've had trouble with.

Last night's discussion helped a bit. I think I can see her point of view better. But I don't think she understands mine.

I've always wanted to excel as a provider for my family. To make sure they had everything, and more. To do that, I've made sacrifices. I've moved into areas of work that, to be honest, I'm not totally comfortable with. I don't think Marcie really appreciates that, and I'm not sure how to explain it to her. When I try, it sounds like I'm boasting about my success, or whinging about hers.

Hopefully, this won't go on much longer. SuperScan is almost ready for launch, and I'm really excited. It's going to move us into the big league!

OK, maybe I do tend to get a bit obsessive about it. I know Marcie thinks so. But I've invested a lot into this. If it comes off, then I'll have made it, big time. After that, I'll be able to choose my own projects, run them my way! Follow up some interesting ideas, do what I really want to do.

But for now, I need Marcie's support. Something's not quite right, and I've spent too long on the management side of things. If this goes bad, I could be in deeper shit than Marcie ever saw at the sewage farm.

I need her to be 100% behind me on this.

The problem's not just picking up the kids when she's on a late shift. That sort of thing I can cover. Nobody could say I'm not flexible! But I get this feeling that her focus is somewhere else. And this colleague of hers being murdered hasn't helped. I hope it doesn't sound callous, but what would the kids do if something happened to her? What would I do? She gets impatient with me when I worry, but I can't help it. I don't think she appreciates how much I care about her – or how much I need her.

I always knew she was a bit of a free spirit. It was one of the things that attracted me to her in the first place. Pity I didn't realise the implications.

CHAPTER 3

'You'll get fingerprints off that for sure.'

The elderly man spoke with total conviction. Marcie looked at 'that', which was a very well used canvas shopping bag, and silently cursed all TV programmes, especially the ones where SOCOs could get prints from anything at all, providing it was crucial to the plot.

'I'm sorry, Mr Williams.' She aimed for professional politeness, tried to avoid stressed irritation, feared that she was coming over as professionally irritated. 'I'm afraid that that sort of surface won't give us anything.'

Mr Williams blinked indignantly. 'But they've been all through it! Took my pension!'

'Yes, I'm sorry. You said that they came through the kitchen door? Was it locked?'

A guilty look came across Mr Williams face. 'Um – no. I had to leave it open for the cat.'

Marcie looked at the door, and back at Mr Williams. 'But you've got a cat flap.'

'Well, yes. But I nailed it shut.'

'Ah. Right.'

Marcie felt a sense of unreality creeping over her. And this was only the first job of what was looking like a very busy day. 'So – why did you nail it shut?'

'Because my neighbour got broken into.' Mr Williams noticed the bemused expression on Marcie's face, and took the explanation further. 'They reached through the cat flap with a stick, hooked the keys off her kitchen table while she was watching telly in the front room.'

'I... see.' Marcie considered asking where he kept his keys, but decided that she was far enough into the twilight zone. 'Well, I'll do what I can, Mr Williams.' She set to work with a brush and black powder, examining the edge of the door for any prints.

CAN OF WORMS

It was turning into one of those days. And it had started out so promisingly....

The atmosphere in the office had been definitely lighter that morning. Perhaps it had been The Prof's speech yesterday, or some sense that the investigation was making progress. Either way, things had seemed quite relaxed. Ali in particular had made a determined effort to get back to her normal persona, and had turned up that morning with her hair a startling shade of iridescent pink.

New colours were no unusual thing for Ali. She changed so often that there was now some speculation as to her natural shade. But this was a little over the top even for her.

'What do you think?' asked Doug. 'Criminal Damage, or Assault?'

'Oh, Assault, definitely!' Mac decided. 'Possibly GBH.'

'You philistines should know that this cost me fifty pounds!' Ali retorted.

'What! You *paid* for it!' Doug gasped.

'Doesn't that make it extortion?' Sanjay suggested.

Ali, caught between amusement and exasperation, turned to Marcie for sisterly support. 'Tell them Marcie – this was from Tardani's, the most exclusive hairdressers in the city!'

'Well, if that's what they told you, it's Obtaining Money by Deception,' Marcie answered with cruel betrayal.

The banter was abruptly cut off when Slippery Mick entered the room. He did not look a happy man. He was frowning very hard at Marcie, but before he could say anything he caught sight of Ali's hair.

'A word, Alison.' he snapped. 'My office.'

Apprehensively, Ali followed him out. When she returned a few minutes later, her face was the same colour as her hair.

'That *shit head*!' she muttered. 'That *burk*! That – that...' Unusually, words failed her.

'I take it he didn't approve?' Marcie observed.

'He gave me a load of bullshit about dress code and proper image – like my hair colour makes a *difference* to finding fingerprints!' She looked around at the room. 'I'd stay out of his way.

'Right,' Doug agreed. 'Well, there's a lot of work to do – I think I'll get going.'

The office emptied.

After five minutes with the brush, Mr Williams's door was looking filthy, and Marcie had found exactly what she expected – which was nothing of any value. However, the poor man looked so downcast that she had him empty his bag out.

'Is that how you found it, then? They tipped it all out on the table like this?'

Mr Williams nodded vigorously. 'That's right. And then they must have sorted through it – took me pension money out of the wallet!'

Marcie gave him her best sympathetic look. The pile on the table was even less promising, forensically, than the door. Battered leather wallet, packet of tissues, old spectacle case, sweets, etc.

'And you put it all back in your bag yourself?'

'That's right.' He agreed. 'All except the envelope that they opened – I threw that away.'

Marcie's ear's pricked up. 'Envelope? What envelope?'

'I had a card for my nephew's birthday. Put a fiver in with it. The bastards opened the envelope and took that too!'

She mentally crossed her fingers. 'And what did you do with the envelope?'

He blinked. 'Like I said, I threw it away. Did you want it?'

'Our lab can get fingerprints off paper, with the right chemical treatment. If the offenders held it firmly enough to tear it open, there's a good chance they left some useful impressions.'

Mr Williams went over to his kitchen bin. 'I haven't emptied it yet – it should be on top.'

'Let me!' said Marcie quickly, jumping in front of him.

'There – that blue one.'

Shortly afterwards she left the house with the envelope and a full set of Mr Williams' fingerprints for elimination purposes. She also left the old man in a much more cheerful frame of mind – he was positively beaming as she drove off.

On her way to the next job, Marcie reflected that she'd taken forty minutes on a scene that Ben would have wrapped up in five. But he probably have missed the envelope, and he would have left Mr Williams upset. Ben had never been strong on the public relations side of the job.

She caught hold of that thought, and wondered why she was thinking about what Ben would have done. It wasn't something that had concerned her while he was alive. Why should it be on her mind now?

Perhaps it was the fact that she was driving Ben's van.

Officially no one had a particular vehicle – but people developed preferences, and this one was Ben's. Nobody had cared to dispute it with him. For a start, it was one of the old Escorts. Most of them had been phased out, but Ben had stuck with his, though it was pretty much knackered. The steering was cranky, the gears grated, and the clutch was so loose you had to have your knee in your face before it bit. As Doug had once put it, the van was as rough and difficult to work with as Ben himself.

Plus which, Ben's habit of chain smoking the cheapest cigarettes he could find while he drove had filled the van with a distinctive aroma. Marcie was forced to keep the windows down, cold day though it was. It was impossible not to be reminded of him. Even dead, he was still winding people up.

The eastern edge of Faringham was a long strip of housing estates – Forest Heights, Tolliver Ridge, Rushe Valley. Marcie was steadily working her way northwards. By lunchtime she was in Rushe Valley, not far from Northdale. On impulse, she headed west, and drove past Callahan's. It was locked up and deserted. Nothing more to see there, anyway.

Looking for a quiet spot to park up for lunch, Marcie continued into Northdale. Without consciously planning it, she found herself turning down Cyrus Street.

Number 34 was on the right. The gates were closed. Slowing down as she passed, Marcie looked up at the blank top-storey windows, wondering what was behind them.

She pulled in to the kerb a little further down the street. She could eat her sandwiches here. Watch the house, see if...

If what? If anyone came in or out? What was she likely to discover in half-an-hours surveillance?

One of the CCTV cameras above the gate whirred round to look in her direction.

'Shit!' Marcie slammed the van into gear, nearly stalled it with the dodgy clutch, and took off down the road. Where had she left her brains today? Parking outside the house in a marked-up van? Had she forgotten the CCTV cameras? Unbidden, her imagination produced a vision of Maddox staring balefully at a monitor, his right hand clenched in his pocket. She could feel the stare all the way down Cyrus Street.

At the end of the shift, she entered the office warily. Mick, however, was nowhere in sight.

'How did it go?' asked Doug, looking up from a computer.

'Cleared my sheet!' she announced with satisfaction. 'And recovered some useful stuff – should get some idents from it.'

'Better than me then. All negative, or No Reply To Knocking. By the way, there's a message on the board for you.'

'Oh?' Marcie took down the sheet of paper with her name on it. Mick's handwriting, she noticed with apprehension.

'Bollocking?' Doug guessed. 'Or an appointment for one?'

'Worse, I think. It's Maddox.'

'What? Your friend from yesterday?'

'Apparently.' Marcie showed him the note, which just said, 'Phone Mr Maddox ASAP' and gave a mobile phone number. 'Oh heck! He must have seen me!'

'Seen you?' Doug raised his eyebrows.

'I – er – happened to go by there today.'

'You just *happened* to go by there?'

'I was looking for somewhere to park up for lunch,' she said defensively.

'Yeah. Sure, Marcie.' Doug peered at the note again. 'Well, if it was lunchtime, it's not about that. Look, Mick's timed the message – ten fifteen this morning.'

'Well, that's a relief.'

'It doesn't mean that Maddox didn't see you.'

Marcie nodded. 'I'd better find out what he wants.' She picked up a phone and dialled the number. 'Hello? Mr Maddox?'

To her relief, the voice that answered wasn't the one she remembered from yesterday. It was calmer, pleasanter, more cultured. Not the same Maddox.

'Jonathan Maddox.'

'I'm Marcia Kelshaw. Police, Scenes of Crime department. I understand you wanted to speak to me?'

'Ah, yes, indeed. Your switchboard tells me that you examined my car – a Cavalier? And I presume it was you who spoke to my brother yesterday?'

Ah. A brother.

'Yes – that's right. What can I do for you, Mr Maddox?'

'Apparently you told my brother Vincent that you'd found a digital camera flash card in the car.'

'That's right. He said it wasn't his, though.'

'Yes, I know. The thing is, ah, Miss Kelshaw...'

'Mrs.'

'Oh, I'm sorry. Well, Mrs Kelshaw, my brother was rather embarrassed to see that card. He had thought it was completely destroyed in the fire, you see.'

'Are you now claiming that it *is* yours, Mr Maddox?'

'No, not mine – Vince's. The problem was though – my brother had, perhaps foolishly, allowed some pictures to be taken of him in a... shall we say, a *compromising* situation?'

'Compromising.' Marcie could now see where this was leading, but didn't feel inclined to help Maddox out.

'Yes. There was a rather wild party – a young lady, a little the worse for drink – that sort of thing.'

From her brief encounter with Vince Maddox, Marcie didn't really see him as a party type.

'I'm sure you appreciate, Mrs Kelshaw, that Vince wouldn't want his wife to become aware of these photographs.'

'Mmm.' Marcie decided to remain neutral.

'So Vince's first thought was to deny all knowledge. He panicked. But when he'd had a chance to think about it, it did seem that it would be better if we could have the card back in our possession. I'm sure you understand, Mrs Kelshaw.'

'You want it to be returned?'

'Yes, please. It is our – Vince's – property. Of course, we do apologise for the inconvenience we've caused you. But now you know the circumstances, I'm sure you understand. And we would like it back as soon as possible.'

'I see.' Marcie thought fast. 'The problem is, Mr Maddox, that the card has been recovered as evidence in a crime.'

'Yes, of course.' An impatient note cut through the cultured voice. 'But I can't see how it could possibly help you find the car thief. So there is no reason for you not to return it, is there? Or should I be discussing this with your superior officer?'

Was there a trace of threat in that? Unfortunately, Maddox was right. If it was his, (or his brother's) Marcie had no justification for keeping it.

'I understand your point, of course.' Marcie assumed a conciliatory tone. 'And I certainly wouldn't want to cause your brother any embarrassment. But the card has already been sent up to our technical department at HQ. I shall have to contact them to arrange its return. It may take a little while.'

'How long?'

'I'll call them now and find out the situation, then get back to you. As soon as possible.' She hung up, and sat thinking for a moment.

Doug looked enquiringly at her, but she ignored him, picked up the phone again, and called HQ.

'Sam – that flash card I sent up yesterday?'

'Sorry, Marcie – I haven't had time to look at it yet. They've got us working on Ben's murder. We're running through CCTV footage from every surveillance camera in the city, trying to get a lead on that Mondeo's movements. It's going to take a while.'

'OK, Sam, thanks. Whenever you can. If you get anything, send it straight to me, OK?'

'Sure, Marcie.'

She hung up. Aware of Doug's stare, and still ignoring it, she rang Maddox's number again.

'Mr Maddox – yes, Marcia Kelshaw. I've just spoken to our technical people. Apparently the flash card was too damaged to be of use – the data was irretrievable. So, it was destroyed.'

There was a pause. 'Are you *quite* sure of that, Mrs Kelshaw?' There was a definite edge to Jonathan Maddox's voice now. Marcie wondered if the two brothers were really all that different.

'Absolutely. It's standard practice. The item was unclaimed, at the time, and of no evidential value. We destroy such things as a matter of course.' Hopefully, Maddox would have no idea about the storeroom jammed with recovered but useless items that they had no authority to dispose of.

'Very well then. In that case, Mrs Kelshaw, I'll consider the matter closed.'

'Certainly.'

The line went abruptly dead. Not one for long farewells, Marcie thought. She looked up and finally met Doug's gaze.

'What?' she asked.

'I hope you know what you're doing, Marcie.' Doug said softly.

She nodded. 'So do I.' She wasn't entirely sure that she did.

*

Apart from the marked-up vans, the department's fleet also included a number of unmarked cars. They didn't carry the equipment for major crime scenes, but had adequate supplies for run-of-the-mill burglaries, assaults and car-crime. As well as working out cheaper, they had the advantage of being much less conspicuous. In some parts of the city that might avoid a brick through the windscreen.

They were also easier to drive than the vans, which made them popular with SOCOs. Marcie laid claim to one by slipping the keys into her desk drawer before she went home.

She also made sure that she got in early the next morning, in order to pick up the Northdale sheet – and incidentally to avoid Mick.

After a busy few hours consoling students over the loss of their laptops ('Did you have much work on it?' 'Yeah, sure, – but there was this really cool game I was playing!') she turned into the bottom end of Cyrus Street, and crept stealthily up until Number 34 was just in sight.

It was, she conceded to herself, a pointless and possibly stupid thing to be doing. But her misgivings were intellectual. On a deeper level, she felt convinced of the need to be doing something. And for the moment, this was all she could think of to do.

Vince Maddox had lied about the flash card. Marcie had thought so at the time, and Jonathan Maddox had confirmed it. She also thought that Jonathan Maddox was lying about his brother's motives. Whether or not there was a link to Ben's murder, something dodgy was going on behind that gate.

It was a bright day for November. Cyrus Street looked almost cheerful in the sunshine. Marcie took out her sandwiches, and began to eat, writing up a scene report from the last job as she did so. She kept glancing up the street, but nothing moved at 34. Or anywhere else. Cyrus Street was the quietest residential neighbourhood she'd ever seen.

Her mobile rang just as she'd started on her apple.

'Marcie Kelshaw.'

'Marcie – it's Doug. Are you busy?'

'Just having lunch.'

'OK, sorry to interrupt, but I could do with a bit of help. I'm at the Health Centre on Longmile. The place has been trashed. Looks like they've broken down every door in the place, smashed every cupboard open.'

'Looking for drugs?'

'Probably. Thing is, they can't get the place cleaned up and open for patients until we've finished, and it's a big job for one – can you give me a dig out?'

'No problem, Doug. I'll be there in ten.'

'Thanks, Marcie. Where are you now then?'

'Northdale.'

'I know that.' Doug's voice took on a suspicious tone. 'You wouldn't be anywhere near Cyrus Street, would you?'

There was a pause while Marcie tried to think of an honest but misleading answer – which was sufficient answer in itself.

'Marcie – I *really* hope you know what you're doing.' Doug said wearily.

'Look, Doug, I – *OH SHIT!*'

Distracted by the conversation, Marcie had failed to notice the big gates open. The Mercedes was already turning down the street. Heading towards her.

'Marcie? What's up? Marcie!'

She didn't have time to answer him.

Her first panicked reaction was to throw herself down on the seats, out of sight; but it was already too late for that, and nothing could look more suspicious. Instead, she grabbed her scene report and held it up to her face, with the phone to her ear.

The Merc shot by, accelerating hard down the street. Vince Maddox was driving, dark eyes staring – thankfully – straight ahead. Next to him, a glimpse of someone younger, fair haired.

Then they were past, and Doug was yelling in her ear.

'Marcie – *Marcie* – answer me, dammit – MARCIE!'

'It's OK, Doug. I'm OK. Relax.'

She watched the Merc in the mirror. Something caught her eye. She twisted in her seat for a direct view, dropped the phone and snatched up a pen to scribble down the registration number, just as the car disappeared round the corner.

'Marcie?' Doug's voice came plaintively from the foot well. 'What the heck is going on?'

She picked up the phone again. 'Vince Maddox drove by, that's all.'

'That's *all*?' A pause, whilst Doug absorbed this. 'Did he see you?'

'No. I don't think so. I was pretending to read something. He didn't even look my way.'

'Heck, Marcie – you scared the shit out of me.'

'Me too, if it's any consolation. But I think I've got something! The number plate – I'm sure it's different from the one I saw on that car before.'

'Different?'

'Yeah. It was a G-plate when I saw it on the Maddox's drive. But now it's an H. H591 RRK. Doug, if I can run it through PNC, and it comes back as false, would that give grounds for a search?'

'It might,' he said slowly. 'But you'd need a better reason to request the PNC check in the first place.'

'What? Why? It's different, Doug – it's got to be dodgy!'

'No – listen, Marcie. The car's not been involved in anything. Maddox isn't, as far as we know. You've got the number in the course of an unofficial surveillance, and all you've got is a vague recollection of one different letter.'

'Yes – but...'

Doug interrupted remorselessly. 'And even if the plate is different now, you can't be sure that the present plate is wrong and the one you saw first is false. If it came back legit, you'd have nothing to justify the search.'

'Oh.'

'Oh indeed. And think about this as well – making an illegitimate request for PNC checks could get you sacked. You need more to go on.'

She thought about it. 'Isn't there some reason I could give?'

'Don't even think about it.'

'You're too sensible, Doug.'

'But I'm right. I'll go over it again for you when you get here!'

'Yeah. OK. On my way.'

Marcie started the engine, slipped into gear – then a thought struck her. She stopped, dug out a notebook, and wrote down the Mercedes registration. After a moment's consideration, she also wrote down the time, circumstances, description, and everything she could remember about the occupants. Was the fair haired one Jonathan Maddox?

She dated the page and put the notebook away. If she was going to do this surveillance, however daft it might be, she'd at least do it properly.

*

The following day – Thursday – she contrived to be back on Cyrus Street, at the same time, in the same car. This time she was armed not only with her notebook, but also a digital camera she'd brought from home. Lunchtime, however, passed uneventfully. There was no activity at 34. Marcie extended her lunch break beyond her official thirty-five minutes, and observed a women going into the house she had parked outside. And a cat going about its own business. None of which seemed to further her cause.

Slippery Mick hadn't spoken to her since the beginning of the week. However, he had apparently noticed that she'd been in the same area every day, because on Friday he saw to it that she took the sheet for Harrick – the other side of town from Northdale. He also commandeered the Fiesta she'd been driving. Marcie wasn't sure if he'd got wind of what she was up to, or was just being his usual self. Nevertheless, she waited until he was out of the office before swapping her van for the identical Fiesta that Doug had taken. Without giving him a chance to discuss it.

'Marcie – are you sure about this?' he asked.

'Of course. I know what I'm doing,' she said cheerfully, and left in a hurry.

Fortunately, the jobs in Harrick proved to be straightforward, and she was able to get up to Cyrus Street for a late lunch. Unfortunately, it was a wasted trip. Cyrus Street was its usual quiet self; nothing moved except the cat, which favoured her with a suspicious stare as it went by. After fifteen minutes, Marcie decided enough was enough.

'Face it, girl, you're wasting your time,' she said to herself. She was off this weekend, so Cyrus Street would get a break from her. Next week – well, she'd see how she felt about it. Perhaps it would be best just to wait for any results back from the flash card.

Jim was the Senior on duty when she got back to the office. He stuck his head round the door as the shift was finishing off paperwork.

'Anyone up for a spot of overtime tomorrow?' he asked brightly. 'Weekend shift's short-handed.'

'Sorry,' said Ali. 'Hot date.'

'With a hairdresser?' asked Mac. Alison's hair had been light brown since her interview with Mick, suggesting that this was at last her real self.

'Piss off,' she told Mac.

'I'm away for the weekend,' said Sanjay.

'I'd love to help,' Doug sounded genuinely regretful. 'But we've got the in-laws coming over. If I duck out, I'll be on bread and water all next week. And I'll have to get it myself!'

'My hot date is with a few lunchtime pints,' Mac informed them. 'Looks like you might have to get out and do some jobs yourself, Jim!'

'I would, but it'd show you up,' Jim explained. 'Marcie – how are you fixed?'

She shook her head. 'The kids are going to my parents' this weekend. I'm hoping to get to know my husband again.'

'A bit indulgent, considering you've only just come back from holiday,' Ali sniffed.

Marcie eyed her. 'Take it from me, two weeks with the kids is not exactly a holiday! And it didn't help that John was on the phone to work half the time. But this weekend will be no kids, no phones – just the two of us, a bottle of wine and a takeaway menu.'

'That's what I call a hot date!' Doug said approvingly. 'I don't suppose your Mum and Dad would like to look after my kids as well?' He noted the look on her face. 'OK. Only asking...'

Jim shrugged in resignation. 'If any of you skivers change your mind, just come in anyhow. Plenty of fun for all!'

Marcie had arranged with her parents to do the pick-up from Julie's. Consequently, she headed directly for Ashford, and was home in good time. As she drove through the gates, she saw the BMW already there, and broke into a smile. This withered abruptly when she saw that the boot was open and John was putting a suitcase into it. He looked up, half guilty and half defiant, as she parked next to him.

She got out. 'If this is a surprise weekend away, that's wonderful, but I'd prefer to pack myself. If it's anything else, John, I'm going to hack your heart out with the bluntest knife in the kitchen.'

'I'm really sorry, Marcie.'

'You're sorry? *Damn* you, John, this was supposed to be a weekend for *us*!' She turned for the house. He reached out and caught her arm, pulled her back towards him. They were both surprised to find that she was crying.

'Marcie, I don't have a choice. If you'll just listen for a moment. Please?'

She glared at his blurry image. 'So tell me then.' And before he could say anything, she continued, vehemently. 'You've been working every hour. I've hardly seen you, the kids haven't seen you – and don't tell me about your programme launch, you said that was sorted, you had an action plan, it was all right!'

He shook his head. 'Yes, we did – but there are problems – the plan hasn't entirely worked.'

'You screwed up, you mean!' she snapped at him. 'You screwed up, and I get a weekend alone while you go and sort the mess out! Are you the only bugger they've got, now? Or just the only one who's got nothing important to do!'

She could hear the tightness in his voice, the effort he was making to stay calm. 'It's not just me. The whole team have been called down to London, group headquarters. That's right from the top. We've got to get it sorted this weekend or the whole project is down the pan. The word is that we get together with the HQ people and we stay with it until they're satisfied.' He shrugged helplessly. 'Marcie – if this goes pear-shaped it could be – well, I could go with it.'

Marcie wiped her eyes and looked at him. John had the look of a man under pressure, and not just from a hysterical wife. 'They'd sack you over this?'

He winced. 'Perhaps not sacked. Perhaps re-graded. Or moved sideways.' He sighed, ran his hands through his hair. 'Or yes, perhaps sacked. Because this was my project, Marcie. My big chance, my opportunity to come up with a winner. If it doesn't perform to spec on the launch date, then the company loses heavily – and I'm the one responsible. They won't be very understanding.'

Reluctantly, Marcie allowed her self-righteous anger to slip away, and allowed a little guilt to creep in. Had she been too focused on her own little project to notice how stressed John had been getting? If he lost his job, it would mean more than a big drop in income. The blow to his self-image would be enormous. She forced a smile.

'Well, I suppose it's up to your wife to provide the understanding, then.'

She reached out and hugged him tight. The hug he returned felt like a drowning man grabbing at a lifeguard.

After a long moment, they pulled free.

'Marcie – thank you. You're – you're...'

'Wonderful?' she suggested.

'Absolutely. And I don't deserve you.'

'No argument there.' She managed a smile. 'Go on then. The traffic's going to be lousy. Better get moving'

'I really am sorry about this, Marcie. I was looking forward to the weekend myself. I will make it up to you, I promise.' He turned away to shut the boot, and looked back at her. 'You could go and join the kids for the weekend.'

She shook her head. 'You know Mum and Dad. They've been planning this for weeks – it'll be a tightly scheduled, fully booked and totally organised chain of theme parks, cinemas and junk food. If I turn up they'll be thrown right off their stride. Plus which they'll ask awkward questions.'

'So what will you do with yourself?'

'I'll assemble a collection of blunt knives.' She laughed at the wary expression on his face. 'Just joking. I'll probably go and do some overtime, they've been asking for help this weekend.'

He nodded. 'Ok, don't overdo it. I really am sorry, Marcie.'

A few minutes later the BMW was disappearing out of the drive, and Marcie was wondering which bottle of wine to open first.

CHAPTER 4

With only a few SOCO's on duty that Saturday, there was no question of working just one area. Marcie got a warm greeting from the overstretched shift, and a job sheet that took her all over the city.

'We've had to prioritise.' Jim explained. 'There's an industrial premises in Ash Ridge that CID are keen for us to get to – they're linking it to a string of others that they've no forensic on, so anything you can recover from there would be useful. After that it's all Burglary Dwellings – down in South Herrick first, and then across the river. There was a lot last night, all the way up through River Heights and Market Green. And if you've got time after that, there's another one up at Stanhope.'

'I've got time,' said Marcie. 'I've got time-and-a-half! But looking at this, I'd be better off being paid by the mile.'

'Pull all these in and I'll pay you by the yard.' Jim answered cheerfully, heading out of the door.

It was going to be a long day, she thought. But it wasn't as if she had anything else on. And she wasn't especially keen to go home to an empty house. Last night had been bad enough. She'd got a take-away, watched a film, drank some wine, and told herself several times how peaceful it was on her own. Her head was still muzzy from all the peace.

It was a bright, sharp day, and the fresh air helped to clear her mind. The industrial burglary also got her off to a good start. The offenders had been kind enough to cut themselves. The near-certainty of a DNA hit from the blood should make CID happy.

South Herrick was a short and unprofitable experience. ('No, dear, nothing's been taken. I'm afraid I panicked a bit when I saw the window open this morning – but I think I might have left it open last night.') Across the river, in the very up-market River Heights, things went better, and by lunchtime Marcie had collected a nice assortment of fingerprints, footprints and a discarded glove.

'On to Market Green,' she muttered to herself. Then, without conscious planning she took a left instead of a right and headed back into the city.

'It is lunchtime,' she told herself. 'And there's a great little cob shop in Northdale.' There were several just as good in Market Green, but that, of course, wasn't the point.

Twenty minutes later, Marcie was parking up in her usual spot on Cyrus Street, and anticipating another quiet lunch.

There was a sharp rap on the window.

Marcie jumped and let out an unprofessional word.

'Put your window down, young lady! I want a word with you!'

An elderly lady with a determined expression was peering into the car. She raised her walking stick to hit the window again; Marcie hastily pressed the button to lower it.

'Can I help you?'

'You can tell me what your business is, thank you very much! You've been parked outside my house every day this week – don't try and deny it; I see everything that goes on here! I don't know what you're up to, but if it carries on I shall call the police.'

Marcie held up her ID card. 'Madam,' she said in her most official tones, 'I *am* the police.'

She'd wanted to say that ever since she started the job.

'Oh.' The woman examined the card suspiciously, looked intently at Marcie to make sure the photograph matched. 'Oh – I see.' She sounded rather disappointed. Marcie suspected she'd been looking forward to moving someone on. But she rallied quickly. 'So are you here on *official* business?'

'I was having my lunch.' Marcie looked ruefully at the mangled remains of her cob, which she had dropped on the floor. She could only imagine what it had picked up from its sojourn on the dirty carpet in her car..

Her interrogator let out a sniff. 'Well, if that's all, I don't see why you have to have it here every day.'

'It's a very peaceful street,' Marcie explained, somewhat lamely. A thought struck her, and she put on her best smile. 'Of course, I expect you could tell me differently, Mrs...?'

'Doctor,' said the lady with a glare. '*Doctor* Routley, if you don't mind. I was the GP in this part of town for over twenty years, and I always respected my patients' privacy. I would expect a similar attitude from the police. After all, since you're not here officially, then it's really none of your business what goes on here, is it?'

'Indeed not,' Marcie agreed, thinking fast. 'You're quite right, of course. No concern of mine what goes on along this street.' She leaned forward, and dropped her voice. 'Officially, that is. But *unofficially* – we might be quite interested if anyone had seen anything happening at Number 34?'

There was a subtle change in Dr Routley's attitude. A wariness in her eyes, interest in her voice. "Number 34... but you say this is unofficial?'

Marcie gave her a conspiratorial look. 'Sometimes we prefer to keep things – unofficial – for a while... more discreet, you understand.'

'Oh. I see.' Dr Routley gathered her thoughts. 'So what is your unofficial interest in Number 34?'

Marcie shrugged. 'Well, I can't say too much, because that would make it official. But that fence and gate seems like excessive security, don't you think?'

Dr Routley nodded. 'I have wondered about that. I made a few enquiries when it went up – I still have some friends on the council. It seems that they do have planning permission. 'Reasons of extra security related to objects of exceptional value'. But I would expect the police to know that already?'

Marcie smiled knowingly. 'Well, quite. And has there been any contact with the neighbours?'

Dr Routley shook her head. 'None at all. I did go over to introduce myself, but they just told me to go away. Very rudely, as well. They never go out except in their cars – or in that big van – and the way they drive, coming out of there at full pelt! Nearly ran me over once while I was walking my dog past there. And the driver, a man with a black beard, he gave me such a glare, like it was my fault!'

Ah, thought Marcie. That would be Vince, then. 'Have you seen any other people going in or out, apart from the one with the beard?'

Dr Routley thought it over. 'Well, now, let me see. There's one who always seems to wear a suit, looks a little like the bearded one, only clean-shaven. Always smart.'

Sounds like Jonathan, Marcie decided.

'Then there's a tall young lad, blonde hair. I've often seen him driving the van.'

Marcie recalled the passenger she'd glimpsed in the Mercedes, and put another tick on her mental list.

'And sometimes I've seen another man – short, burly, a bit older than the others – at least, he seems to be balding.' the Doctor concluded.

'Thank you – those are very good descriptions, very useful.' A thought struck Marcie. 'But have you ever seen any women there? Any wives or girlfriends?'

'Do you know, I've wondered about that! You'd have thought there might be – but I've never seen anyone in or out but those four men!'

Lied to me again, Jonathan! Marcie thought. Vince isn't married – so what's on that flash card that's such a worry for him? 'What vehicles have you seen at the house, Dr Routley?'

'Now let me think... I'm not so good on such things, more a people person... but there's that van, and a big white car, and there used to be... Oh! Oh my goodness!'

Marcie had started scribbling notes on her pad: she looked up to see her informant scuttling back into her house and slamming the door behind her. 'What's got into her?' Marcie asked aloud. She looked up the street, and saw Vince Maddox striding towards her, face radiating fury and barely suppressed violence.

Abruptly, her stomach clenched tight with pure fear. She fumbled with the keys, started the engine – but he was already there, standing right in front of the car, hands braced on the bonnet and glaring at her through the windscreen. Daring her to run over him.

She tried to go into reverse, and stalled. Hit the door lock, started to raise the window, but he'd come round to the side, had his hands over the edge of the glass, face just inches from hers – and her last reserves of courage drained away. She took her finger off the button, and stared dumbly at him, quivering.

She expected violence. She could see it in him, the desire to smash her face, to break bone and tear flesh. She expected him to shout, to swear, to blast obscenities at her. She flinched as he reached out his hand. But he merely held her chin, firmly, but almost gently. And he spoke in a very low voice.

'You are a *stupid* little bitch.'

'I...' Marcie gasped. 'I...'

He shook his head. 'Did you think we wouldn't notice you? Parked up in the same place every day? Or did you think that we wouldn't know a police car, just because it's unmarked? And now you're talking to the neighbours. Very stupid to think that we wouldn't see.'

'I was having my lunch.'

His hand clenched a little tighter on her chin. 'Oh, no, don't bother saying anything. I don't want to hear it. Just listen, right?'

'Mmm.'

'That'll do for a yes.' He pulled her head closer to the window, turned it so he could speak directly into her ear. 'Now, if my brother were here, he'd threaten you with charges of harassment. Because that's the way he works. He's the nice one. But that's not me. What I do is, I make a phone call. Just one is all it takes, because I already know your name, Marcia Kelshaw. One call, with your name, and then I'll know *all* about you. I'll know where you live, who you live with. I'll know when you go out, when you get back, where you drink, where you shop. If you've got kids, I'll know about them. I'll know what school they go to. If you've got family, I'll know about them. Just one phone call and you can never be safe again. Not you, not your family, not your friends, not even your pets.'

'No. Please.' Some distant part of Marcie observed with amazement that she was crying.

'Well then, if you don't want that, here's what you do, Marcia Kelshaw.' He squeezed her chin even tighter, still just short of painful, but enough so that she knew he could hurt her if he chose. 'You go away from here, and you don't – ever – come – back. You don't park here for lunch, you don't drive by, you don't walk down the street, you don't talk to the neighbours. Clear?'

'Y –yes.'

'Good. Because if I ever see you again, I'll make my call. And very bad things will happen. Got it?' He let go of her chin at last.

Not trusting herself to speak, she nodded.

He smiled. Not pleasantly. 'So, even a stupid bitch like you can learn, eh? Bye bye.'

He turned away and was striding briskly down the street.

Sobbing and shaking, Marcie somehow managed to start the car, and drove off as fast as she could. Drove blindly, barely seeing through the tears, barely aware of where she was. Hardly noticing the horns blaring and lights flashing as she shot out of the end of the street, without looking. Not even registering the thirty m.p.h. speed limit as she floored the accelerator, thinking only of getting away from Cyrus Street, as far and fast as possible.

When she had regained some control, and slowed down, she was numbly surprised to find herself driving by Callahan's. Still locked up and empty. She pulled in to the side of the road opposite, and rested her head on the wheel.

Vince Maddox had been right, she realised. She had been stupid. Out of her depth. She had opened a can of worms, just as Jim had warned – but not the one he'd had in mind. This was much worse.

One thing was clear; her vague suspicions about the Maddox's were fully justified. Unless it was all bluff – which she couldn't believe – Vince's threats indicated a depth of criminal involvement beyond anything in her experience. He had contacts, he had access to information and resources, and he would use any means necessary to gain his ends.

There was no doubt at all in Marcie's mind that Vince Maddox was capable of murder. He'd totally convinced her of that. Which meant that he would have been capable of Ben's murder.

So there it was, out in the open. Something that she'd felt in her gut ever since her first meeting with Maddox. A man like that, linked by the car, the Cavalier with Ben's blood on it.

Tenuous, perhaps. But possible. It *felt* possible.

Well, now it was time to stop acting on gut instinct, and start thinking. Because, if she was stupid again, Vince would carry out his threat.

Thinking about that brought a renewed wave of fear – but something else as well.

Anger. A surge of pure fury swept over her. 'Bastard!' she said vehemently. Then she shouted it. *'Bastard!'*

'He threatened me – he threatened my family – You BASTARD....' She slammed her hands against the wheel, screaming obscenities. 'You won't do this – you can't...'

With an effort, she regained control, feeling weak and shaking from an excess of emotion. 'Calm, Marcie, calm,' she said to herself. She had to be in control if she was to find a way out of this situation.

Vince had been in control. One of the most frightening things about him was how much he had been in control, in spite of his rage. For him anger was not an emotion but a tool. A weapon he could use with the destructive force of a bomb or the precision of a scalpel.

Thinking of that reminded Marcie of the way his hand had felt as he'd held her chin. Logically, it was better than a fist in the face – but it felt almost as bad. An assault in a deeper and more subtle way than pure violence.

A touch, she remembered, of his bare hand.

The same hand with which he'd held on to the window as she tried to raise it.

A slow smile spread across Marcie's face as she looked at the window – still in the same position as it had been when Vince had gripped it.

'Stupid little bitch, am I, Vince?' she said to herself. 'Well, perhaps you're not so bright either.'

Carefully not touching the window, she got out of the car, went to the boot, opened her case, took out a pot of aluminium powder and a brush.

'Let's see, shall we?' With just a touch of powder on the brush, she began to dust the window, inside and out.

One of the things she liked best about a SOCO's job was the way fingerprints could appear, as if by magic, on apparently clean surfaces, when you applied the powder. To see a beautiful, clear fingerprint develop was always a thrill for her, making up for all the smudgy marks and negative results. Vince Maddox's prints on her car window were as sharp and fresh as any she'd seen: thumbprint on the outside, full set of fingers inside. Pointing down, showing clearly how he'd gripped the glass.

Marcie took out a roll of lifting tape – like Sellotape, but much clearer, stickier, and more expensive. She cut off a length and, holding her breath, carefully smoothed it over the thumbprint. Then repeated the procedure on the inside.

The last stage could be the trickiest. Every SOCO could tell tragic tales of how perfect fingerprints had been lost because the tape tore. Or a sudden gust of wind wrapped it round their fingers.

Very carefully, she peeled the tape away from the glass, laid it down on a sheet of clear acetate, sliced off the excess with a scalpel blade.

Did it again on the inside.

Held the results up to examine.

The skin ridge detail was brilliantly sharp. Textbook stuff. She could see cores, she could see deltas, she could see ridge-endings and bifurcations in abundance. More than enough for a fingerprint expert to work on.

'Got you, Vince,' she said softly. 'Got you, you bastard.'

Let's see you make your phone call from a cell, she thought, as she drove back to Ash Ridge. Threaten me then – and meanwhile, we'll see what else these prints tell us about you. Because I'm damn sure you must be in the frame for more than one crime.

Back at the station, Marcie rushed up the stairs and burst into the Seniors office.

'Jim, I...' she stopped abruptly as Slippery Mick looked up from the desk.

'Jim's off,' he explained. 'We've split the shift. And I'd appreciate it if you knocked?'

'Oh. Sorry.'

'But since you're here – what's the problem?'

Marcie took a deep breath. She would have preferred to talk to Jim about this, but really it shouldn't make a difference. Mick would surely not let an assault on a SOCO go by. He'd be professional about it, whatever their differences in the past.

'I've been assaulted,' she said bluntly. 'By Vincent Maddox, of 34 Cyrus Street.'

Mick sat up sharply. 'What! What happened? Are you hurt?'

She shook her head. 'No. But he threatened and verbally abused me. It's got to be assault, Mick! And he can't deny it; I lifted his prints from where he touched the car.'

Mick ran his hands through his hair, and sat back again. 'Right – well – sit down, Marcie. You'd better tell me the whole thing.'

Starting from her conversation with Dr Routley, Marcie went through the sequence of events, keeping it as professional and factual as possible. Annoyingly, her voice started to quaver as she described Vince's threats. She kept control, and finished off. 'So his prints were all over the window, Mick, and I've got a good lift. It'll be interesting to see who they come back to – I'll bet he's got form!'

Mick was leaning back in his chair, frowning. 'Not so fast on that. Let me get this straight. You've been parking on Cyrus Street regularly? Watching number 34?'

'Well – yes – but only during my lunch break.' Marcie started to get a bad feeling. This wasn't the reaction she'd hoped for.

'And you asked this neighbour some questions about number 34, and about the people who live there?'

'Yes! That's how I know it was a lie about him being married!'

'His wife doesn't have to live at the same address.' Mick pointed out. 'But that's not really the issue. Have you actually called this in, yet? Reported it to the Control Room?'

Marcie shook her head. 'No. I wanted to run it past Jim – or you – first. I wasn't sure of the best way to go about it.'

Mick nodded. 'Good. That's the first intelligent thing you've done, so far.'

Marcie felt her jaw drop.

'So I'm going to do you a favour.' Mick continued. 'I'm going to forget that this conversation ever took place, and that this incident ever happened.'

'But – s*hit*, Mick, he threatened me! He threatened my family!'

'Ah, yes. But it's only your word on that, isn't it?'

Marcie couldn't believe what she was hearing. 'What? Don't you believe me?'

Mick shrugged. 'That's not really the issue, is it?' He raised his hands to forestall an outburst. 'OK – I'm sure he did threaten you – though it may not have been as bad as you think – probably just bluff, anyway.'

'You weren't there, dammit!' Marcie snapped at him, anger rising. 'How the heck would you know?'

'That's just the point, Marcie!' Mick snapped back. '*No one* else was there! Sure you can prove he touched the car – but that means nothing. Did anyone else actually hear what he said?'

Vince had spoken very quietly, Marcie remembered. Now she understood why he hadn't ranted and screamed at her.

'He touched me...'

'Who saw it? This Dr Routley – was she watching?'

Marcie shook her head. 'I don't know. I – I don't think she could have seen inside the car from her house. Not with Maddox standing where he was.'

'Right,' said Mick.

'But there's other houses. Someone might have seen something!'

'Might have,' Mick agreed. 'Or might not. It's a long shot. And even so – what would they have seen? He touched you – yes, technically assault, but no injuries, no bruising. And what you have to remember is, if this is made official, if it goes further – what's going to come out?'

'What's that supposed to mean?' Marcie asked. She had the feeling that a hole was opening up under her chair, and she was dropping into it.

'OK – so you accuse Maddox of assault. There's an enquiry – perhaps he gets arrested. And it comes out that you were carrying out an unofficial, unauthorised surveillance on his property. That you were making unsanctioned enquiries, asking his neighbours questions. Can you imagine how much trouble you'd be in?'

'But – there's so much to link him to Ben's murder – if we could just get him inside, run some checks!'

'There's sod-all to link him to Ben – except in your imagination!'

Fury was rising in Marcie, overcoming her self control. 'Isn't this more about covering your own back – because you screwed up the investigation in the first place?'

Mick flushed a deep red. 'Enough of that!'

'You spineless shit!' Marcie stormed. 'You let one of your people be assaulted, and abused, and won't lift a finger – should I be surprised? You don't give a damn about finding Ben's killer!'

'ENOUGH I SAID!' Mick had jumped to his feet, and slammed his hands down on his desk. 'ONE more word, Kelshaw, just one more word and you're over the line!'

Marcie was standing as well now. With an effort, she shut her mouth, and they glared at each other over the desk.

'I'll overlook this,' Mick grated, 'because I appreciate that you've had a distressing experience. I'll put it down to shock. But I will not tolerate insubordination, and I will *not* have you tell me my job! Is that clear?'

Not trusting herself to speak, Marcie looked away and nodded curtly.

'Very well. Now then, I'm going to make this easy for you. From now on you do not, under *any* circumstances, go to, park on, or even drive down Cyrus Street. In fact, you do not even take any jobs in the vicinity. Got that? No jobs in Old Northdale. That is a direct order. Do you understand?'

'Yes,' Marcie spat.

'Good. That should keep you out of Maddox's way, and avoid any threats he may make or may have made. But just to be on the safe side, destroy that lift you took, to avoid any temptation to try and run it. In fact, give it to me, and I'll destroy it myself.' He held out his hand.

'It's in the office.' Marcie said.

'Then put it in my tray before you leave. I *will* check.'

'Right.'

'And while I think of it, from now on, stay out of the unmarked cars. If you're in a marked-up van you might be less tempted to play detective. You can use Ben's old one – no one else wants it.'

'Thanks.'

'Welcome. You'd better get off home. If you managed to do any of your proper work today, sort the paperwork out Monday.'

'I've got exhibits to submit.'

'Do that then. But don't hang around.'

Marcie left without goodbyes. Mercifully, the main office was empty. She was able to swear to herself without interruption, which she did for at least ten minutes. Then she tried to call Doug, but his mobile was switched off. He only used that phone when he was at work or on call, she remembered. He didn't like to be contactable when he didn't have to be.

Early on in her career, when she'd just started the job and Doug was her mentor, he'd made a special exception and given her his home number, just in case she ran into something difficult and no one else was around. She'd never had to use it, but ferreting around in her desk, she found the number still there. She dialled it on the office phone.

Doug's wife didn't sound pleased, but she fetched Doug anyway. Doug sounded happy to get a break from the in-laws, so Marcie poured out the whole story.

He was furious. At Maddox for his threats, at Mick for his attitude, but finally (and less satisfyingly) at Marcie for getting herself into the situation in the first place.

'What the heck did you think you were doing, anyway?' he asked.

'Just trying to find out what's going on! OK, so it went a bit pear shaped, but if Mick would only back me up, I might get something back from those lifts! In fact, I've half a mind to go ahead and report it anyway. Mick couldn't stop me, could he?'

'No,' Doug agreed. 'But half a mind would be right.'

'Oh, thanks – I thought you were on my side!'

'I am, Marcie. Which is why I'm telling you this, for your own good. Though I hate to admit it, Mick has a point. You can't bring charges against Maddox without getting yourself into *deep* doodoo. And there's no guarantee that *he'd* be in any trouble. With a good lawyer, it wouldn't even get to court.'

Doug paused, waiting for an answer. Marcie couldn't find anything to say, so he pressed on.

'And you have to think of your safety as well. If you make a charge against him and it doesn't stick – well, you'd still have his threats to deal with.'

'Mick thinks he's bluffing.'

'Do you?'

Marcie remembered Maddox's face, inches from her own. There had been no suggestion of bluff, no hint of uncertainty. Marcie was convinced, down to her stomach, that Maddox could and would do everything that he had threatened.

'No,' she said quietly. Her guts were knotting up again at the thought.

'Not worth the chance, anyhow,' Doug continued. 'Leave it, Marcie. Walk away. Sure, it's crap, but you daren't take it any further.'

'But – heck, Doug – I can't just let him get away with it! There must be something we can do!'

Doug sighed. 'Look, I'll have a word with some people I know in CID. Ask if Maddox has come up on their radar at all.'

'OK. Thanks.' It wasn't what Marcie had hoped for, but it was clearly the best she'd get. And it was a lot safer than trying a head-to-head with Vince Maddox. 'Run 34 Cyrus street past them as well,' she suggested. 'The place has got more security than Fort Knox. There's got to be a reason for that. Perhaps someone's noticed?'

'OK, I'll do that.' Doug paused, listening to a conversation Marcie couldn't hear. 'I've got to go. A small war just broke out between the kids, I have to enforce the peace. Go home and get some rest, Marcie. Put it behind you. See you Monday.'

'Bye Doug. And thanks.'

Marcie hung up. Talking to Doug had helped get some perspective, and she had to agree that he made sense. But she felt defeated. Depressed, empty, tired – but most of all, beaten. She would do what Vince Maddox had told her. She would do what Slippery Mick had ordered her. And she would do what Doug had asked her to, because she couldn't think of any alternatives. Not acceptable ones.

Paperwork completed, exhibits submitted, she took out the lifts from the car, went over to Mick's tray and dropped them in.

As she did, she had a rebellious thought.

She'd told Mick she'd got a lift. She hadn't mentioned that there were two of them.

She picked the lifts out again: looked at them, and dropped one back in. She kept the best one: the fingers, inverted, from the inside of the window. Slipped it into the bottom of her drawer, and locked it away.

What she'd do with it, she had no idea. But the small act of defiance gave her back a modicum of self-respect. Clinging tightly to it, she went home.

Doug

After Marcie's phone call, I spent the rest of the weekend worrying about what she might have got herself into – and what she might do next. You just can't tell with her. She's got this sort of stubborn wildness in her. And it shows itself at the most inconvenient times.

I was planning to talk to her about it on Monday. We were on the two-ten shift, and I thought we should be able to get chance for a quiet word. As it happened I was late getting in, and found the place in chaos. Marcie and Mac had already been sent up north on some urgent murder enquiry. Ali and Sanjay were busy trying to prioritise the other jobs, I was about to pitch in and help, when Slippery Mick collared me.

'Doug – we've got the Post Mortem. City Hospital – we need to be there in thirty minutes, so chop chop!'

For Mick, that was quite pleasant.

On the way, it turned out he had other things on his mind.

'You and Marcie – you're quite close, aren't you.'

I gave him a sideways look – all I could spare, as I was driving, and the traffic was heavy. I wondered what he was getting at. He wasn't meeting my eye, but that was normal.

'I mentored her when she joined the department,' I explained 'We work well together.' Mick already knew that of course. I started to get a bit worried about where this was going.

'Yes, good.' He paused, staring out of the window. 'Well, we're all quite fond of her, of course.'

News to me that Mick was fond of anyone apart from Mick.

'Only I'm a little worried. She seems to becoming a bit obsessed with this job she's picked up.'

'Which job would that be, Mick?' I asked, knowing perfectly well what he meant.

'This thing at Cyrus Street, connected to that car at the garage.'

'The one linked to Ben's murder, you mean?' I asked innocently.

Mick shifted uncomfortably. 'No such link has been made,' he said firmly. 'And it would not be helpful to the investigation to postulate any.'

'So you're sure that it's not connected, then?'

'If it is, then the investigation – the proper investigation – will find it. What we can't have is one of our officers muddying the waters with her own unofficial enquiries.' He lowered his voice a touch. 'Confidentially, Doug – and do keep this to yourself – Marcia had something of a confrontation last week.'

'No! Really?' I exclaimed, all wide eyed innocence.

Mick nodded sadly. 'I'm afraid so. It seems she's been carrying out some sort of surveillance operation of her own, and a member of the public took exception to it. Of course, I'm sure she blew the whole thing way out of proportion, but it is worrying. Not only could she have got herself into a lot of trouble, but it would reflect badly on the department. On all of us, Doug.'

I didn't trust myself to reply, so I kept my attention on the traffic and gave a non-committal grunt.

'So,' he continued, 'Since you probably know her best, I would like you to keep an eye on her. Make sure she drops this Cyrus Street thing. Let me know if she has any more problems with it.'

'I hope you're not asking me to spy on her?' My voice was sharper than I had intended.

'No! Oh, no, not at all.' Mick, backpedalling, was one of the fastest objects in the known universe. 'For her own good, that's all. Don't let her get into any more trouble.'

What you really mean, I thought, was make sure she doesn't cause you any problems. It was on the tip of my tongue to tell him to get lost, and it would have been very satisfying as well.

What stopped me was the thought that unfortunately Mick was right – although for the wrong reasons. Marcie was in danger of getting herself into all sorts of trouble. Of course, I had no intention of letting

Mick know how much I knew, and if she came up with something solid I'd back her all the way. The heck with the department's image!

But in the meantime, trying to keep Marcie out of the shit was something I'd do anyway, with or without Mick's prompting. That being the case, it would be better to be diplomatic.

So... 'I'll do that.' I agreed.

Mick gave me a satisfied nod, and I drove on to the mortuary, feeling like I'd just made a pact with the Devil.

CHAPTER 5

The Torford Canal joins the river several miles north of Faringham, and runs off towards the north-west. Never a great success in its commercial years, it had proved much more popular for fishermen, walkers, and narrow boat holidaymakers.

Early on Monday morning, a man out walking his dog on the towpath passed a moored narrow boat. A common sight, which he gave little attention to. His dog, however, found it much more interesting. Barking wildly, it leapt into the cockpit and paid furious attention to the partially open cabin door.

Cursing, his owner jumped after him, ready to make quick apologies to anyone who came out. However, seeing a hand poking out of the door caused him to revise his plans. Cautiously opening the door, he found the hand attached to the body of a young woman, with a large and bloody hole in her chest.

Seconds later, he was racing down the towpath as fast as his wellies would take him. His dog – delighted at the unusual amount of excitement in this morning's walk – followed along, barking joyfully.

Geographically, the Torford Canal was in Northern Division, but divisional areas are often ignored for major incidents. Coming in for the late shift, Marcie found herself and Mac dispatched immediately up to the canal boat crime scene, with instructions to take over from the Northern SOCO's, who had been there all day.

'It's a weird one!' said Pat Manning in greeting. Pat was one of the Northern Division Seniors, and the Crime Scene Manager for this case. A tall, silver-haired women, she'd put in twenty years as a copper before transferring to Scenes Of Crime.

'I'm sure it is, Pat,' Mac agreed cheerfully. 'But leaving aside your personal problems, what's happening here?'

Pat favoured him with a sour smile. 'Spare me your dysfunctional humour, Mac. I've had a long day. What we've got is three bodies, two female. All white, early twenties. Two with gunshot wounds, one dead of unknown causes. Bodies have gone to autopsy. Everything's been photographed. Now we're going through the boat for DNA and fingerprints. Any firearms or ammunition, of course, plus any paperwork. None of the bodies have been identified as yet.'

'Where's the boat from?' asked Marcie. She was looking at the writing on the side. '*Happy Holidays Ltd*. How appropriate.'

'It's a company based at the other end of the canal, in Torford,' Pat explained. 'The police up there are onto it, but the last we heard was that the offices are closed and they haven't traced the owners yet. Mac, I want you checking the drawers, cupboards and any other storage areas in the main cabin. We've finished the kitchen.'

'Galley. It's a boat.' Mac had a naval background, and liked to get the terminology right.

'Whatever. Marcie, you start on the table. It's got bottles, cans, cigarette ends. DNA first, then dust for prints. Brought your sandwiches? Good – you're going to be here a while! Get suited up.'

Fully kitted out in white disposable overalls, gloves and masks, Marcie and Mac entered the crime scene – carefully stepping over the pool of dried blood on the steps. The main cabin table was, as Pat had warned, a major job in itself. Bottles, cans, cigarette ends and ash, dirty plates, scummy mugs, crisp packets, chocolate wrappers...

Marcie sighed, and got to work.

Like most parts of a police investigation, crime scene examinations lack glamour. Marcie had been in the job long enough not to be surprised. All the same, she thought to herself, fingering her way through the debris of other people's dirty habits wasn't her favourite part of it.

On the other hand, the meticulous precision required for a major crime scene had a satisfaction all of its own, and Marcie became absorbed. Carefully diagramming the table, she measured everything before starting to recover and package each cigarette end.

As she got into a work rhythm, her concentration eased a little, and part of her mind began replaying the events of the weekend.

*

Compared to Saturday, Sunday had been a blast..

She'd slept in, and had been pleasantly woken up by John's early return – all problems solved, all parties satisfied, and programme back on track. Apparently, John had been largely responsible for the turn-around, so he'd gone from designated scapegoat to Man of the Match, and was bubbling with pride and relief. Marcie wasn't keen to talk about her own adventures. Fortunately, John didn't ask

They'd had a pleasant pub lunch, a relaxed afternoon, and were refreshed and ready to welcome Rory and Kady back that evening. The kids were in their usual state after a weekend with the grandparents, bubbling with stories of zoos, cinemas and theme parks, stuffed with sugar, hyperactive, over-excited and totally exhausted. Marcie was pleased at how well she'd coped with the tears and tantrums that resulted, and it all helped to put Maddox and Cyrus Street well on the back burner.

*

Work on the barge crime scene continued steadily. By about nine that evening, when she had nearly finished the table, Doug turned up. He had been assisting Slippery Jim with the post mortem's down at City Hospital and he brought pizza and news. The pizza was welcome, the news somewhat less so.

'They've arrested someone.' he announced cheerfully. 'At a boat yard in Torford – where it was hired from.'

'They found the owners, then.' Mac was barely intelligible through a mouthful of cheese and pepperoni, but Doug got the gist and nodded.

'They gave descriptions that matched our three corpses, plus one other person. They also pointed out the car that all four had arrived in. The local boys put a watch on it, and sure enough, along comes our missing boater. They arrested him climbing into the car. Sawn-off shotgun under his coat, pocket full of pills, and high as a kite on whatever he'd been using.'

'So this is all for nothing?' Marcie moaned, looking at her pile of packaged cigarette ends.

'Don't fret – you'll still get paid!' Doug reassured her.

'Ah, but Marcie doesn't do it for the money – she does it for fun!' Mac sniggered.

Marcie gave him a sharp look. Ben Drummond had once accused her of 'playing at the job' – like it was just a hobby to her. She felt she'd proved her commitment since then and realised that Mac was just making a clumsy joke. But the fact that she didn't *have* to work was still a sensitive issue.

Doug stepped in quickly. 'Anyhow, the word is to wrap things up for tonight. All exhibits back to HQ, since that's closer than any of the Divisional Scenes of Crime offices.'

Mac finished his pizza and went back to the barge, complaining that all the bending over had brought on his back trouble.

'I did offer to swap,' Marcie told Doug. 'But his back's not *that* bad!'

Doug smiled. 'He didn't mean it, you know. And even if he did, you don't have to prove anything.'

She shook her head sharply, irritated at her own sensitivity. 'Forget it. I'm tired, that's all. Help me get these exhibits in the van.'

Doug collected an armful of carefully labelled rubbish. 'By the way, I've had an e-mail from my friendly Detective Constable. About Cyrus Street.'

Something knotted itself in Marcie's guts. 'And?'

'Nothing's come up about the premises. But apparently there's rumours going round that the local lads – burglars and suchlike – have been warned off 34 Cyrus Street.'

'Warned off? What does that mean, exactly?'

Doug shrugged. 'Not clear about that. Nobody will say anything specific. But apparently the word has gone round that anyone trying to pull a job there will regret it.'

Marcie thought about Vince Maddox. 'I can believe it. That man could put the frighteners on anyone.'

'There's more.' Doug reached the van and dumped the exhibits inside. 'Does the name Jason Deeley ring any bells?'

'Vaguely.' Marcie frowned. 'I got an ident on him, months back. Stolen car, I think.'

'That's the lad. Well-known local TWOC'er – very prolific, not very bright. Gets caught a lot, doesn't learn from it. Or didn't. Apparently he's dropped out of sight in recent weeks. And the word is that he nicked the wrong car.'

'Wrong car? *The Cavalier?*'

Doug held up his hand. 'That's speculation, Marcie. We can't be sure about that. *You* can't be sure – so don't go there, alright?'

She nodded. 'Of course not, Doug. You know me.'

'Exactly. So don't go storming off to Cyrus Street shouting "Murder!" We don't know what's happened to this lad, or if it's anything to do with the Maddoxes.'

'OK,' Marcie agreed. 'After all, all we've got is a warning-off in the criminal community, which could only come from some very serious players. And a missing car thief, who is rumoured to have been connected with a stolen car. A car which Ben was examining when he was shot. And at least one very dodgy, very scary person, from the warned off address, who certainly fits the bill of a serious player in the criminal world. And don't forget that flash card, found in the aforesaid car, which the serious players first denied all knowledge of, then wanted back.' She paused for breath. 'And that's all.'

Doug shrugged. 'I hear what you're saying. But the fact is, Marcie, there's not a shred of real evidence in any of it.'

'I know. I know. But if nothing else, it's interesting. Don't you think?'

*

The month became damp, grey and chilly. City Scenes of Crime hit a quiet patch.

'Stands to reason,' Doug said, looking at a near-empty job sheet. 'Why should burglars go out in this weather? They're self-employed, after all.'

The full story of the 'Torford Canal Murders' (or the 'Barge Bloodbath', depending on which newspaper you read) was made public. The barge had been hired by the four people for a weekend of sex, drugs and booze. Having steered an increasingly erratic course down the canal, they finally moored up, too stoned to go any further. The murderer had gone off to get food. On his return, he found his girlfriend dead from an overdose. The other two hadn't even noticed. An argument followed, a gun was produced, and then there were three bodies. Being incapable of logical thought by this time, the survivor had set off on foot, back to his car in Torford, finally arriving just in time to be arrested.

Doug had contacts in Torford, and supplied further details. 'Apparently he was so out of his head that he'd forgotten that he still had the gun on him. The coppers said that when they took it off him, the first thing he said was 'That can't be mine! I dropped mine in the canal miles back!'

'Pity they aren't all that easy,' said Sanjay.

Marcie snorted. 'Trust me – it wasn't that easy!'

As things continued to be quiet, Sanjay went on leave. Ali hit a lamp-post: 'I was just looking for a house number,' she explained. 'You know how hard it is to see them some times.'

'And the lamp-post leapt out in front of you?' asked Mac gently.

She gave him a dirty look. 'I must have clipped the curb or something... stupid place to put a lamppost anyway.'

Unhurt, except in her pride, Ali still took some time off due to 'stress'. Marcie wasn't sure if this was caused by the accident or by the ribbing she'd got from her colleagues.

Even with two people short on the shift, the work load continued to be low. Marcie made the most of the time by giving Ben's van – now her van – a thorough clean out and re-stock. The air-fresheners she'd bought hadn't cleared the atmosphere much. Looking under the seats, she found out why.

'It's like a crime scene under there,' she complained to Doug later. 'Ben must have been using it as an ashtray for years.'

Doug shuddered. 'I wouldn't even go there! Why don't you take it over to Forest Heights, leave the keys in, and go for a short walk. The local lads will soon sort it for you.'

'Aye,' agreed Mac. 'Burnt out wreck equals brand new van.'

'Careless misuse of vehicle equals disciplinary action,' Marcie sighed. 'I really can't afford to piss Mick off any more.'

Slippery Mick had hardly spoken to her recently. Which suited Marcie fine, but she knew he had a reputation for holding grudges, and was being careful not to give him any excuses.

Borrowing an industrial strength vacuum cleaner from the station caretaker, she went back to her assault on the van. The storage racks were a revelation. Ben had never thrown anything out and had made sure he was never short of anything. There were piles of old report forms, of a type that had gone out of use years ago, and the department's chronic shortage of evidence bag labels was explained by the huge stock that Ben had squirrelled away. By the time she'd cleared the clutter, and put the excess supplies back in the store, the inside of the van looked twice the size.

'Might improve performance as well,' she muttered to herself. 'It must be half a ton lighter.'

Ben had left more than rubbish behind. Marcie had unearthed three large files of old scene reports, witness statements and other paperwork, most of which should have been filed or submitted somewhere months or even years ago.

'If they think I'm going to sort this lot out...' Marcie started to shovel it all into a rubbish bag, but her eye was caught by a dog-eared folder marked 'Erica Nolan'.

That name rang a bell. She opened the folder. It was the usual mass of unorganised paper: the first thing she pulled out was an old newspaper clipping, reporting the tragic rape and murder of a young women from River Heights. She vaguely remembered it. It had been before her time in Scenes of Crime, and as far as she knew had never been solved.

The body had been found in parkland down near the lake. Ben, it seemed, had been the first SOCO on the scene, and he'd stayed close to the case throughout. A suspect had been arrested, but was never charged due to lack of evidence. The file included copies of correspondence between Ben and various CID officers. Marcie was surprised to see that the most recent was dated just a few weeks before Ben's murder.

In it, Ben suggested that a handkerchief he had recovered from the scene should be submitted for DNA analysis. Recently developed techniques made it more likely that a profile could be obtained. The handkerchief had already been linked to the dead girl by fibres from her pullover found on it, and relatives had stated that it wasn't hers. Ben had kept track of all this, listed all the points concisely, and concluded that a good DNA hit could finally close the case.

Marcie took the whole file up to Jim. 'I'm not sure what to do with this,' she explained. 'It might be worth following up.'

Jim leafed through the file. 'Oh, yes. I remember this one. Very nasty. Ben was all over it – just his sort of thing.'

Marcie pointed out the latest letter. A technical article about the new technique had been attached, with relevant points highlighted. 'I didn't know Ben gave a stuff about new techniques.'

Jim laughed. 'He liked to come over as an old dinosaur. But the fact was, if he thought something might help with a case, he'd dig out any information he could. It was amazing what he came up with sometimes. He would refer to cases from all over the world to try and get something done, or acquire some equipment... even caught the Prof out sometimes.'

Marcie shook her head. 'I never knew about that.'

'Well, he didn't advertise it – it wasn't good for his image.' Jim tapped the letter. 'Thanks for showing me this. It explains something. DCI Morgan from HQ – Major Crime Squad – has been on to the Prof, asking to get that hankie referred for exactly this treatment. Since it's going to put a big hole in the budget, the Prof wanted to know how he'd found out about it. He doesn't want every DC on the force digging out unsolved crimes from the last ten years and sending them up.'

'So they might get a result on this?'

'There's a fair chance. Ben was right. It would be good for this situation.' Jim shook his head. 'Can you believe it? Still on the case, even though he's dead!'

'He always was stubborn,' Marcie agreed.

'That reminds me,' Jim went on. 'They've finally released the body. Funeral's next Monday. Put the word round, will you? I'll go over the details later, but everyone needs to keep it clear.'

*

Ben's funeral turned out to be a bigger affair than Marcie had expected. The family – families, Ben had been divorced twice – had declined a funeral procession, but the service was held in St. Mary's, the largest church in the city. And it was packed. Not only all of City Scenes of Crime were present, but a surprising number of other SOCO's, even some from other Forces. Ben, if not exactly popular, proved to be surprisingly well known – and even respected. Marcie thought that that would be easier for those who didn't actually have to work with him, and then felt ashamed.

Nearly all the Force's senior officers were present, from the Chief Constable down, and all in full uniform. The Prof was there as well, and most of the Senior SOCO's. That was expected, but more remarkable were the numbers of reporters – even TV cameras from national stations – and members of public, all crammed into ancient wood pews between stained glass windows and dark panelled walls. The murder of a SOCO was still news, it seemed. It was a pity that there were no arrests to report. Officially the CID was 'following up leads'. Unofficially, the investigation had stalled. The word had gone around that they were *not* to talk to the press about it.

The formal service seemed to Marcie to be stilted, somehow unrelated to Ben Drummond, the nominal focus of it all. Her imagination tried to fit the real Ben, the man she'd known, into this context. The best she could manage was an untidy ghost who shambled in, snorted at the waste of time and money, and smirked sarcastically at the eulogy given by the Chief Constable.

Had Ben really been such a key figure in so many high priority investigations? Marcie knew he never cared much for 'wasting time' on low-level crime. She hadn't realised he put so much more effort into major crime – to hear the Chief, and then the Prof talk about him, half of the county's biggest cases had been solved with Ben's help.

Her eyes were drawn to the family pews, across the aisle from the SOCO's. There was a brother, a sister, several nieces and nephews, two ex-wives and an assortment of sons and daughters. Even a baby grandson. The only one who looked at all sad was a fifteen year old lad who kept wiping his eyes. According to talk in the office, he had been born after Ben's last marriage broke up, and had hardly known his father.

Marcie thought that that was the saddest part of the ceremony.

The service dragged to an end. The family went on to a private cremation. The Chief Constable and other officers followed them out. The public, reporters and cameras dispersed. In her mind, Marcie saw a big, shabby man scratch his bottom, spit on the floor, and slouch off for a pie and a pint.

'Bye, Ben,' she muttered.

*

The SOCO's met, by prior arrangement, in a city centre pub reputed to be one of Ben's favourite watering holes. Mac, hoping for a free drink to toast Ben's memory, explained the occasion to the barman. The barman presented him with Ben's unpaid tab.

That detail attended to, they took over a corner and sat down to swap stories. Doug looked mournfully at what remained in his wallet. 'I knew Ben liked a free drink, but I didn't think we'd still be paying for him. Mind you,' he went on, 'that's typical. He did a job at a pub one Sunday, and talked himself into a full lunch, roast beef, Yorkshires, potatoes and two veg. Sponge pudding and custard. Didn't pay a penny – and this was before he even did the job! Which only took him ten minutes. Wrote it up as a negative. Told me he'd only taken the job because he knew they did a good meal there!'

'He was a champion at getting something for nothing.' Marcie shook her head. 'I was out at a job with him once. He said to this woman who had just been burgled – she'd been telling us everything that had been taken – 'Did they take your kettle as well, luv?'

'No,' she told him.

'Good. You can make us a cup of tea.' Ben told her. She did as well! I couldn't believe his cheek.'

'I couldn't believe all that stuff the Chief said.' Ali (her hair appropriately black) settled back with her drink. 'I thought Ben spent more time avoiding jobs than doing them.'

'Oh, aye,' said Mac. 'It was true enough, when you cut through the bullshit. Ben wouldn't stir himself for a burglary – not without a direct order – but if there was something serious going on, he was your man.'

'He had an instinct for it,' put in Mike Vancy, a SOCO from South Division, and another contemporary of Ben and Mac. 'Remember that job down at The Carter's Arms, Mac?'

'Down in Obley, wasn't it?'

'That's the one.' Mike took a sip of his pint. 'Everyone took it to be an accident. Landlord's wife fell down the cellar steps, bashed her head in. No reason to suspect otherwise. Ben was only supposed to be there to photograph the scene, but he started looking around. Found a patch on the floor, near the billiards table, which looked a bit cleaner than the rest. Hunted a bit more, found a broken cue in the dustbin, with traces of blood still on it. Found the other half, with the landlord's fingerprints. Of course, the blood came back to the wife. Turned out that they'd had an argument, he'd hit her with the cue, then tossed her down the steps when he found she was dead. Cleaned up the blood patch near the billiards table, and thought he'd got away with it. Would have, except for Ben.'

'He wouldn't touch crap jobs, though, would he?' Doug said. 'Ever get him to go to an Attempted Burglary?' There were smiles and chuckles all round, recollecting the legendary three day battle Slippery Mick had had with Ben, trying to get him to do just that.

In the end, Doug had done it himself. 'If that was all that was on, he wouldn't stir out of the office. He'd rather sit in front of the screen, drinking tea and waiting for something worth his time to come up.'

'He was terrible for cherry-picking the good jobs,' Sanjay added. 'Sometimes he'd lift them from right under your nose. I went to a big break at a factory in South Herrick once. I'd taken it off the computer that morning, but I'd gone to City Hospital first for some urgent injury photos. When I got to the factory, I met Ben coming out, with an armful of exhibits!'

'What did you say?' asked Marcie.

'I said 'Ben, that was my job!' 'Not quick enough mate!' he said to me and went off laughing. Got some good identifications from it as well!'

'On the other hand....' Ali began. She stopped, and blushed as everyone looked at her. 'I know, I didn't get on with Ben any better than anyone. Worse, in fact. But, to set it straight, when you really needed help, he'd back you up.' She paused for a drink. 'When I was new on the job, I was doing a break at Market Green. Big house, ransacked, lots of stuff to look at. And I ran out of lifting tape, didn't I? No spare in my kit, none in my van. This was on a late shift, and the only person I could get hold of was Ben. He was at a job all the way over in Forest Heights: but he dropped everything, came over and bailed me out. Even stopped to help me with the job.' She smiled. 'Cursed me the whole time, though. Called me a woolly minded ... well you can guess! Never let me forget it, either!'

Marcie laughed with the rest of them. 'One thing, Ben would never run out of anything – not from what I found in his van! Enough to supply the whole department.' She went on to tell them about the file. 'He was persistent, wasn't he?'

Mac nodded. 'Never gave up on a job. Let's have a toast.' He lifted his pint. 'Ben – you were an obnoxious old bastard, and a pain in the neck to work with; but you were a heck of a good SOCO. And that's all you ever cared about anyhow.'

They all drank to that.

Mac

I'm finding nowadays that it takes me about four or five pints to remember Ben clearly. Which is a bit of a coincidence, because that's about what it used to take me to start liking him.

Everybody thinks that we were good mates, having been in the job together for so long. Truth was, Ben had no mates, and didn't want any. We used to go out drinking together, sure, but that only started after his second divorce. It was about the same time that my Alice passed on. I needed a bit of company, and he just liked to have someone to talk to. Or talk at. He wasn't much good at listening, but he did have a whole lot of stuff to unload.

So we used to go out for a few pints, and I'd listen while Ben moaned – about the weather, about politics, about sport, but mostly about work. Didn't have many interests or much life outside the job, and to hear him talk, he didn't even like the job much.

After four or five pints, I used to start feeling sorry for him. When I felt sorrier for him than I did for myself, that's when I liked him. Almost.

Ben wasn't always that bad. I remember when he started – always a bit intense, always keen to get a job wrapped up, but he was still married then, had wider interests. True, he had a sharp edge to him, dead sarcastic even when he was trying to be nice, but he wasn't as single-mindedly obnoxious as he became later.

I reckon he just started taking it too personally. It wasn't about getting 'Justice for the Victims' or about 'Making the Streets Safe'. For Ben, it was a contest, if not a war, between him and the offender(s). If he didn't get a result, it was like an insult. Perhaps even a threat. Whatever, he couldn't bear to think of them getting away with it. Dog with a bone didn't even come close.

It was a lesson to me, anyhow. After I'd got over Alice – as much as I ever could, or wanted to – I made sure I had some other things in life outside the job. Joined some clubs, got some hobbies. Didn't take my work home with me. Didn't go out drinking with Ben so often. Even with four or five pints, there was only so much of him I could take.

He was the best SOCO I've ever known. And the saddest man.

CHAPTER 6

Business picked up.

Mac proposed the theory that the local villains had returned from their holidays and were now busy working to pay for it. Whatever the cause, burglaries and car crime were increasing.

Marcie had a day dealing with cars. It brought to mind the missing TWOC'er: she wondered if that was a line of enquiry she could pursue. No obvious way came to mind, and Doug was firmly negative when she mentioned it to him.

'No way, Marcie! What the heck are you thinking of doing? Interviewing his car-nicking mates? Dammit, you're not CID!'

'OK – I know – but....'

'But nothing!' Doug shook his head. 'Marcie – you're getting too involved in this. And it's dangerous! You wouldn't want to run up against Maddox again, would you? And there are others out there just as bad. Start poking around on your own, asking questions....' He threw up his hands. 'I don't want to be visiting you in hospital to take pictures of your assault injuries!'

Marcie smiled. 'Glad to hear it! And thanks for your concern. Really.'

'So give it up, OK?'

'Ben didn't give up, did he? Remember some of those stories we swapped about him?'

'Yes. But you're not Ben. Thank goodness. And don't try to be him. For one thing, you'd have to put on about twenty stone!'

She patted her stomach, ruefully. 'I've made a start on it! But I get the point.'

Mac strolled into the office, whistling.

'You're cheerful!' Marcie observed. 'Spent the day in the pub?'

'Cheeky young lady... as a matter of fact, I've been up at HQ all day.'

'Ah, in the canteen, then!' Marcie winked at Doug.

'If you must know, I've been sorting exhibits for disposal, and it was not a pleasant job! You wouldn't believe the junk that was stored up there.' He gave Marcie a hard stare. 'Actually, you might, considering that a lot of it was yours!'

'Come off it Mac,' Doug put in. 'She's not been here that long!'

'No,' Mac agreed. 'Perhaps not – but you have, Doug, and I saw your name on some rubbish! What the heck did you recover a steering wheel for?'

'Oh. That.' Doug looked sheepish, with reason. Contrary to popular belief, steering wheels were not good sources of fingerprints. Even if the surface had been good in the first place, constant handling would quickly smear any marks. 'I remember that job. Not my fault, I had a DC breathing over my shoulder the whole time, saying 'Get that! Better have this! Take that, will you!' None of it ever got used, of course.'

Mac put on a sarcastic tone. 'Oh, the DC made you do it! But all the same, a steering wheel?'

'It was in the boot: the DC deduced that it had been moved, so he insisted. Anyhow, if you've had such a bad day, how come you're so cheerful?'

'Because I'm off for the next week, and I am going to spend a lot of it in the pub. Starting now, so I'll see you... oh, and not that you deserve it, Marcie, but I've got some mail for you.'

He tossed a manila envelope on her desk. She regarded it with suspicion.

'What's this – another urgent statement request?'

Mac shrugged. 'Couldn't say. Sam the Techie Man gave it me. Said you'd been waiting for it. Now, if you'll excuse me...' He walked off, whistling cheerfully.

Marcie didn't watch him go. She was too busy tearing open the envelope. A sheaf of 6x4 photographs fell out, with a note. She snatched it up.

'Marcie,

Sorry it's taken a while. As you see, we've managed to get some results, but not very good ones. As far as I can tell, the memory chips are undamaged, but the contacts were affected by smoke and heat. I cleaned them up as much as possible, but the images are badly degraded, and I suspect that there are a lot more that I couldn't recover at all.

There are techniques that would access the chips directly and would probably produce much better results. Unfortunately, we don't have the facilities to do this in-house. Submission to other labs would be possible, but expensive, and this would need approval from Professor Hubert-Hulme. To be frank, that's not likely to be forthcoming for a minor crime like TWOC. However, if you think you've got a case for submission, put it to him. I'll keep the card up here for the time being.

Regards, Sam.

Doug was hovering curiously over her shoulder. She handed him the memo without comment, and spread the photos out on the desk.

There were six of them. She picked up the first and examined it.

'Doesn't look like much.' Doug commented.

Out of a mottled grey background, an oblong shape loomed. 'Could be a block of flats?' Marcie suggested. 'Or an office block. Perhaps.'

Doug shrugged. 'Or a Lego brick. There's nothing to give scale.'

'But it's some sort of building, don't you think?' Marcie persisted hopefully.

'Maybe.'

'Be positive, Doug. Look, this one's better. Definitely a street, somewhere.'

'In a fog, apparently.'

Marcie frowned at him. 'What did I just say about positive? You can see some houses there – quite large ones – and isn't that a car?'

'Or a van. A red one.' Doug produced a magnifying glass, and studied the picture closely. 'I think it could be a Post Office van.'

'See – that's something identifiable.'

'Oh sure! Now we know it's a street with a postal service! Narrows it down to somewhere in the UK!'

'You're no help at all! What about the houses?'

Doug nodded sagely. 'You're right, Marcie. They are houses. Apart from that....'

Marcie sighed. 'OK, let's look at the others.'

It didn't take long. Of the remaining four, two might have been large houses, or possibly the same house from different angles. Another was an ornate set of iron gates, with an indistinct background. The final photo showed a cluster of low buildings behind some trees. That was the best quality picture, and as Doug gloomily pointed out, it was none too good. 'I don't think we've got enough there to identify any locations, Marcie.'

She shook her head in frustration. 'But it must mean something! Why all these photographs of buildings? What was Maddox up to?'

'Perhaps he's moving into real estate?' Doug caught her look, and held up his hands. 'OK, sorry, Marcie. But what did you expect? A picture of Maddox standing over a body with a gun in his hands?'

She laughed. 'Point taken. But let's not give up yet. Is there any way we can enhance these?'

'I'm sure Sam would have done his best on that already.'

'Could we get a licence number for that postie van?'

'Not a hope.'

'I can try.' Marcie went to her case, rummaged round and produced a fingerprint glass. This was a small, powerful, magnifying glass, mostly used by fingerprint experts for detailed examination of recovered marks. It was mounted in a stand that kept it at an optimum distance from the subject.

'I never use those things,' Doug said. 'Every mark I ever found looked crap under that amount of magnification!'

'Every mark you ever found *was* crap!' Marcie retorted. She put the glass on the photo, and peered hopefully. 'Dammit!'

Doug smiled happily. 'I don't usually say 'I told you so', but after your last remark, I can't help myself! Nothing there, I assume?'

'Just magnified blur.' Marcie agreed ruefully.

'I told you so.'

'I hate it when you're right.'

'You should be used to it. And I don't think you'll get much from the others, either.' Doug paused, and picked up the one with the gate. 'Hang on though – try this one.'

Marcie took the photo. 'What am I looking for?'

'Just to the side of the gate. There's a bit of the wall that looks different. Flatter, perhaps? Could be a notice board?'

Not daring to be hopeful, Marcie looked. 'Hmm – I think you're right. There's writing on it... but the contrast's lousy. I think the first letter might be an 'S'. Then there's a gap – and that could be a 'C'.'

'Is that all?'

'The rest is in lower case. There's another line underneath, though. Two words. Beginning with upper case again... could be a 'C' or a 'G'. The other one's an 'A', I think.'

Doug frowned, thinking hard. 'S – C? How many letters?'

She peered at it again. 'Looks like there might be one, after the 'S'. Then a space. Not sure how many after the 'C'.'

'Could it be 'S' – small 't'? As in Saint something?'

Marcie nodded. 'Yes! That would work! A church?'

'There's a St Cuthbert's in Herrick.'

She took another look. 'I don't think so. It looks too short for 'Cuthbert's'.'

'St Cyril's? St Cedric's?'

'Perhaps. What about the 'C-A' or 'G-A'?'

He shrugged. 'Sorry, I never was any good at crosswords.'

Marcie pondered. 'If that second 'C' is 'Church' – what's the 'A'.'

'Church 'All?' Doug ducked as Marcie threw a pen at him. 'Sorry, but this is just off the top of my head, you know.'

'More like the bottom of the barrel. Now think... suppose the second 'C' is 'Catholic'?'

'Catholic Association?'

'*Much* better! See, you can do it if you try!'

Encouraged, Doug bent over the photo and looked through the glass. 'Perhaps the second line is an address?' he suggested. 'May be it's something like 'St Cedric's, Colton Abbot?'

'Is there a St Cedric's in Colton Abbot?'

'I don't even know if there's a Colton Abbot!' Doug confessed. 'Face it, Marcie, we're reaching a bit here. And it's getting late. I'm afraid I've got to leave you to it – I'm on call tonight, I need to get home for a shower and a bite to eat in case things turn nasty.'

'Oh heck – you're right, look at the time, this'll cost me a fortune in childminder overtime. But think about it, OK?'

'Sure. See you tomorrow.' Doug was already heading out of the door.

In spite of the time, Marcie lingered a moment, casting another glance over the photos. Perhaps John could work out how to enhance them? He certainly had access to more computer power and expertise at his workplace than she did at hers.

On second thoughts, taking exhibits home was a good way to lose her job. In fact, considering that she'd told Maddox the card had been destroyed, just having the photographs put her on thin ice. Best not to push it.

She slipped the photos back into the envelope, dropped it in her drawer, and left.

As feared, she was seriously late picking up the kids. It earned Marcie a raised eyebrow from Julie – which was a mild reaction considering how often it was happening. The tension between child care and work demands was the hardest part of the job. If anything caused her to give up being a SOCO that would probably be it. She got off less lightly with a very tired Kady, who had an uncharacteristic tantrum as she was strapped into her child seat. It left Marcie feeling ready for a tantrum herself – restrained mostly by the knowledge that it was her fault.

It was a dark, drizzly evening, and the journey home was fraught with heavy traffic and sibling warfare in the back seat. Marcie braced herself for a sharp words from John about her lateness. Instead he had hugs, kisses, and the kids tea all ready.

'Thanks, love. I do appreciate this!' she told him as he loaded the dishwasher. He'd been unusually tolerant and easy-going lately. The pressure was off at work, and he was riding high on a crest of senior management approval and junior staff admiration.

'No problem.' He smiled at her. 'But, thing is, Marcie, I've got to go out again.'

She raised an eyebrow. 'Ah, so all this was just a softening up exercise? Keep the little woman sweet?'

He looked embarrassed. 'Well, not really, it's more like...'

She laughed. 'Stop squirming, John. It's fine by me – go out every night if you have to, just as long as you pay your dues in advance.'

'Oh – really?'

'Well, maybe not every night. What is it, a meeting?'

'More of a celebration.' He noted that Marcie had raised the eyebrow again. 'Things are on a bit a roll, since we cracked that last little problem. There's some new development contracts in the pipeline, and some of the people at work thought it was time we – ah – celebrated. I would have taken you along, of course, but it's a bit impromptu. It was only decided this afternoon, and there was no time to get a baby sitter.'

She shrugged. 'OK. I wouldn't enjoy it much anyway, sitting listening to you talking shop. Once you start getting technical I can't understand one word in ten!'

'Right. Good. I'll get going then.'

'Ah, not quite just yet... if you're off to celebrate, you can do the bedtime stories first! Deal?'

He grinned. 'You drive a hard bargain! OK, as long as Kady doesn't want 'Princess Tootles' again. I know every word off by heart!'

'She always wants 'Princess Tootles', you know that. Fortunately for you, she's nearly asleep already. I'll put her to bed, you see to Rory. He'll want something you'll appreciate – he's into that 'Digital Dragons' series just now.'

'Digital Dragons?' John's face brightened with interest.

Three quarters of an hour later, and after reading two chapters more than Rory's normal bedtime allocation, John finally left for his celebration. With the kids asleep and the house to herself, Marcie contemplated mixed motivations. She might have felt slightly resentful of John, rushing out to celebrate without her, but she was also relieved that they hadn't had a renewed argument over her job and being late home. Especially as she was still feeling guilty about that. It hadn't been fair on Kady to let her get so tired. Or on Julie, for that matter.

Apart from which, she had thought of something else she could do with the evening. Not bringing her work home exactly – but it would be better done without John around. No point in stretching his new tolerance too far.

She went into the study, and switched on the PC. It was a top-of-the range model, as befitted someone in John's line of work, but it hardly got used nowadays. John tended to use the more high-tech equipment at the office, or his laptop. Marcie didn't have his fascination for gadgets. She could use a computer when she had to, but didn't think of it as fun.

She went on-line, opened Google, and tried a search on St. C. It brought back over ninety five million results: and a brief scan of the first few pages showed nothing that looked helpful. After pondering for a moment, she ran the search again, restricting it to UK websites. This reduced it to around seven million. A move in the right direction, she thought. But there were a depressing number of false leads and irrelevant hits. A surprising number of them had no obvious connection with any Saints at all.

She spent a frustrating hour trying to refine her search to give her what she wanted, without any significant success. John, of course, would have known exactly how to tweak it. He'd have found what she wanted in ten minutes. But John was off out celebrating.

She sat back, yawning. Another approach was needed. She thought for a while, then put in a search on St Cedric. And then on St Cyrus. Lots of sites. None of value.

In desperation she ran a search on 'Saints', and learned a great deal about Southampton Football Club. Various other clubs and institutions came up, but none of any relevance. Eventually, however, she ran across a list of various Christian Saints, and this gave her new ammunition.

Many of the St. C's were too long – Cuthbert, Cyprian (either of Bulgaria or Carthage), Clement and Columba. St Clare (of Assisi, like St Francis) was more hopeful, but a long search produced nothing definite.

Marcie's eyes were aching, as was her back and her wrist. She glanced at the clock: it was nearly ten. 'Enough of this!' she said to herself. 'I'll try one more Saint, then I'm off to bed.'

St. Celia, she decided. It was about the right length.

St Celia, she learned, was the mother of St Gregory. Purcell had written an Ode for St Celia's day. Britten had written a 'Hymn to St Celia'.

And somewhere in North London was St Celia's Girls Academy.

By the time she found it, Marcie was in a mentally numb state: her finger's moved automatically, taking her past the reference and on to the next page before it penetrated.

'S – C – G – A?'

Suddenly awake she clicked back, and searched the page frantically.

It was a reference from a site on architecture – specifically, great British buildings which the author thought should be owned by the National Trust, or similar.

'A wonderful example of a late eighteenth century building on the grand scale', the author enthused, 'with particularly fine additions from the early nineteenth century. Set in extensive grounds, it was built as a home for the wealthy Buscombe family and was sold when their fortunes failed in the Depression of the nineteen thirties. Currently it is an extremely exclusive girls' school, and as such access for the public is almost non-existent. I myself was roughly handled whilst merely taking a few photographs for the benefit of all those with an interest in architecture! It is scandalous that such a national treasure should be restricted to such a small minority of staff and students...'

The writer continued to vent his indignation for several paragraphs. Marcie was more interested in the small collection of photographs. The building was indeed impressive, but unfortunately none of them showed the gates.

She printed out the article and the pictures, and switched off. Stood up and stretched. Every muscle ached, but she was smiling. It was a step forward. Just a small one – she could already anticipate Doug's scepticism – but it was going in the right direction. Finally.

*

Driving to work next morning, Marcie rehearsed answers to Doug's most likely objections.

'Q: What possible link could there be between a girls' school in London and a burnt out Cavalier in Faringham?'

'A: That's just the point! There isn't any obvious connection, so it's suspicious!'

'Q: What if there is a legitimate connection?'

'A: Name one first, and I'll think about the 'what if'.'

'Q: Can you name any illegal connections, then?'

'A: Checking out burglary targets?'

'Q: Isn't that a bit speculative?'

'A. Sure it is. So what? It's possible.'

'Q: But how do you even know that that photo is of this girls' school? It's not clear enough to be sure.'

'A: Agreed, but it's the best lead I've got yet. And I'm working on it!'

Rehearsed and confident, Marcie marched briskly into the office. Only to find her effort wasted. Doug was off sick. And Sanjay had been sent to help with a major incident on South Division, which left a big workload for the rest of the shift. Marcie was itching to get the photos out of her drawer for another look, but Slippery Mick was hanging around the office, making sure everyone looked busy. The last thing she wanted was awkward questions from that source. She put together a job sheet, and headed for South Herrick. Hopefully, Mick would be out of the way when she got back.

As it happened, he was, but she still wasn't able to follow up on St Celia's Girls Academy. A straightforward attempted car-theft suddenly got more complicated, when the owner happened to mention, in passing, the knife he'd found nearby.

'Wasn't sure if it was connected, because it wasn't actually on my drive – just out in the street. Saw it when I went looking for whoever set the car alarm off. Thing is, though, it's got blood on it, and there weren't any blood on the car.'

Marcie had just come from examining blood stains at a pub three streets away, where a fight outside had apparently involved a knife – but none had been found. Making the connection brought her effusive thanks from the Detective Sergeant on the case, but sorting it all out took time. And she couldn't afford to run late again.

Ah, well, she thought, it's not been a bad day for all that... try again tomorrow.

The kids – picked up, taken home and fed on schedule – were more tractable than the previous night. Moreover, John showed his gratitude for being allowed off the leash by going above and beyond the call of duty. He not only read three more chapters of 'Digital Dragons' for Rory, but even read 'Princess Tootles' to Kady.

'That makes it about ninety times she's heard that story,' he told Marcie. He pointed out the five bar gates that he had been marking on the inside of the back cover. There wasn't much room left. 'Doesn't she ever get tired of it?'

'It's probably twice that number. I don't bother keeping track. And no, she doesn't get tired of it. Maybe in another six months. Or a year!'

Marcie was feeling relaxed and comfortable, in spite of the day's frustrations. But as John continued to bustle around – loading the dishwasher again, wiping the table, pouring her a glass of wine and being generally attentive, her suspicions were aroused. This might be more than just his way of saying thank you.

'Darling,' he said as he sat down beside her on the sofa, 'did you have any special plans for the weekend?'

Marcie, suspicions confirmed, turned to him and raised an eyebrow. 'Well, that depends.'

'Only, they're doing a big product launch for SuperScan. Saturday evening. Major publicity thing, big hotel, lots of top names, people from big organisations, Government as well. And they want me there. After all, it's largely my project.'

'Of course.'

'And the invitation is for wives and partners as well.'

'Ha! I knew that was where you were going!'

John gave her a pained smile. 'Please Marcie, hear me out. This is important! It goes well with the corporate image. They want to see you there. And there'll be a bit of a party as well. It could be fun!' he added hopefully.

Marcie gave him an irritated glance, only a degree or two short of a glare. 'Like I told you last night, John, mixing with people I don't know, talking about things I don't understand over fancy drinks I don't like isn't my idea of fun!'

'It won't be just shop talk. There'll be entertainment as well. And some really important people.'

She snorted. 'I don't give a stuff about 'important people'. It's not my thing, John. Go if you have to, I understand that, but don't drag me along as the token wife!'

'Please Marcie. I'd really like you to be there. Not as a token wife. Honestly, I'd enjoy it a lot more myself if you were with me.' He peered earnestly into her eyes.

Softening a little, she smiled. 'You're a sweet talker when you want something! But I can't, anyway. I'm on call Saturday.'

He groaned. 'Can't you get out of it? I thought we'd take the kids down, make a weekend of it. The hotel has childcare facilities, all laid on at company expense. And we could go early, show them London!'

A relay clicked in Marcie's head. 'It's in London?'

'Yes. Didn't I say?'

'Ah. Well, I suppose if I did a shift for someone on Friday, when I'm supposed to be off, they'd cover for me on Saturday.'

John's face lit up. 'Brilliant! Thanks. Marcie – you're wonderful!'

She nodded wisely. 'Very true. Bear it in mind. And how had you planned to travel down?'

'I thought we'd take the train.'

'Can we drive down?'

'I suppose so. Why?'

Marcie shrugged. 'You've got that huge great BMW, but you always drive on your own. It'd be nice to give the other seats some use! And perhaps we can take the scenic route?'

John shrugged. He wasn't well placed to argue the point, after all. 'Certainly, love. Whatever you want!'

The following morning, Marcie continued to make use of her strong domestic position by getting John to take the kids to Julie's. She left early and got to the office before anyone else. In particular, before Jim. She was aware that she was now working to a tight schedule. She needed to find out more about St Celia's before the weekend.

Unfortunately, St Celia's was not forthcoming with information. She'd already established that if it had a website, it wasn't listed on any search engine she knew of. She now discovered that it didn't have a telephone number either, unless it was ex-directory.

The architectural enthusiast's website had described it as 'North London, near Epping Forest.' She thought that that might put it in the Metropolitan Police area.

A little research put it near Chingford, just inside the M25. A call to the Faringham Police switchboard got her a connection to the Met's main switchboard, who put her through to Tarford Police

Station, who re-directed her to a local station, where the desk clerk (after a short delay) put her on to a PC who knew the area.

'Hello. June Cheston. How can I help?'

Brisk, but friendly, Marcie thought.

'Hi. Marcie Kelshaw – Faringham Scenes of Crime. I'm trying to find out about a place called St Celia's Girls Academy – do you know it?'

Laughter. 'I know *of* it, certainly. Can't say that I *know* it though. Not likely to, either, unless I win the lottery – on a big rollover!'

'Yes – I got the impression it was a bit exclusive!'

'Absolutely,' June agreed. 'It caters exclusively for daughters of the super-rich, the ultra-rich, and the filthy-rich. If you have to ask how much, you can't afford it.' She paused. 'But what's the connection with Faringham?'

The question wasn't hostile, Marcie thought. But professionally suspicious, and perfectly reasonable. If it was connected with her beat, June wanted to know what was going on. Any copper would. She decided to tell her as much as she could.

'I recovered some photographs from a stolen car. One of them seems to show the entrance to St Celia's. We believe the owner of the car may be involved in various crimes. I'm trying to find out if anything's happened at the school which may be connected.'

'I see.' June paused for a moment. 'Well – I'm afraid you're going to have problems with that. It's rather difficult to find out anything about St Celia's.'

'I know it's exclusive,' said Marcie, slightly puzzled. 'but there must be some contact with them.'

'Remarkably little, I'm afraid. The thing is, the enormous fees at St Celia's are for more than just good teaching and facilities. They also pay for privacy. They've got their own security staff, a lot of them ex-army. Very serious people, if you get my drift? And they do not encourage outsiders! The rich and famous don't want their daughters bothered by paparazzi, or fortune-hunters – or the police.'

'But if a crime was committed, surely they'd report it?'

'Hmm. Maybe. In theory. In practice, though, it hasn't worked out that way. For example... about six months ago, we had someone come into the station here, complaining that he'd been robbed and assaulted at St Celia's. I went over there with him to sort it out. Turned out that he'd been trespassing. He was some sort of architecture nut, and he'd sneaked in to take pictures of their buildings. Security found him, took his camera and tossed him out. Not very gently either. But they didn't call us. Even with me there, they didn't want to talk about it, and they wouldn't let us any further in than the gatehouse. In the end, he got agreed not to pursue the matter, they returned his camera and made no charges against him.'

Marcie thought of the website that had led her to St Celia's. She now understood the author's attitude.

'Anyhow,' June continued 'I haven't heard anything, but that's not significant. I'll ask around, but I doubt if anyone else here has either.'

'Thanks.' A thought struck Marcie. 'Don't these people have any contact with the outside world?'

'Not a lot. It's not quite a prison, but they keep themselves to themselves. The girls are allowed out locally, and further afield on organised trips, but their security keeps an eye on things there as well. The locals are all on their side, because St Celia's pays to keep them that way. They're a close-mouthed bunch anyway, and they definitely won't discuss the school.'

'I see. You wouldn't have a telephone number would you? There's nothing listed.'

'No, there wouldn't be. I asked for a number when I was there, in case any follow up was needed. They gave me the switchboard number, but I think it's manned by security. I've never got beyond the operator, even when I'm warning them about local crime waves!'

There was a brief pause, accompanied by the sound of paper shuffling, before June came back with the number and, after a further request from Marcie, directions.

'The main gate's about half-a-mile down the road from a pub – 'The Green Man'. On your left if you're going in towards London,' she concluded. 'Best of luck. And if you do come up with anything...'

'Of course. I'll let you know. Thanks again.'

Marcie hung up, and sat back, thinking.

The office was filling up now, as the rest of the shift drifted in. Doug sat down at the desk opposite, and raised an interrogative eyebrow.

'I've tracked it down!' Marcie informed him smugly. 'S-C-G-A: St Celia's Girls Academy. Just north of London. Very expensive, very exclusive girls' public school.' She went on to summarise her conversation with PC Cheston.

'Mmm – yes, good work, Marcie.' Doug said, hesitantly. 'But, you know this doesn't prove that the photo is of this place? And even if it is, what possible connection...'

'Don't bother, Doug. We've already had this conversation.' Marcie sat back and enjoyed his puzzlement.

'We have? When? I was off all day yesterday.'

'I know. Don't worry, I took your part for you, and you agreed it was worth pursuing. How are you, by the way?'

'Fine. Just some twenty four hour bug I picked up from the kids. Thanks for covering for me!'

'No problem. Is Mick in yet?'

'Gone to HQ.' Sanjay called from the other side of the office. 'Seniors meeting. Back lunchtime.'

'Good! Then I've got time for another phone call.' Marcie took a breath, gathered her thoughts, and dialled the number that June had given her.

'St. Celia's Girls Academy. How can I help you?'

The male voice that answered was calm but expressionless. Unreadable. Polite, but not going to go out of his way to be helpful, thought Marcie. She sensed that this might be uphill work.

'I'd like to speak to the Head Teacher, please.' She did her best to sound confident and authoritative.

'That's not possible.' No apologies, excuses or exclamations, Marcie noted. 'If you want to leave a message, I'll see that it's passed on. Or if you state the nature of your business, perhaps I can help you.'

'Who am I talking to?'

'Duty Security Officer. And you are?'

'Faringham Police, Scenes Of Crime.' If you don't have a name, I don't, Marcie thought.

'I need a name.'

OK, she decided, I'll try a trade. 'Marcie Kelshaw. And your name is?'

'What is the nature of your enquiry?'

Not playing fair! The Security Officer's manner made her feel defensive and off-balance. She'd hoped to get beyond the switchboard operator, but it didn't seem likely to happen. She pressed on.

'Have there been any suspicious events at St Celia's lately?'

'No.'

The flat, unhesitating answer left no room for doubt and discouraged further enquiry. But she wasn't ready to give up just yet.

'Anyone found trespassing? Any unusual activity in the area? Anyone seen taking photographs of the premises?'

'Nothing of that nature.'

Nervous and needing answers, Marcie felt her patience slipping. 'Well, Mr Duty Security Officer, perhaps you'd better put me on to someone who might have more knowledge. Can I speak to your supervisor?'

'Not available. I assure you, there has been no incidents of such a nature at St. Celia's, and nothing that would involve the police.'

'Really?' Time to play her trump card. 'Are you sure about that? Because St. Celia's has not always been very good at reporting such things, has it?'

There was a pause. 'What's that supposed to mean?' For the first time, the security officer sounded a little less sure of himself.

'There was an incident at St Celia's – a photographer in your grounds? Who had to go to the police to get his camera back? The incident you didn't report? Are you aware of it or do I need to speak to someone else after all?'

There was another pause, but when the security officer spoke again he was once more relaxed and confident. 'That was hardly recent, and was satisfactorily dealt with by the local police. I don't see what connection it has with Faringham.'

Marcie felt herself back on the defensive: her counter-attack had run out of ammunition.

'We are pursuing enquiries,' she said carefully 'in which a possible link with St Celia's has been established.'

'What link is that? What crime is involved?'

'At this stage, we can't be certain,' she admitted. 'But it is possible that certain criminal elements here have shown an interest in St Celia's.'

'Well, that's a little vague, isn't it?' The security officer sounded amused. 'And if this is an active investigation, how come inquiries are being made by Scenes Of Crime? Perhaps you do things differently in Faringham, but in most forces it would be a matter for C.I.D. So what exactly is your involvement, Ms. Kelshaw?'

With a sinking feeling, Marcie realised that she'd overplayed her hand. This security officer knew quite well how police forces operated, and what the proper remit of a SOCO was. Very likely he was an ex-copper himself: which left Marcie out on a limb, and feeling somewhat foolish.

'Things haven't reached that stage yet,' she answered, with as much confidence as she could muster. 'I'm simply following up on evidence I recovered from a crime scene. I want to confirm the link to St Celia's before I pass it on to C.I.D.' Which might sound plausible, to anyone who didn't know about normal police practices. 'So, has there been any suspicious or unusual activity at St Celia's lately?'

'As I said before, no, there hasn't. And I would suggest, Ms Kelshaw, that if you have any information regarding criminal activities you should pass it on to the appropriate department. So that a competent investigation can be carried out.'

He hung up, without the courtesy of a goodbye.

'Patronising git!' Marcie snarled, slamming down the phone.

'Not good, then?' asked Doug.

Reluctantly, Marcie relayed the gist of the conversation to him.

'Ouch!' he winced as she finished. 'Put down by a security officer! Rude of him, but...'

'If you dare say 'he's got a point', I'll ram this phone down your throat! Then I'll dial his number so he can listen to you choke! A lesson for you and a warning for him!'

Doug clamped his mouth firmly shut, and with a helpless shrug, left the office.

Marcie sat back, replaying the conversation. She'd made a fool of herself, going in to it without thinking it through and not really knowing what she was after. But perhaps there had been something?

Just for a moment, the security officer had sounded a little off balance. Worried, even.

It had been when she suggested that St Celia's didn't report things that they should. When she'd gone on to talk about the photographer, the security officer had been back in control. Because he'd known, then, that she was on the wrong track.

But that implied that there was a right track.

It was tenuous. Far too faint a clue to mention, even to Doug. But Marcie felt certain. 'Something has happened at St Celia's,' she said quietly. 'And they're keeping it to themselves.'

CHAPTER 7

'It's hard to believe that there's this much green inside the M25.'

'I know.' Marcie agreed. 'There are suburbs just a few miles in every direction, but we could be right out in the country.'

An overcast day, but unusually mild for the time of year, with an occasional flicker of watery sunlight leaking through the clouds. John was driving the BMW, Rory and Kady were fast asleep in the back. They were on a narrow road, following the winding course of a small river. Beyond the river on their right were fields and grazing horses, on their left rose a wooded hillside.

'I don't know why you chose this route,' John continued, 'but it's certainly an improvement on the motorway.'

'I thought it would make a change,' Marcie agreed – not without a twinge of guilt at her deception. 'Left at the next junction, I think.'

After the turn, they passed a small group of houses and 'The Green Man' pub. To Marcie's relief, this matched the directions she'd been given by PC Cheston. A few minutes later they were driving alongside a high brick wall on their left. St Celia's outer perimeter, thought Marcie.

'I wonder what's behind that wall?' John mused. 'Whatever it is, they don't want trespassers. See those black globes?'

'Like that one?' About a foot in diameter, they stood several feet above the wall on metal poles, at fifty yard intervals.

'Yep. That's top-of-the-line, state-of-the-art, security surveillance. Proteus Systems Series Fifty. Digital CCTV, infra-red, microwave movement sensors, automated tracking... if they've got the full system installed, there'll be pressure sensitive strips along the walls, and a linked access control for all the doors and windows. It's the most advanced security system on the market. So sensitive, you can set it to tell you every time a fly crosses the wall.'

'How come you know so much about it?'

CAN OF WORMS

John looked smug. 'We wrote the control software for it. Or rather, re-wrote it. The prototype system was too sensitive. It really did tell you every time a fly came in range! Lots of false alarms. And the links to the access controls didn't work either, so you could enter legitimately and still set off the alarm.'

'So they came to you?'

'That's it. They'd tried to do it all in-house, but then ran up against a deadline and needed some specialist help. So we sorted out the link problem, and then built in an image database with a recognition and learning package which...'

'OK, enough!' Marcie interrupted. 'You're about to slip from impressive to boring!'

John laughed. 'Alright! Anyhow, the point is, it's a very expensive system. We looked at using it ourselves, but couldn't afford it! So whoever this place belongs to is seriously well off – and possibly a touch paranoid.'

'Looks like an entrance coming up.' Marcie pointed along the road, trying to hide her tension. 'Slow down a bit as we go past – perhaps we can see what the place is.'

John obediently dropped down to a sedate thirty, then to a crawl as the wall pulled back from the road. A short driveway led to a closed iron gate that looked both elegant and strong. It was flanked by squat stone towers, each topped by a Proteus globe. Behind the gates a tall man in a maroon jacket stood watching them.

It was nothing like the blurry picture from the flash card.

Marcie sank back in her seat, disappointment flooding through her.

'Well that's a surprise,' said John.

'What is?' Marcie asked, without much interest.

'So much security for a girls' school.' John glanced at her, as he sped up again. 'Didn't you see the sign?'

Marcie shook her head. 'No – I was looking at the gate.'

'It was at the road end of the drive – quite small, actually. Discreet. They don't want visitors and they don't need to advertise.'

'What did it say?' she asked, already knowing.

'St Celia's Girls Academy. Never heard of it, but the fees must be sky-high if they've got Proteus Fifty fully installed! Why would they need it? Girls sneaking out at night to visit their boyfriends? Or super-rich parents afraid their girls will get kidnapped for ransom?'

Marcie sat bolt upright. '*What* did you say?'

John looked at her in surprise. 'Only that it's hard to see why they'd need so much security at a girls' school. They even had a live security guard at the gate – or that's what he looked like.'

Marcie's head was whirling. 'Rich kids get kidnapped, don't they?'

'So I hear. But that's more your area than mine!'

She rubbed her eyes, and grabbed at another thought as it tried to slip by. 'Do you think that there might be another entrance?'

'Well, I'd expect so.' John gave her a puzzled glance. 'A place this size has probably got a side entrance for tradesmen. Why?'

Marcie shrugged. 'No particular reason. Slow down again, I think we're coming into a village.'

A picturesque group of cottages clustered round a small green, with a church on one side and 'The Oak Leaf' pub conveniently opposite. The effect was somewhat spoiled by the broad plate glass windows of a mini-supermarket and post office next to the pub. The main road took a leisurely turn round the green and carried on south. A side road ran off to the left, flanking The Oak Leaf.

'Stop here a moment, please John,' Marcie asked.

'What for?' He pulled in to the side.

'Admiring the view.' Wondering if that side road ran past St Celia's southern boundary.

'It's straight on to London,' John said, pointing out the signpost.

'What's down there to the left?'

'St Celia's side gate.'

Marcie looked up in astonishment. 'Does it say that?'

'No. But there's a giggle of girls in a rather smart maroon uniform coming down from that direction. Elementary, my dear Watson!'

Marcie's view up the lane was obscured by foliage, but a moment later she saw what John had seen. About half-a-dozen girls, looking to be aged from twelve to sixteen, and all identically dressed, were walking down towards the green.

'So they are allowed out, then,' John said. 'But only on a short leash. Here come the minders!'

Two adults, a man and a woman, were following the group. They were also wearing maroon jackets, but without the gold badges Marcie could now see on the girls.

Leaving the lane, the schoolgirls went across the front of the pub and into the shop. The woman followed them; the man stayed outside, and stood where he could see the whole green. He gave their BMW a long stare.

'Whoops, I think we've been clocked,' said John lightly. 'A bit overprotective, aren't they?'

'More than a bit,' Marcie agreed. June Cheston had said something about the pupils being allowed out locally, but she hadn't mentioned the security presence. 'Isn't that a radio he's holding?'

'To call in reinforcements?' John speculated. 'In case the girls start a fight in the post office?'

A big Mercedes 4x4 came down the road from behind them. It slowed right down as it passed them. The windows were heavily tinted, so Marcie couldn't see the occupants – but she felt sure they'd got a good look at them.

'I think the reinforcements just arrived,' she said.

The Merc – no insignia, but the same familiar shade of St Celia's maroon – parked in front of the pub. The man in front of the shop walked over to the driver's door. The window slid down, revealing the driver to be a man in dark glasses and the expected maroon jacket. They exchanged a few words and both looked at Marcie and John.

'This is weird,' John muttered. 'I feel like a suspect or something. Can we get out of here, Marcie?'

'OK. Go left, up that lane.'

He gave her a startled look. 'Why?'

She grinned. 'I just want to rattle their chain!'

John shook his head. 'What are you like... OK then. If they pull out pistols and open fire, let your last thought be of me saying 'I told you so!"

He pulled away, indicated left and headed up the lane. In a few moments they had past the last houses, and St Celia's wall – marked as such by the now familiar black globes of the Proteus Fifty – came up on their left.

John glanced in his mirror. 'We're being followed,' he announced.

Marcie looked back. The Merc was coming up the lane behind them. Not trying to catch up, but staying in sight.

'I hope we don't meet another of them,' she said. 'There's no room to pass.'

'That had occurred to me as well,' John agreed. 'Cheerful thought. Have your phone handy in case we need to call the police.'

'You're joking?' Marcie asked hopefully.

'Almost certainly.' John didn't sound worried, but he was frowning as he looked in the mirror again. 'I'm sure they're just being very careful, but it's disconcerting to have so much attention, just for driving past. Ah – look, another gate. That answers your earlier question.'

Marcie crossed her fingers, then breathed a quiet sigh of relief as they passed. John hadn't slowed down this time – Marcie hadn't even thought of asking him to – but the glimpse was sufficient: it was clearly the same as the flash card image. She'd even seen the sign set in the wall. All the words she'd puzzled over were now clear and obvious – 'St Celia's Girls Academy'.

It was confirmation that she had the right place. Maddox had been here, had driven along this lane. A disquieting thought.

About half-a-mile from the village, the road angled away to the right, leaving St Celia's behind.

'Our shadow has stopped.' John sounded a touch relieved.

'Seen us off the premises,' Marcie commented. 'No problem here, just two lost tourists.'

They reached a main road, and turned towards London.

'Enough exciting detours, Marcie,' John pleaded. 'Let's just get to the hotel, alright?'

'Works for me,' she agreed. She'd found out what she'd wanted to know. and more besides. The level of security at St Celia's was far beyond what she'd expected, and supported her suspicions that something had happened there.

Moreover, John's chance remark had opened up a whole new area for consideration. Kidnapping? It certainly fitted with the Maddoxes interest in a school for girls. Girls with excessively rich parents.

If St Celia's *had* had a girl go missing, that would explain their paranoid level of security. But was it credible?

Marcie frowned to herself as she thought it through. Even given the school's reluctance to talk to anyone, something as serious as a kidnapping *must* have been reported! If not by the school, then by the parents. She couldn't imagine that they wouldn't tell them.

Perhaps there had been a failed attempt?

Or perhaps there had been a successful kidnap, which was now being investigated with utmost secrecy. That could make sense. Marcie knew that such operations were handled by special police units, and kept as low-key as possible.

She could now put together a pretty good picture of what might have happened, but frustratingly nothing could be proved. Like the flash card image, the vital parts were fuzzy.

John's laugh broke her train of thought. 'What?' she asked.

'I think I've just figured out how that place can afford so many Proteus Fifties.'

'Well, it is a rich school, for rich people's daughters.'

'Even so, if they've got the scanners all round the perimeter, as seems likely – and it's a good size perimeter – the cost would be astronomical. And that many security staff as well? But – perhaps they got a discount.'

'How?'

They were entering suburban London now, and traffic was building. John was silent for a moment, as he made a late lane change, and then stopped at a red light.

'The boss of Proteus Systems' he said, looking across at her, 'Is Brian Reardon. Heard of him?'

Marcie frowned. 'Is that *Sir* Brian Reardon?'

'As of the last honours list, yes. Knighted for services to industry. Or contributions to the Government's last election campaign, if you're a cynic.'

'Surely not!' exclaimed Marcie in horror. 'The lights have changed.'

'As I said,' John continued, driving on, 'only a cynic would make such an allegation. But, the point is, Sir Brian is the sort of person who likes to show off his success. Get into conversation with him, and the topic will be his houses – Sussex, Scotland, France, and probably one or two other places by now. And he'll also want to tell you about his yacht, his cars, his racehorses... and his knighthood, of course.'

'What an interesting man!'

John snorted. 'He could bore for England. His only subject is 'me, and how well I'm doing'. Except that, rumour has it, he isn't doing as well as all that. Some of his businesses – he owns more than just Proteus – are struggling, and those campaign contributions were *huge*. Allegedly! Not that that would slow him down. For Brian Reardon, keeping up appearances is everything.'

'I spend, therefore I am?'

'Pretty much. But, here's the point. He has two daughters. And it would be typical of him to have them in the most expensive, exclusive school possible. '

'A school which just *happens* to have a new security system made by *his* company?' Marcie suggested.

John flashed her a grin. 'Exactly! If Sir Brian was a bit strapped for cash, perhaps he paid the fees in kind! Put in Proteus Fifty, at a reduced price – perhaps even at cost – and he gets something else to boast about!'

'That sounds plausible,' Marcie agreed. 'It would be interesting to find out where his daughters do go to school.'

'You might be able to ask him. As a high-profile past customer of ours, he's been invited to tonight's little event, and it's the sort of thing he likes to turn up at. To see and be seen. And to tell everyone what he's bought this week.'

'Perhaps I will,' Marcie said thoughtfully. 'It would give me something to do while you talked incomprehensible computer stuff to your mates. Yes, I might do that.'

They reached the hotel without further incident. By a miracle of good timing, Rory and Kady woke up just as they did so, wanting food and drink and the toilet, not necessarily in that order. After satisfying these immediate needs, John took them all out on what he called the 'Grand Tour' of London.

Marcie would have preferred to sit down for a while and think through what she'd learned from the morning. But John had been planning this family trip for several days, and she didn't have the heart to disappoint him. So, after a frantic rush for the Underground, they made it down to Greenwich Observatory for the one o'clock time ball. John spent several minutes explaining its significance to Rory. Rory wanted to go back on the Underground, which he and Kady had both thought was great fun.

Instead, according to the carefully worked out itinerary, they took a boat trip to see the Thames barrier, and then back to Greenwich to tour the Cutty Sark, before finally visiting the Tower of London.

This wasn't the end of the planned tour, but Marcie decided it was time to put her foot down. Both she and the kids were toured out. John was a little disappointed, but having to carry Kady on his shoulders for the last fifteen minutes helped to convince him.

'We'll save the rest for another time.' he agreed, and they settled for ice-creams by the river – resolutely ignoring the light misty rain that had started to fall.

'This Sir Brian Proteus,' Marcie began, pursuing a line of thought that she'd been trying to follow all afternoon

'Sir Brian Reardon,' John corrected with a grin. 'Proteus is his company – and his product.'

'Yes, of course. I knew that. Whatever. But Sir Brian – what would be the best way to get him talking about St Celia's? Would it be a good idea to mention that we'd seen his security system there?'

John considered it. 'Perhaps not. If he did get admissions on the cheap, he might be a bit sensitive about it. And he can be quite nasty if he doesn't like the way a conversation is going.' He gave her a look. 'But why would you want him to talk about St Celia's in particular?'

'Just curious.'

'Well, I'd just let him ramble on. As long as someone's listening, he'll talk! If he has got daughters at St Celia's, it'll come up sooner or later. You may need a lot of stamina though!'

'Perhaps I could work in a short cut? Ask him what school he'd recommend for Kady?'

'Might work, I suppose. I'm sure he'd love to give his recommendations.' John's face took on a wary look. 'I hope you're not seriously thinking along those lines, Marcie. There's no way we can afford St Celia's!'

'You don't know what their fees are,' Marcie pointed out.

'If it's equivalent to the cost of a Proteus Fifty system, then it's far too much! Besides, I don't much like the idea of our kids going to a boarding school. We don't see enough of them as it is.'

'Yes, alright! Relax, John. I haven't got the slightest intention of sending Kady – or Rory either – off to a boarding school, even if we could afford it.'

'Good.' John relaxed. 'So why are you so interested in this school? Don't tell me it's just idle curiosity about where Sir Brian sends his daughters. You don't normally have any interest in 'Life Styles of the Rich and Famous'.'

His tone was light, but there was the tiniest bit of an edge to it. He was looking at her with a slightly guarded, slightly worried expression. As if his subconscious was telling him something his conscious didn't want to hear.

Marcie had been about to say something flippant about making conversation, but seeing that look made her think again.

'Well,' she began hesitantly. 'Actually, St Celia's may be connected with a job I worked on. I thought I might be able to get a bit of background information from Sir Brian.'

She looked at him, trying to gauge his reaction. Thinking he might be angry. Or disappointed. Or perhaps even amused.

Instead he closed his eyes for a long moment, and when he opened them, he looked lonely.

'Well, that explains our little side trip, doesn't it?' he said quietly. 'And why you were so ready to put yourself out to come down with me. Fool that I am, I thought you were proud of me. I thought you wanted to come and support me. Big day for me. Big day for us, I thought. But it just worked out convenient for you, didn't it?'

Marcie felt his pain as her own pain, felt the shock of his words, even worse, the way he was looking. But not looking at her. She reached out, hesitantly, to touch him.

'John – I'm sorry – it's not like that, really. OK, so I used the side trip to get a look at the school. We – I – needed some confirmation. To see if it was the same place as – as a photograph we had. But it doesn't mean that I didn't want to come! Please don't take it this way! I am proud of you! This was just a chance to check something out. In passing.'

'So why didn't you tell me?'

'Because, well, it wasn't that important. And the way you are about my work. About me working at all. I didn't mention it because I didn't want it to be an issue. That's all.'

'Well, I think you got that wrong, didn't you? Looks like an issue to me.'

'Only because you're making it one!' Marcie could feel her guilt turning to anger. With an effort, she fought it down. 'What is the issue, really? That I brought some work home with me? Sort of. Haven't you done that often enough?'

'I never tried to sneak it past you! That's the issue here, Marcie! Honesty and trust! Things we're supposed to have in a marriage! Aren't we?'

'Of course. Of course. John, I'm really sorry that – that it's come over this way to you. I honestly didn't think it was that big a thing. I didn't think that – well, perhaps I just didn't think. I didn't see your point of view. And I'm truly sorry.'

John looked at her, silent.

'I'm *sorry!* Look, if it'll make things better, forget about Sir Brian, OK? Forget the introductions, forget I ever mentioned him. I'll drop the whole thing. Alright?'

John opened his mouth to answer, but then his gaze moved beyond Marcie.

'Rory! Rory – no! Put your sister down before you drop her in the Thames.' He jumped up and ran over to the kids. 'I don't care what she wants to see – you don't try and lift her over the railings! Come on now – it's time we were getting back.'

On the way back to the hotel, they talked only to, or through, the kids.

The silence persisted while they fed them, bathed them, and put them to bed. While they themselves got ready for the evening, they spoke only when entirely necessary. A pared down minimalism of communication. Tight lipped and mutually painful. Not for the words, but for what was being said in the silences.

It wasn't until they'd left the room (with the hotel-provided baby sitter installed) and were waiting in the lobby, did John turn and look directly at her.

'You're looking terrific.'

Not, as a rule, someone who much enjoyed dressing up, Marcie had made a special effort. New dress. Make up, planned and applied with careful precision. She'd even had her hair done – yesterday, actually, though it seemed that John had only just noticed.

'Thanks,' she said with a tentative smile. 'You've cleaned up pretty good as well.'

He smiled back. 'Suit and tie I can cope with, but this... full-dress uniform stuff!' He grimaced, and tugged at his collar.

'You look very smart. Distinguished.'

John winced. 'Distinguished? Isn't that another word for going grey?'

'Don't worry, it's not obvious. Except to me!'

They shared another smile. It had more of relief than humour to it, as they both felt the tension between them easing.

John took a deep breath. 'Marcie. This afternoon, I may have been a bit OTT. I over-reacted. I'm sorry about that.'

Marcie touched his arm. 'Oh, John – you're always the first to apologise, aren't you? Really, it was my fault, and I'm sorry. This is the biggest day of your career, and I'm running my own agenda. Of course you're upset! You've every right to be. I should have...' She hesitated, and he reached out and touched her lips with a fingertip.

'Enough!' he commanded gently. 'I may be always the first to apologise, but your apologies are always longer! Let's forget it, OK? Look – here's the taxi.'

They shared a kiss, and went out. But as they settled into the taxi, Marcie was thinking of her uncompleted sentence.

'I should have known better,' she'd been about to say. But she'd hesitated, because the truth was, she had known better. She'd known he'd be hurt by it. But she'd gone ahead anyway, hoping to sneak it by him. Hoping he wouldn't notice.

The evening was a great success. Marcie enjoyed it more than she'd expected to – which had been not at all! She had her criticisms: the food portions were too small and the presentation too fussy. Still, it made a nice change from limp sandwiches in a SOCO van.

Even the speeches weren't overly long, and she was pleasantly surprised by the enthusiastic greeting that John received when he stood up to speak. The fulsome introduction he'd been given may have helped, but Marcie heard the sincerity in it, and saw the respect in the faces of his colleagues.

With sudden insight, and a rush of pride, she realised that John was immensely valued by the people he worked with. Had always been, but even more so since he'd saved their project almost single-handed..

And it was a good speech as well.

She made a point of saying so, as soon as he had returned to his seat.

'I think I finally understand what SuperScan is all about,' she whispered, during the 'Closing Remarks' from Someone Important. 'You made it so clear!'

He pulled a face. 'Thanks. But someone else wrote that speech. I just read it.'

'Oh. Well, you read it really well!'

'That's something, anyhow.'

'John – I'm proud of you!' she said fiercely.

He looked at her, surprised by the force in her voice. And pleased.

'And I love you!' she added, and kissed him.

'I love you too!' he gasped. They had drawn amused glances from their neighbours, and a slight frown from 'Closing Remarks'.

Speeches over, the gathering began to drift away into the adjoining rooms, where drinks were laid out amidst groups of computer workstations, all running SuperScan to demonstrate that it could do all that had been claimed of it.

'Now the real work starts,' John told her, a little glumly. 'I'll have to explain it all over again to everybody.'

'Everybody?'

'Just about, but all in different ways, according to who they are.' He snagged a couple of drinks as they passed a tray, handed one to Marcie, and nodded at several people already trying to catch his eye. 'The media will want to know what it does. The business people will want to know what it does for *them*. The accountants will want to know how much it costs, the politicians will want to know who pays for it, and the academics will want someone else to pay for it.'

'Wow. Does that cover it?'

'Not at all. There's at least a dozen computer specialists and software experts – nerds and geeks to you – who will want to know why we didn't do it *their* way. And there's even a few poor lost souls – such as you, love – who would rather talk about the real world! Sorry, but I won't have time for that!'

'OK. I'll just smile and nod.'

'Or you could go and talk to Sir Brian. If this St Celia's thing is connected with something important, it would be a pity to waste the chance.'

She looked up at him. 'Thank you,' she said softly.

He smiled. 'It's all right. You're going to be bored stiff this evening anyhow, so you might as well be bored for a purpose. And thinking about it, I'd rather you were bored with Brian Reardon than with me! He's over there, in that group of people whose eyes are already glazing.'

'What – that charming gentlemen with the fake tan and flowing grey hair?'

'Yes. Distinguished looking, isn't he? But the tan will be genuine! Mediterranean or Caribbean, I expect. Don't make that mistake!'

'I won't.' She squeezed his hand and left him to his own fate.

*

As she made her way across the room, Marcie noticed that the gathering had split into two distinct groups. The computer buffs and others actually interested in SuperScan were coalescing around the workstations. The rest were congregating at the bars.

Sir Brian Reardon was at the centre of one of these latter groups, talking animatedly and emphasising his points with short, punchy jabs of his left hand. The right hand, holding his drink, was rock steady.

Marcie drifted into the fringes. The current topic of conversation was politics and economics. Sir Brian was explaining to everyone how he'd put the Chancellor right on various issues, and how valuable Sir Brian's help had been. He had, it seemed, also given valuable advice to various leaders of industry and to several peers of the realm. All of whom were very good friends of his.

Marcie was impressed by Sir Brian's technique. He was more subtle than she'd expected. Without dominating the conversation, he still managed to control the topic. It wasn't a monologue. He gave other people opportunity to make their contribution, and he listened attentively when they did. But his next remark invariably brought them back to his main theme – the deeds, possessions, achievements and contacts of Sir Brian Reardon.

Viewed objectively, it was a remarkable performance. No matter what the subject, Sir Brian could put himself at the centre of it. And he spoke quite well, with a rich voice, good eye contact, and some interesting anecdotes. The problem was that after a while you could have too much of Sir Brian as the centre of every story. Listening to him became first boring, then irritating. It was, thought Marcie, a fine example of presentation being let down by content.

The result of this was that Sir Brian's audience was steadily diminishing, as people reached saturation point and slipped away to talk about computers instead. By the time the conversation had come round to 'home is where the heart is', only two people were left apart from Marcie – a short man with a faint resemblance to Sir Brian, and a slender blonde woman who looked to be in her early forties.

Sir Brian's heart seemed to be split between several homes. There was Reardon Hall, situated in the better part of Sussex, Reardon Lodge up in Scotland, the Chateau in France, a place in New York – 'just a modest little apartment, for when I'm over on business ... but the décor is rather fine! Designed by DeHarne, who did such a good job for some of my friends over in Hollywood...'

Marcie smiled brightly and looking fascinated. Sir Brian paused to take a drink and Marcie dived into the gap.

'Sir Brian! Marcie Kelshaw. So glad to meet you! My husband, John, has told me so much about you!'

Sir Brian shook her hands, beaming with genuine pleasure. 'John Kelshaw's wife! *Very* pleased to meet you! *Fine* speech he made this evening!'

'Yes, thank you – I thought so as well.'

'I have to say, though, I'm not surprised. First time I met him, I knew he was someone to watch. I'm a pretty good judge of people, you know, and when he came and did a bit of work for me, I could tell he'd be an achiever.'

'Oh - yes, thank you, Sir Brian.....'

'Had to have a little word with him, though. Give him a bit of advice – older and wiser head, sort of thing! Glad to see he's taken heed!'

Intrigued by this, Marcie was deflected from her main agenda. 'Advice – what advice was that?'

Sir Brian smiled genially. 'I told him to stay out of the management side, and stick to the programming and technical stuff. 'Not that you can't do it,' I said. 'You've got the brains. But it's not where your heart is. You'll be successful but unhappy. Stick to what excites you! Leave the balance sheets and the marketing and the board meetings to boring old farts like me, who actually like that stuff!'

'You told him that?' It had taken Marcie years to realise why John was becoming increasingly miserable, the higher he rose in the business. It had taken the SuperScan crisis to get him back to doing what he did best, and loved most – tinkering with software. Sir Brian had seen it in one meeting. Mentally, she apologised. He wasn't just an empty bore, he had real perception about people. But then, he was a very successful businessman.

'Oh yes! I can read people very well, you know.' Sir Brian confirmed her revised opinion of him. 'Got a knack for what makes them tick! For example, that actor fellah, O'Dowd...'

'Darius O'Dowd?'

'That's him! Had him over to dinner one night, after that big film of his flopped. The 'Gangster Romance' thing. I told him, laddie, you don't belong on the screen. You're brilliant on stage, but you need that live audience, you need that feedback. Took me up on it too. Biggest thing on Broadway at the moment, I hear!'

Marcie realised she was missing her chance. Sir Brian was getting deep into the world of show business, in which he was (of course) a pivotal figure. Risking rudeness, she interrupted.

'Actually, Sir Brian, I was hoping you might give *me* some advice.'

'Oh, yes, certainly. Glad to help if I can!' Sir Brian switched tracks smoothly. 'What's the problem?'

'Not so much a problem, but I've been wondering how best to plan for our children's future education. I have a daughter, and John tells me you have daughters yourself. He told me 'Sir Brian is the person to speak to; he'll know the best place! Wherever he's sending his girls, that'll be the place to look at!'

Sir Brian fairly beamed. 'Why of course, of course - delighted to help. My girls – Andrea and Georgina, thirteen and eleven now – they're at St Celia's.'

Yes! Marcie thought, with a surge of triumph.

'Wonderful place!' Sir Brian continued enthusiastically. 'Brilliant facilities and absolutely top-notch staff. Recruited from all over the world. Very exclusive, of course. You'll need a recommendation. By all means use my name. I'd be honoured! I was very glad to be recommended by my old friend Lady Alice – Lady Alice Carstairs, that is, who gave that wonderful speech in the House of Lords last week. I was able to give her some help on that, particularly with regard to...'

'I was a bit concerned about security...' Marcie risked another interruption.

'No problem there at all – I know that for a fact! I've seen to it personally! Top of the range Proteus security system, nothing better on the market! You know, we've sold that system, that same model that St Celia's has, to some of the most security conscious world leaders. In fact, only last month I was with the Sultan of Andraman, and he was telling me how much peace of mind he has since he bought Proteus. Of course, his little country has a lot of problems with terrorists and so on. As I told him...'

Trying to guide Sir Brian's conversation, Marcie decided, was like trying to deflect a compass needle. She had hoped to get more, but at least she had confirmation that Sir Brian had daughters at St Celia's. Better yet, she had his permission to use his name. That should give her some leverage with the school.

At the next opportunity, she slipped in with 'Oh, excuse me, there's someone I *must* speak to...' and made her escape.

Not that it was much of an escape. Apart from John, the only people she knew were some of his colleagues, all of whom were busy demonstrating, discussing, or trying to sell SuperScan. John himself was deeply embedded in an enthusiastic group round one of the workstations, and clearly wouldn't be free for some time yet.

With a sigh, Marcie got another drink and resigned herself to a boring few hours making empty conversation with people she didn't know. The price to be paid, she decided. She had wanted to come for her own reasons, and now had to live with the consequences!

'Excuse me...'

Marcie turned round: it was the blonde woman who had been next to Sir Brian.

'Sorry to chase after you like this, but I just thought I ought to say something. Only you may not have realised, from what was said, but St Celia's is really *very* expensive. Far too expensive, really.'

Marcie raised an eyebrow. 'Far too expensive for me, you mean?'

A look of horror went across the woman's face. 'Oh goodness – I'm sorry! That sounded so patronizing, didn't it! I really didn't mean it like that. Of course it's none of my business. It's just that Brian's enthusiasm can run away with him sometimes – he just doesn't *think* – I'd hate for you to have the idea that he'd deceived you. About the cost, I mean.'

'Brian? Sir Brian you mean? And you are?'

The woman smiled and held out her hand.

'I'm Janice Reardon. Brian's wife.'

Marcie took the hand, but raised both eyebrows. 'Lady Reardon?'

Lady Reardon winced. 'Yes, technically I suppose, but I hate using the title. Brian likes that sort of thing. I don't. I used to call myself a socialist, even voted Labour, back when I thought there was a difference! Just call me Janice, OK? Or better yet, Jan!'

Marcie smiled. 'Jan it is, then. And I'm Marcie. But what was it you were saying about St Celia's?'

Jan shrugged. 'It's a good school, right enough – all the facilities, excellent staff, and so on. But even so, it's far more expensive than it needs to be. You pay through the nose for the snob value – it's just another way for the wealthy to show off how very wealthy they are. And Brian, bless him, is a sucker for that sort of thing. But the fees are horrendous. To be honest, if he hadn't worked out some sort of deal over their security system, the girls wouldn't have got in there.' She gave Marcie a worried look. 'But please keep that to yourself. Brian would be really upset if it got out.'

Marcie thought of saying 'I already knew,' but she didn't have the heart. Instead, she did some more fishing.

'Do they have security issues, then?'

'Not particularly. But some of the richest people in the world send their girls there, so security's always an issue.'

'Your girls haven't heard of any problems, then?'

'Oh, they're not my girls. I'm Brian's second wife.' Jan saw the polite look on Marcie's face. 'No, don't get the wrong idea. Brian was devoted to Beth. I liked her too. Everyone did, she was a really warm, kind, woman. It was a tragedy when she died, a few years ago. Cancer. Terrible thing.'

Marcie nodded, and made sympathetic noises.

'I was Brian's PA for ten, eleven years. When Beth became ill, and after she died, I just started doing more and more to help him. And the family. It just followed on from that. I know people think I'm a gold digger, but it was never like that.'

Marcie put her hand out and touched Jan's arm. 'It's OK. You don't have to tell me – but I believe you anyway.'

Jan smiled gratefully. 'Thanks. It doesn't normally bother me – but I'm no good at these social things that Brian likes so much, and I always feel a bit guilty, like an impostor here in Beth's place.'

'Do the girls have trouble with it?'

'A bit. They've accepted me, but we're not close. David – that's Brian and Beth's son, he's the one who was with me and Brian while you were talking to us... Well, we get on OK. We have a sort of conspiracy, to keep Brian from getting too carried away with all his big talk!'

Jan looked across the room. 'I know he's a terrible bore and he can be a snob, but he's also the most kind hearted man I've ever known.' Marcie followed her gaze, to where Sir Brian was talking to his son, the only audience he had left. 'People think he's in financial difficulties because he donated so much money to the Government. If they only knew how much he gives to charities! But that's the one thing he never talks about.'

Sir Brian was looking around as if wondering where everyone had gone. 'I'd better go back and give David a break.' Jan sighed. 'It's been nice to meet you, Marcie.'

'Likewise.'

Janice Reardon turned to go, and then suddenly turned back again. 'I've just remembered something I heard about St Celia's. Not from the girls, it was another parent who I met at one of Brian's occasions. Apparently they did have a bit of a security scare, not long ago. One of the girls went missing. There was a big panic, but then it turned out she'd simply gone home, unofficially. The interesting thing is, St Celia's have never said a word to any of the parents. This other person I met had only heard about it from her daughter! It was several days before they even told the girls what had happened to their classmate. That's another thing I don't like about St Celia's: they go beyond security minded into downright secretive!'

'I wonder who it was?' Marcie speculated. 'Could it have been someone famous – or their daughter? Perhaps that's why they're keeping it so quiet?'

Jan shrugged. 'Maybe. I didn't hear a name. Just rumours. Bye, now!'

'Bye.'

Marcie went to find John. Boredom had been replaced with a deep satisfaction.

'Went home unofficially, did she? Or is that just a cover up story? I'll have to look into this a bit more...'

CHAPTER 8

Part of the price Marcie had paid for cover on Saturday was a swap to night shift on Monday. In fact, this worked well for her, as it gave her time to make plans.

John was working from home, putting together a proposal for his next big project. With SuperScan off to such a good start, his stock was sky high, and he'd been given carte blanche to follow up any brainwaves he wanted.

'I just don't know what it should be,' he confessed to Marcie. 'I've been so focused on SuperScan, it's like tunnel vision. So there's no shortage of ideas, I just need a bit of time to think it through.'

He was still on a high from the launch, inebriated with his new freedom, intoxicated with possibilities. It was just a matter of choosing which radical, revolutionary, world-changing piece of inspiration would be best to start with.

Marcie saw the excitement in his voice, the energy in his eyes, and loved it. Loved him for it. Which made it all the more difficult to make plans to deceive him.

Actually, she told herself, it wasn't really about deceiving him. It was just that she couldn't tell him why she had to go to St Celia's herself, using Sir Brian's name as an introduction, to try and discover what had happened there. Because if she started to tell him, then other things might come out, like Vince Maddox, and his threats to her and her family. She couldn't imagine how she'd tell John about that, but he was too intelligent to be fobbed off with half a story. And he would certainly not understand why she had to do this.

But she did have to do it.

The more she thought about it, the more certain she was that the key to the whole thing lay at St Celia's. If she could just show that a crime had occurred, then everything would fall into place. Her chain of tenuous links, bits of gossip and smudgy photos would become evidence, which someone else would then do something about.

Just a little more, she thought. Just this one thing, and that's it. Then I can back off and leave it to CID or whoever.

There was another reason. A nagging little thought that meant she had to follow this up.

It had started as a vague worry at the back of her mind the first time John had mentioned 'kidnap', and had been steadily gnawing its way through to her conscious thinking. Now it couldn't be ignored.

Somewhere in 34 Cyrus Street, there could be a kidnap victim.

Her imagination was developing an increasingly vivid picture. Some young girl in St Celia's uniform. Tied to a chair, or strapped down to a bed. Frightened – no, terrified. Because they were at the mercy of Vince Maddox, and the mere idea of that terrified Marcie. The thought of Kady in such a situation made her stomach twist.

Marcie couldn't leave it now. It was no longer just about Ben's murder; it was the possibility that an awful crime was still taking place.

She made plans.

John helped, by disappearing into his home office after breakfast. When Marcie dropped in on him after the school run, he had the PC and his laptop both running, with the desk and floor littered with rough notes and technical manuals. Plus, he was on the phone, discussing something deeply technical while tapping at both keyboards. He looked totally absorbed and utterly happy.

She watched him from the door, asked him if he wanted a cup of tea. He grunted something, without looking up. She made the tea, put it on the desk and did some housework. An hour later, she took it away, cold and untouched.

'Thanks love,' he mumbled vaguely, switching attention between the two screens but not her.

Marcie made her first call of the day to the office, where Jim was on the day shift. He was quite happy to grant her request for a day's leave.

'Can't be Wednesday, though,' he said. 'Doug's already off that day, and Ali's in court. Would Thursday do?'

Thursday was fine.

'I'll put it in the duties book, then. Sort out the paperwork when you get in, OK?'

The next part was more of a challenge. Taking a deep breath, Marcie punched in the number.

'St Celia's. How may I help you?' The voice was different, the tone identical.

'Jane Lawrence.' Marcie rarely admitted to her middle name, but now found it useful. Along with her maiden name, she had an instant false identity. 'I'm considering St Celia's for my daughter. Sir Brian Reardon recommended you.' She'd been practising her manner. Self-assured, busy, expecting compliance as a matter of course.

'One moment please. I'll put you through to our admissions office.'

No messing around with the security staff this time, Marcie thought with satisfaction.

'Good morning, St Celia's, Office of Admissions. This is Sarah Anderton, Director of Admissions. How can I help you, Ms Lawrence?'

Marcie put on a posher voice than she normally used. 'I am looking at the options for my daughter,' she said firmly. 'Sir Brian Reardon suggested that St Celia's might suit my requirements.'

'Well, I'm sure....'

Marcie, well into character by now, interrupted. 'I shall be in London this Thursday, and I will want to look at the school then. Eleven o'clock would be convenient.'

'I'll check my schedule...'

'It can't be later than one pm. I need to be back by evening.'

'Yes, I see.'

'And I'll need to talk to someone.'

'Of course.'

'The Head Teacher, preferably.'

There was a brief pause. 'If you mean the Chancellor, I'm afraid she won't be available.'

Chancellor? Marcie took the phone from her ear, looked at it incredulously.

'Pretentious cow!' she whispered, as loudly as she dared, then put the phone back to her ear. 'Oh, the *Chancellor*. My apologies, I had understood that the title 'Chancellor' referred to the administrative head of a university. Of course, I am delighted to hear that St Celia's has achieved university status, but somewhat surprised that Sir Brian failed to mention that pertinent fact to me."

There was a short pause. "St Celia's is a very old and very prestigious institution, which has its own traditions."

Sarah Anderton sounded annoyed and a little defensive, which suited Marcie very well.

"But it is, in fact a school? Rather than a university? Since my daughter is not yet of university age, I consider this something that requires clarification. Or perhaps I need to talk to Sir Brian again?"

"I'm sure that's not necessary," Anderton assured her. "St. Celia's is a school, and we admit girls from the ages of..."

"Good, I'm glad my information was accurate after all. Well, if the 'Chancellor' is not available, can I assume that *someone* with knowledge of the school will be?'

'Yes – certainly – I'm sure something can be arranged!' Anderton hurried to re-assure her. 'If no one else is on hand, I'm sure I can be free to meet you at one.'

Marcie was rather proud of the expressive sigh she produced. 'Very well, then. Thursday at one.' And hung up.

She hoped she hadn't overdone her role. She had been enjoying herself more than she should have. Clearly, she had natural talent as a Rich Bitch.

'It's what I was destined for,' she told herself.

But a Rich Bitch was not going to look impressive turning up in a Focus. It wouldn't suit the image she wanted to give. She could probably borrow John's BMW, but St Celia's Security had had a good look at it on Saturday. They might even have recorded the registration number, perhaps tagged it as suspicious. Better not to have any connection.

And besides, it would be something else she'd have to explain to John.

So she needed another car, and one that looked the part.

That might be a problem, Marcie thought. Where could she get something suitable? Some of John's colleagues drove some pretty up-market vehicles, but she didn't know any of them well enough to borrow a car with no questions asked. Perhaps a hire car something? Marcie didn't know much about hire vehicles, but you could get Rolls-Royces or Mercedes' for weddings, couldn't you? That would be suitably up-market, but they mostly came with chauffeurs, and that would cause complications.

Perhaps she could take a car for an extended test drive?

A few minutes research with the Yellow Pages opened her eyes to a whole new world of car hire. It wasn't just bog-standard Mondeos and Vectras. There were companies offering luxury cars, prestige cars, sports cars, classic cars – anything you might want on wheels was for hire, it seemed. At a price.

Noting an address not far from Ash Ridge, Marcie made another phone call, and shortly afterwards had booked herself the use of an Aston Martin DB7 Vantage for Thursday. That, she thought with satisfaction, would not look out of place arriving at the gates of St Celia's.

The price had been a bit of a blow. Five hundred pounds for a day's hire! She was offered a more reasonable three hundred and fifty a day, if she'd took it for a week. She turned that down. One day of being a Rich Bitch was all she could afford.

Fortunately, she had kept her own bank account after she'd married John. Most family finances went through their joint account, but in the early days, when money had been a bit tight, she'd squirrelled away odd amounts and used them for surprise presents or family treats. They hadn't had to do that for a while, but she'd kept the habit, and the account held enough to do what she needed, without leaving awkward items on the next joint-account statement.

One more thing remained, which would be a lot harder. For this one, she wouldn't be able to hide behind a Rich Bitch alter-ego.

John finally emerged, intending to grab a quick sandwich for lunch. He was pleasantly surprised to find that Marcie had laid on a small buffet

'Would you be able to do me a favour this week, as you're at home anyway?' Marcie asked casually, as he was finishing off a slice of cheesecake.

John gave her a wary look. 'Possibly. But I am still working, you know.'

'I know, but I've had a long term invitation from an old friend of mine, to meet up with her for a day out sometime. I've been putting her off for months, but I thought this might be a good time to do it. If you could do the school run this Thursday? And the evening routine?'

John shrugged. 'I don't see why not.' He smiled. 'I expect you could do with letting your hair down a bit!'

She shrugged. 'It won't be anything wild, I promise. Just a bit of lunch, some shopping, perhaps a show or something in the evening. Maybe a few drinks.'

'Well, don't stint yourself. Make the most of it, stay over!'

'I've only booked Thursday off, so I'll have to be back that evening.'

'OK. But if it turns out too much fun to get away from, don't worry! I'll cover for you, work-wise. Who's this mystery friend, anyhow?' He gave her a mock-suspicious look. 'We're not talking about an old boyfriend, are we?'

Marcie laughed. 'Don't worry, love. None of my old boyfriends were ever any competition for you. This is Angela Vidderson.' A name at random out of her memory. 'She was at school with me. I don't think you've ever met her. Apparently she's kept in touch with a lot of the old crowd, and tries to put little reunions together quite often.' Marcie was improvising wildly now. 'She's been trying to drag me in for ages, so I'm sure she'll be delighted if I can come down. She lives in London now. I thought of her last weekend... if you're sure it's OK?'

'Sure, no problem. How are you travelling?'

By Aston Martin, Marcie thought. 'By train,' she said. 'If we're going to be drinking... I can leave the Focus in the Ash Ridge car park, and get a bus to the railway station.'

'OK, have fun. And thanks for the lunch! Do I get it like this every day?'

'Will you change your mind if you don't?'

John chuckled. 'Relax, I'll be OK with a sandwich. Mmm – some more of that cheesecake would be nice though!'

'You've got it, love.' Marcie smiled sweetly at him, and ignored her guilty conscience.

One more problem occurred to her while she was driving in to work that afternoon. Suppose the security guards recognised her? Several of them had seen her, and the one in the car had given them a particularly long look.

Maybe she should do something to disguise her appearance. Well, that could be arranged.

*

The office at shift change was always busy. Early shift getting ready to go home, day shift sorting out paperwork and exhibits, evening shift filing in and waiting to get on a computer to pick up their jobs.

Alison was just packing her bag. 'Hey – Ali!' Marcie called across the room, anxious to get her before she could leave. 'How do you think I'd look as a blonde?'

That brought the office to a standstill.

Ali was, of course, more than happy to share the benefit of her considerable experience on the subject. Even to the extent of calling the manageress of her favourite salon at home and booking Marcie in for first thing Thursday morning. She was disappointed that Marcie only wanted a straightforward dye. It was only with great difficulty that she was persuaded not to arrange a complete makeover.

What John might think of it, Marcie preferred not to think. She might put it down to wanting to surprise her friends. It would certainly surprise him.

When she finally got down to work, Marcie found herself dealing with a spate of burglaries in the University Halls of Residence. She took the jobs and went out to her van without much enthusiasm since she had a good idea what she would find.

Ground floor windows left open a crack for fresh air. The university central heating was always too high. Laptops on the desks beneath the windows. The windows would only open a few inches, not enough for someone to climb in. But quite enough for put a bit of wire in, hook on to the laptop's wires, and drag it to the gap. Once within reach, it was easy to yank out the wires, fold the laptop, and pull it out.

It happened with monotonous regularity. New intakes of students in September were easy targets for a few months, until they wised up. If they ever did. She just hoped they all had insurance, and had backed up their work.

On arrival, Marcie's worst fears were realised. The steady drizzle that had been falling all day, and the fact that the offenders had never actually entered the rooms, made her job virtually impossible. She tried a little powder on the inner window frames, hoping for some upward pointing fingerprints, indicative of a hand reaching in from outside and pushing up. But the frames were wooden, heavily grained, the paint was old and had lost its gloss finish. The only marks she found were vague smudges, lacking all detail. Entirely useless.

'I'm sorry, it's a poor surface.' It always seemed a feeble excuse, even though it was true. After using it for the fifth time, it sounded even worse. The evening threatened to be wet, boring and thoroughly unproductive.

Marcie had found that, at times like this – when the job threatened her will to live – the only remedy was a kebab. Or a few glasses of wine, but she was driving. Fortunately, she knew a suitable place, not far away in Northdale. A bit close to Cyrus Street, but she had no intention of actually going down there. And where she chose to eat was none of Mick's business.

Traffic in Northdale was quiet at this time of night. It only took her five minutes to reach her destination, a row of shops and fast-food places set back from the street behind a parking area and a row of trees. There were a few additional parking spaces tucked away at the far end, out of sight. Marcie parked there, as she normally did. If you wanted a quiet meal whilst in a marked up police van, it was best to be as inconspicuous as possible. Or you ran the risk of being interrupted by someone wanting legal advice.

She got out of the van and locked it behind her. The kebab shop was at this end of the row, just past a boutique and a newsagents, both closed. Further down, past the post office and the video shop, was Jake's Pizza Parlour and a fried chicken place. Not Colonel

Sanders – more like Private Pigeon, according to office rumour. In any case, Marcie's heart was set on a kebab.

A vehicle entered the far end of the car park, lights on full beam, directly in Marcie's face. Dazzled, she swore at the driver's lack of consideration.

The vehicle, a dark-coloured van, pulled into a parking space further up the row. As the driver opened the door and the internal light came on, Marcie got a brief glimpse of fair hair – the face was in shadow, but there was something familiar...

The lights of a passing car flickered through the trees. For a fraction of a second Marcie saw his face clearly.

The last time she'd seen him he'd been sitting next to Vince Maddox, in a Mercedes, going down Cyrus Street.

A cold twist of fear wrenched at her guts, and she ducked into the shadowed doorway of the newsagents, frantically scanning the van for Maddox.

Maddox didn't appear. The fair-haired man ambled towards the Pizza Parlour. In the light from its window she could see that he was quite young, late teens or twenty at the most, with an expression of bored truculence.

Marcie's heart rate began to slow to a more normal level. Still no sign of Maddox. She hadn't seen anyone else in the van. There were no windows in the back, but he wouldn't be sitting there, would he?

The driver passed out of her field of view. She edged out of the doorway in time to see him go into the pizza takeaway.

Plucking up her courage, she stepped away from the doorway, and walked slowly towards the van. A Transit.

She'd seen a Transit at Cyrus Street, but that had been white. Perhaps they had two?

Mick had told her to stay away from there. And away from Maddox. But she wasn't on Cyrus Street, and Maddox wasn't here.

Mick would probably think her interpretation of his orders rather too literal, but Mick wasn't here either. Marcie continued to approach the Transit. A glance at Jake's Pizza Parlour showed the driver queuing behind two young women, probably students. If he hadn't phoned in his order, he might be there fifteen or twenty minutes.

Or if he had, he could be back in five.

She had to take the chance. She needed a closer look at that van.

She changed course, walking briskly towards the road. Once there she stood behind a tree, and checked the Pizza Parlour again. No change. Using the trees for cover, she approached the Transit.

Ducking behind the bonnet, she ran her hands along the paintwork. It felt rougher than it should be. Marcie fished in her pocket, pulled out two essentials of the SOC business - a torch and a disposable scalpel blade.

A quick look round, showed that she was alone. She unsheathed the blade, and began scraping at the paint.

It flaked away easily. The surface underneath shone white in the torchlight. It was the same van.

'So, you've had a paint job done, eh? And why was that I wonder?'

Another look at Jake's showed the blond man still studying the menu, and the students apparently awaiting their order. Marcie crept along the side of the van, tried the driver's door. It opened easily. He hadn't bothered to lock it.

'You'd have thought they'd be more careful, after they lost their Cavalier.' Marcie muttered. She climbed in, and started a quick examination by torch light.

It was tidier than she'd expected. No clutter of papers, food wrappers and tools, such as she'd often found in workmen's vehicles. The dashboard was clear. There was a local newspaper on the passenger seat – two days old. Some crushed cigarette ends in the foot well.

Shit! Marcie thought.

Under the seat – empty Coke can. Cig ends and a can were potential DNA sources, if she had grounds to submit them, which she didn't. Shit again.

She checked the door pockets. Some crumpled tissues, a broken pen. Nothing useful. Nothing like an undamaged compact flash card, for example. Perhaps they *had* been more careful, after the Cavalier.

The wing mirror gave her a view of the Pizza Parlour. The students had gone, the van driver was talking to the girl at the counter, jabbing his finger at the menu. She had a few more minutes.

Turning her attention back to the van, Marcie opened the glove box, and peered inside with the torch.

A Transit driver's manual. A bent screwdriver, a pair of cheap sunglasses, scratched and dirty. Nothing of value. Shit, shit, shit!

Looking up, Marcie saw something poking over the edge of the sun visor. A book? She reached up and took it down. Carefully. She'd once casually dropped a large rubber spider on her head whilst examining a car. Doug had been with her, and the story was still one of his favourites.

It was a UK road atlas. She eagerly flipped the pages, looking for the area round St Celia's.

The page was pristine: no markings. No useful lines, circles or notes. No little memo: 'Kidnap girl here'.

'Crap.' Marcie said to herself, by way of a change. She flicked through the book, checked the page for Faringham, checked inside the covers, shook it for any loose pages or odd bits of paper. Still nothing.

Carefully replacing the atlas, Marcie checked Jakes again.

The van driver was no longer in sight.

In a burst of panic, Marcie dived for the door, pushed it open and nearly fell out. Half expecting to hear a shout, feel someone grab at her... she looked back at the Pizza Parlour. The fair haired man was still there. He'd walked along to the end of the counter, was reading a notice on the wall whilst picking his nose.

Feeling weak, Marcie leaned back against the open van door.

'Deep breaths.' She told herself, and looked back inside.

The cargo section of the van was separated from the cab by a plywood partition, but Marcie now noticed something she hadn't seen before. Right up at the top was a small wire grille.

Checking the rear doors would have been a dangerous business, as they were in full view of the Pizza Parlour: but perhaps she could still get a look in the back?

She got back in the cab and climbed up to peer through. The grill was set inconveniently high, but by pushing her head painfully up against the roof, and squeezing her torch next to her eye, she could just make out the rear doors and floor.

Empty. Bare metal. Not even a wood covering to the floor. In fact, what she could see of it looked stripped. Anything that might have been there was gone.

Words no longer sufficed, not even bad ones.

Checking the mirror, she slipped out of the door and shut it behind her. There was nothing more to be done here, she told herself. Disappointing, but there it was.

Then another thought occurred to her. She'd had some suspicion that the Maddoxes car had been on false plates, and the Transit had definitely been repainted! Perhaps it was on false plates as well?

She bent down by the front number plate, and examined it carefully.

There were different ways of falsifying number plates. The simplest was to add strips of black insulating tape to change – for example – a 'zero' into an 'eight'. Quick, crude and easily detected.

Especially when – as in one case Marcie had dealt with – the criminal masterminds involved made different alterations to the front and rear plates. She didn't expect anything so obvious from the Maddoxes, and she was right.

Another quick way to change plates was to stick a second set over top of the first: but the Transit had just the single set, properly screwed on.

And the registration matched that on the tax disc in the windscreen. All legitimate as far as Marcie could tell.

There was one more thing she could do, but there were problems involved. And risks. She could call up the Control Room, ask for a check against the Police National Computer database. That should reveal if the number plate was false, or if the vehicle had been involved in anything criminal. But calling in a PNC check without good reason was not just against the rules, it was actually illegal. At the very least, Marcie's job could be at risk.

She moved away from the van, keeping it in sight. The driver was still waiting for his order. She fingered her radio: then quickly – before she had time to think too much about it – she pressed the button.

'X-ray Mike One Three to Control.' She felt a mild panic at what she was doing.

'Go ahead, One Three.'

'I'm at the shopping area off Stacey Street. I've just observed a dark blue Transit van parked here. The driver's acting in a suspicious manner round some of the closed shops. Vehicle registration is Tango Nine Eight Three Juliet Mike Papa.'

'Ten-Four. I'll check PNC.' Thanks, thought Marcie. I didn't actually ask. 'Do you still have the driver in sight, One Three?'

'Negative.' Marcie replied.

'Understood. Tango Golf Five Two, what's your current location and commitment, over?'

Tango Golf Five Two, a Police patrol car from the Deeson Street station, came back at once. 'Five Two. At the station, over.'

'Five Two, could you turn out to Stacey Street, please. SOCO on scene there, reporting man acting suspiciously.'

'Ten Four, Control. Show me travelling.'

Oh bugger. Marcie thought. It was probably only five minutes from Deeson Street to here. Then she'd have to explain to a copper why she was calling in a man buying pizza as a suspicious activity.

'Control to X-ray Mike One Three.'

'Go ahead.' Marcie responded.

'Tango Golf Five Two is on his way to you.'

'Understood. Any result on PNC?'

'Stand by on that – it's running a little slow tonight.'

Great, thought Marcie.

'X-ray Mike One Three: from the Control Room Inspector, do not, repeat do not approach this suspect. Observe and report only. Do you copy?'

'Yes, yes, understood.' Marcie suppressed a groan. This was turning into a disaster. Now the Inspector was involved! They must be having a slow night. If she wasn't careful she'd have half the coppers on duty turning up. She should call in now and cancel... but.

But PNC might still come back with something. Marcie bit her lip. She was back at the far end of the parking lot now, hiding behind a tree and trying to watch out for the cop car approaching from one direction, whilst also keeping an eye on the Pizza Parlour in the other.

'X-ray Mike One Three?'

'One Three, go ahead, over.'

'You did say this was a dark blue van?'

'Confirm that.'

'PNC comes back to a white Ford Transit, registered to a Jonathan Maddox of 34 Cyrus Street. No reports on it.'

'Copy that, Control.' Marcie felt like pounding her head on the tree. No false plates, just a recent re-spray, which was hardly a crime. The whole risky exercise was for nothing. 'Ah – Control, I've just seen the suspect again. He was coming out of a doorway, doing his flies up – nothing suspicious, cancel the Tango Golf mobile.'

'Ten Four.' The operator sounded disappointed. It really was a slow night. 'Tango Golf Five Two, do you copy?'

'Yes, Yes. I'm half-way there now. Could we get him for urinating in a public place?'

Marcie suppressed a wave of panic. If an officer turned up now and started making accusations... 'Tango Golf Five Two, this is X-ray Mike One Three. The – ah – person concerned is back in his van and is driving off.'

Tango Golf Five Two sounded fed up. 'Understood. In that case, I'm returning to the station. Do you copy, Control.'

'Ten Four,' said the Control Room Operator, apparently suppressing a yawn.

'Apologies for the false alarm,' Marcie added.

'No problem, One Three.' That was Control. The Tango Golf didn't reply. He was probably cursing the feather-brain SOCO who'd dragged him out of his nice warm station into the drizzle.

'X-ray Mike One Three?' Control again – different operator.

'Go ahead.'

'If you're not committed now, would you be free for a job on Norden Rise? Officers have come across a large cannabis growing operation – they'd like photographs of it in situ, ASAP. That's 27 Norden Rise.'

Marcie sighed. She'd pay for her crimes by missing out on her kebab. 'Ten Four. Show me travelling. ETA – about twenty minutes.'

'Thank you, One Three. Control out.'

During this last conversation, the blond man had finally left the Pizza Parlour, laden with boxes. Marcie watched him morosely, as he got in the Transit, started up, and backed out. Lights still on full beam. It looked like he was getting his supper, anyhow – which made her even hungrier.

She turned to head back to her van, then a thought struck her, and she went across to the Pizza Parlour instead.

The girl behind the counter looked up in mild surprise as Marcie burst in, holding out her ID card, with her fingers strategically over the 'Rank' section.

'I'm from the police,' she said. 'Just a quick enquiry. That man who was just in here, do you know him?'

The girl shrugged. 'Never seen him before. What's he done?'

'Driving with his lights full on,' Marcie answered, truthfully. 'He's not a regular, then?'

'Don't think so... hang on I'll see if anyone else knows him. Hey – Bob – did you ever see that bloke before? The blond one who just left?'

Bob emerged from behind the pizza oven. 'No. Not one of our regulars.' He came over to the counter, eyeing Marcie with curiosity.

'OK. Thanks anyhow.' Marcie turned to leave.

'If he comes back, should we let you know?' Bob asked.

Marcie thought about it. 'No thanks,' she decided. 'It's not that important. But if he ever does come back, try and get a name. I may come by sometime, see if he's been around.'

'Sure, no problem. I wouldn't be surprised if he does come back. Young lads like that, with a lot of kids to feed – stands to reason he doesn't want to do much cooking.' He laughed. 'His Mrs probably left him to look after them while she's out with the girls.'

Marcie had been half-way to the door. She stopped, and turned back slowly. 'What did you mean, 'a lot of kids to feed'?'

Bob shrugged. 'His order. Two Xtra-Large Mighty Meat Feast's, with garlic bread and wedges, and three Kiddies' Specials.'

'Three Kiddies' Specials?' Marcie's head was buzzing. 'Three?'

'Yes, definitely three. Nine inch cheese and ham, with dippers and a can of Coke. That's right, isn't it, Cassie?'

The girl confirmed with a nod.

'Fiver each,' Bob continued 'I call that a bargain. Some folks round here don't seem to give their kids anything else. So if he's got three of them to look after, I bet he'll be back.'

CHAPTER 9

'Kidnap victims? Three of them?' Doug shook his head in puzzlement. 'What are you talking about, Marcie?'

Tuesday morning and Marcie was back with her normal shift. Bleary eyed but excited. She'd accosted Doug in the station car park, and started bringing him up to date before he could get out of his car.

'It was the young one, the fair-haired lad who was with Maddox in the car. On Cyrus Street, that time they drove past me. And he was in the Transit, the same one that I saw there! OK, so they've repainted it, but that's suspicious in itself! I wouldn't be surprised if they'd used it to do the actual kidnapping. Probably on false plates then, of course!'

Doug, floundering badly, grasped desperately at a coherent thought as it whirled past.

'Kidnapping? You think that the Maddoxes are kidnappers?'

Marcie nodded brightly. 'Yes, of course! It explains their interest in St Celia's. Girls school, rich parents. Only, I was assuming just one kidnap victim, but three kids' pizzas means three kids, doesn't it?'

Faced with this unassailable logic, Doug could only shrug helplessly. 'I suppose so but why would kidnappers go and get pizza for their victims? I mean, it's not the sort of thing you'd expect from a kidnapper, is it? What do they do next – trip to the cinema and a MacDonald's?'

Marcie gave him an irritated look. 'Be serious about this, Doug. My guess is that the Maddoxes were away somewhere. Left the blond lad in charge. Perhaps the other one was with him – the short bald one Dr Routley mentioned? He did have two big pizzas as well. And maybe they didn't feel like cooking that night, so he went out for pizza. Safe enough, it was just coincidence that I was there and recognized him.'

'Yes, OK. Look, Marcie, why don't you tell me everything? From the beginning. I seem to have missed something crucial.'

'Heck, Doug, weren't you listening? Oh, never mind. I'd better tell you about the weekend as well.'

The full update kept Marcie talking all the way up to the office. As they got there, Doug went past the door, down the corridor and into an empty interview room.

'Well?' Marcie asked impatiently. 'What do you think? It's got to be kidnap, hasn't it?'

'What I think...' Doug looked her straight in the eye. 'What I think is that what you've done is possibly the stupidest thing I ever heard of.'

Marcie's jaw dropped. 'Doug – I ...'

'Think about it, dammit!' Doug was angry. Really angry. She'd never seen him like this, forcing words out through clenched teeth, and a red flush spreading up the back of his neck. 'You entered a vehicle illegally. You called in a PNC check on spurious grounds – also illegal! At the least, either one could be grounds for dismissal. And if that's not enough for you, you then go and tell *me* about it! That makes me an accessory! Did you think of that? Did you?'

Stunned, Marcie shook her head.

'No, you didn't! You're so damned pleased with yourself, playing detective, you never stopped to think of the position you're putting me in, did you!'

Doug slammed his hand against the wall. Marcie jumped.

'Doug – please....'

'Don't 'Doug please' me!' He snapped at her. With an effort, he controlled his voice. 'You've told me about illegal actions that you've committed! I should report you at once! If I don't, and it comes out, then I'm in the shit, right alongside you. I could lose my job for your stupidity! And that's serious stuff, Marcie – unlike you, I *need* this job!'

They stared at each other. Finally Marcie took a deep breath.

'Doug, I'm sorry, I didn't think...'

'No. You didn't!'

'But it's not like anything will come of this, anyhow? Who's going to remember it after a day or two?'

'It doesn't have to be *remembered!* There's a record! You reported a suspicious activity, Control would have created an incident log. The PNC search will be attached to it! Or had *you* forgotten *that*?'

Marcie had forgotten it.

'Of course not!' she answered quickly. 'But it's not likely that anyone will dig it out, is it?' She took a deep breath. Doug's outburst had shaken her. And his remark about needing the job stung deeply. She struggled to think clearly over the wave of mixed emotions. 'OK, I screwed up badly. I acted stupidly. I accept that. But, think for a moment about this, if I'm right there could be three kids being held in that house. Kids in Vince Maddox's care? Can you imagine that?'

'Imagine?' Doug snorted. 'I think you've done enough imagining for both of us!'

'No, listen, it's not just imagination! It fits! And it fits with Ben's murder as well!'

'Ben's murder is being investigated by real detectives,' Doug spat out. '*Experienced* people who have investigated *other* murders and who have *not* come up with any links to Maddox, or St Celia's, or kidnapping, or *pizzas*!'

'No, but they don't have the flash card. They don't know about the Cavalier. Do they?'

'They don't know because there's no link.'

'Of course there is! It's just that Mick won't allow them to make it!' Marcie took a deep breath. 'I'm sorry if I've got you involved against your will. I thought you were with me on this one, Doug. But I'm right. I may be going about it the wrong way, but I am right.'

'So prove it! So far, you've got nothing that could go to court. You don't even know if there has even *been* a kidnapping!'

'I'll deal with that. Thursday. I'm going to St Celia's and I'll find out what happened there. And when I do, that's all I'll need. That's the last piece, Doug. That'll bring it all together – Ben, Maddox, the Cavalier, the photographs – everything! I just need that last link.'

Doug went to the door, opened it and looked back at her. 'Fine, Marcie. You go to St Celia's, you find your evidence, and you solve your case. You do whatever the heck you want to do. But don't involve me, OK? Whatever it is, I don't want to know.'

He went out, disappeared down the corridor.

Marcie shut the door, and slumped down at the table. She stayed there for a while, head in hands. She didn't feel like facing anyone else.

When she finally went to the office, Doug had gone out. Mac and Ali looked at her, and at each other, but said nothing.

Marcie took her jobs off the computer, picked up her kit and left. It wasn't until she was getting into the van, and caught a glimpse of herself in the mirror, that she realised her eyes were red and puffy.

The next two days were miserable. Doug didn't report her. She'd never thought that he would. But neither did he speak to her. The atmosphere in the office was brittle, as everyone pretended nothing had happened.

On Wednesday, Marcie made a point of taking out a short list of jobs, and getting back to the office early. Her pretext was a backlog of paperwork and urgent witness statements. The real reason was an entirely unofficial report.

It covered all her activities relating to the Maddoxes and 34 Cyrus Street. She started from the examination of the Cavalier, and included every incident, observation, and item of evidence. She added her Scene Examination Report for the Cavalier, the set of

Vince Maddox's prints from her car window, the flash card and photographs, and the contact details for PC June Cheston.

After some internal debate, she added the Pizza Parlour incident to the report. As Doug had pointed out, it was on record anyway. She didn't mention her search of the van, which after all had proved fruitless.

She completed the report, signed it, and sealed it in a plain envelope. After some hesitation, she marked it 'Maddox' and dropped it in her drawer. She had thought of passing it to Doug, but that was obviously out of the question now.

On Thursday, she went to St Celia's.

*

Looking back afterwards, she was surprised at how normally the day had started. Rory lingered over his breakfast watching cartoons, until she had to switch off the telly. Kady, decided at the last minute that she no longer liked her pink coat, which she'd refused to take off all summer. John's mind was already lost in cyber-space even while she kissed him goodbye.

'You will remember to pick the kids up from Julie's, won't you?'

'Hmm? Oh – yes – of course! Don't worry about it, love. Go and have a good day.' With a visible effort, he brought his mind back into the real world, and focused on Marcie. 'You're looking great! New outfit?'

'No, love.' The silk blouse was new, but she'd decided that her black suit, with the trousers freshly pressed, would look the part at St Celia's. Smart, stylish, business-like. It suited the image she was trying to project. Not what she'd wear to a girl's day out, but John wouldn't know that.

'Well, it looks good on you, anyhow.'

She smiled and gave him an extra hug. 'Thanks. I might be back in time to collect them anyway. I'll let you know, so don't ignore the phone if it rings, OK?'

'OK, OK! But remember what I said, Marcie. Stop over if you need to.'

'Thanks for letting me do this, John.' She bundled Rory and Kady into the Focus, and headed off into the traffic.

A pretty normal sort of day, until she'd dropped them off at Julie's. But from there, things began to get different.

Instead of going to Ash Ridge nick, she went into town, to keep her appointment with Ali's favourite hair stylist. She emerged an hour later looking very blonde and feeling slightly ridiculous. She just hoped John liked it. But not too much, since she had no intention of staying this way.

Then to Ash Ridge. Leaving her Focus in the car park, she walked to the car hire firm, and shortly afterwards drove a dark green Aston Martin very carefully out into the traffic.

Marcie considered herself a good driver, with a fairly wide experience of different vehicles. But all her years of driving vans and small cars had done little to prepare her for the DB7.

For one thing, it was bigger than she'd expected. Just easing out of the garage had her heart in her mouth as she contemplated the effect a marginal brush against the concrete would have on the gleaming paint work. After the Focus, it felt like a tank. A very fast tank with lightening responses. The acceleration the massive twelve cylinder engine could produce from just a slight depression of the pedal was frightening.

It didn't help that she'd been given a little lecture on the prestige, rarity and enormous cost of the car by the firm's owner, who obviously considered it the flagship of his fleet and was deeply reluctant to see it move any further than the car wash.

In consequence of all this, Marcie drove with extreme caution, hardly daring to relax her concentration long enough to breath. Knuckles white with tension, she worked her way through the streets, grateful that it wasn't rush hour.

Once out of the city, she began to relax. She was getting used to the car now, and could start to enjoy the experience. She could even spare enough attention to admire the luxurious interior.

'Perhaps this is me.' she thought. 'Not the girl from the sewage farm, the Rich Bitch in the Aston Martin.' She considered that, and laughed at herself. 'No, I don't think so!' she said aloud. 'But it helps get into character.'

Let off the leash, the DB7 made short work of the motorways. It was not long after noon that she turned off the M25. Better not to arrive early, Marcie thought. It wouldn't be in keeping with the rich, busy and impatient persona she was trying to project. On impulse, she pulled in to the forecourt of 'The Green Man'. Only ten minutes from St Celia's, and a quiet place at this time of day. Low oak beams, brass ornaments and framed sepia photographs. Lots of atmosphere carefully created. The few locals in the bar probably came from the same place as the brass and photos.

She got a sandwich and a fruit juice from the bar, and then found that her stomach was so knotted up she could hardly eat. Mindful of the barman's curious glances, she forced some down, and drank the fruit juice slowly.

Twelve thirty.

She paid a visit to the loo. Never miss an opportunity, her Dad had once told her. Fancy remembering that just now.

Stepping back outside, she found that a weak winter sun had broken through. It was enough, she decided, to put on her sunglasses and so add an extra level of disguise. She got them out, spent a few minutes playing with the various gadgets on the dashboard.

Twelve fifty-five.

Marcie took a deep breath. She settled her sunglasses comfortably on her nose, firmly put aside thoughts of what Doug or John might say if they could see her now, and focused on the task in hand.

'This is it,' she said quietly. 'Today, I finally nail this one down.'

She put the car in gear and drove on.

The security guard at St Celia's main gate looked familiar, Marcie thought as she turned off the road. She wondered if he'd been on duty the last time she'd gone by, wondered if he might recognise her in spite of all her precautions.

On the other hand, all she'd really seen on that occasion was a tall man in a maroon jacket. All *he* could have seen was a man and a woman in a silver BMW. This guard matched that minimal description, but Marcie was certain that she did not.

The gates swung smoothly open for her. The guard ran an eye over the car, noted the registration, and approached her window.

'Jane Lawrence,' Marcie announced imperiously, using her not-entirely-false identity. 'I have an appointment.'

'Yes, Ma'am. You are expected. If you follow the drive up to the main entrance, and park in the reserved space next to it, the Vice-Chancellor will meet you.'

Vice-Chancellor, eh? Marcie thought. She'd moved up in the world.

An inner gate opened ahead of her. Marcie nodded her thanks to the guard and proceeded as instructed.

It was a longer trip than she'd expected, made so by a number of wide, sweeping curves apparently put in at random. It took her through some well-tended parkland, broken by carefully arranged copses and well-manicured bushes. Side roads ran off here and there, with discreet signs indicating that they led to 'The Maxine Dorage Bio-Sciences Centre' or the 'Lord Arthur Brooks Sports Complex'.

Marcie wondered if there was a road to the 'Sir Brian Reardon Security System'.

A final strip of woodland concealed the main buildings from her until the last bend, which brought her to a vast expanse of gravel, neatly labelled 'Visitors' Car Park'. Beyond was a late eighteenth century edifice on the Grand Scale.

. She'd seen the building in the illicitly taken photographs on the web, but the reality was considerably more impressive. It fully justified the photographer's description, even without sight of the 'particularly fine additions from the nineteenth century'.

The golden-brown stone structure shot up five storeys in a welter of pillars, buttresses, balconies and other architectural extravagances beyond Marcie's technical vocabulary, broken by a series of massive windows. At the top it burst into a frothy concoction of turrets, towers and imitation battlements, before drawing back, catching its breath and proceeding further skyward in a long grey-slate roof, studded with dormer windows.

Dragging her eyes down to earth, Marcie spotted the main doors. They were hard to miss, being on the same scale as the rest of the building and underlined by an enormous semi-circle of stone steps. She drove towards them.

As she pulled up, a smaller and more practical door opened nearby. A short, grey-haired woman stepped briskly out. She was wearing a severely cut suit and an expression of polite but wary welcome.

'Ms Lawrence?' she asked, as she approached. Marcie, climbing out of the DB7, acknowledged the name. '*So* glad to meet you!' Marcie's hand was shaken with enthusiasm. 'I'm Renee Armworthy. Vice-Chancellor.'

Something in her tone conveyed to Marcie that, yes, Vice-Chancellor was what she'd said and the title was not negotiable, no matter what Marcie thought.

'Thank you for meeting me, Vice-Chancellor,' Marcie said, conceding the point. 'There are a few matters I want to discuss.' The sub-text was 'Fine, you can be Vice-Chancellor, *if* we can get straight down to business.'

'Oh – of course – but I thought perhaps you would like a tour of our facilities first? Or some lunch?'

'I've eaten, thank you. I'm sure the tour would be fascinating, but I do have a tight schedule.'

'Oh – certainly.' The Vice-Chancellor looked flustered and off-balance, which was exactly what Marcie had hoped for. 'Shall we go up to my office?'

'That would be satisfactory,' Marcie agreed, and followed her back to the practical door.

They emerged at the side of a vast entrance hall, all marble floor and oak panelling. It was decorated by oil paintings of bad weather in bleak landscapes, alternated with serious men and women in uncomfortable clothing.

'Hogwarts,' thought Marcie, 'Without the magic.'

A wide marble staircase led them to a plush carpeted corridor, and so to an oak door. Beyond it was a small outer office – a secretary there was only the second person Marcie had seen – and into a much larger office beyond.

Vice-Chancellor Armworthy directed her to a chair, and seated herself behind a large desk. More oak, Marcie noticed. The PC monitor on it looked out of place.

Her composure slightly recovered, the Vice Chancellor gave Marcie a warm smile.

'How can I help you, Ms Lawrence??'

Marcie jumped straight in.

'My good friend, Sir Brian – Reardon, that is – has recommended your school. However a certain matter has recently come to his attention that has caused us both some disquiet.'

Renee Armstrong raised an eyebrow. 'I'm very sorry to hear that. What exactly is the problem?'

'We would both like to know how you managed to *lose* one of your pupils!'

Both eyebrows shot up, and a slight flush crept up her cheeks. But the Vice-Chancellor stayed calm.

'Oh, I see. I'm afraid that Sir Brian must have heard one of the wild stories that some of our girls have been circulating.'

'So there's no substance to it?'

'Absolutely not!' The Vice-Chancellor said firmly. 'A girl was withdrawn from the school, rather suddenly, and that's all there was to it. I'm afraid that some of our more imaginative students made rather a lot of it, but in fact nothing untoward occurred.'

'The school hasn't communicated this to anyone, though.'

'There was no need to! It's purely a private matter between St Celia's and – and the parents concerned.'

'But it took several days before the rest of the school was informed? It's not surprising that there was speculation!'

Vice-Chancellor Armworthy bit her lip. 'The school has its own procedures for such situations. The matter was dealt with appropriately.'

'Of course. I understand.' Marcie sat back, smiled, and tried to look relaxed. 'But you do appreciate our concern?'

'Oh, quite!'

Did the Vice-Chancellor look a touch relieved, Marcie wondered? 'Naturally, we are concerned about the security aspects,' she continued.

'Of course. Quite right.' The Vice-Chancellor nodded vigorously.

'Quite apart from personal concerns, Sir Brian has invested a great deal in the school security system. He has a professional interest, as you might say. To some extent, his reputation, and that of his product, is at stake.'

'Of course, absolutely! But you can re-assure Sir Brian on that account. The school's security system was not compromised in any way. It all happened outside the grounds.' The Vice-Chancellor gave Marcie a re-assuring smile. Then a look of alarm crossed her face as she realised what she'd just said.

'Oh, *thank you*!' thought Marcie.

She leaned forward again, frowning. 'Is it normal for students to wander outside the school grounds?'

'Well of course not! What I meant was...'

Marcie decided to take a risk. 'And is it normal,' she interrupted, 'for them to be withdrawn by being bundled into a Transit van?'

Vice-Chancellor Armworthy's jaw dropped. 'How did you...'

'How did I know about the Transit?' I guessed, Marcie thought. 'We have our own sources,' she said. 'Sir Brian's security interests are quite far-ranging. And I'm sure that other parents would be concerned to hear about this incident, as we were. All the more, since you seem to have done nothing and informed no one. Not even the police! It sounds very much like an attempt to cover things up!'

'But there's nothing to cover up!' the Vice-Chancellor protested desperately. 'I assure you, the girl is with her parents and there's no need for concern!'

'I rather think there is!' Marcie snapped. 'To all appearances a child has been kidnapped! And what assurance do I have that she is, in fact, alright, as you claim?'

'I – we – the Chancellor – spoke to her father!'

'And he was not concerned about what had happened?'

'No – well, I mean, I suppose so, but...'

'Perhaps you'd better tell me the full story, Vice-Chancellor Armworthy,' Marcie said severely. 'And I will check against what I already know.'

The Vice-Chancellor wilted. 'I – I must insist that you consider this confidential.'

Marcie frowned again. 'That rather depends on what you tell me. After all, parents have a right to know what's happening at the school.'

'Sir Brian?'

'I expect so. Perhaps Lady Alice as well. Possibly others.'

'Lady Alice – Carstairs?'

Marcie nodded.

Renee Armworthy closed her eyes, sagged back in her chair. 'I said it might come out – but the implications... and really, we *have* had assurance that the girl is safe.'

'The story, please?'

She took a deep breath. 'Some of the girls are – were – allowed to go down to the village shop on their own. It's a quiet little place, and the locals are all friends of the school. Now, of course, they can only go down in organised groups, with security staff.'

'But on this occasion?' Marcie prompted.

'Ju... the girl in question went down to the village with one of her friends. Have you seen the village shop?'

'From the outside.'

'I see. Well – the window is obscured by magazine racks and so on. The girl had made her purchase and gone outside to wait for her friend there. She couldn't be seen from inside. The friend followed her, she was only a little way behind, but the girl wasn't there! All her friend saw was a white van driving off at very high speed. She remembers that the back doors weren't properly shut.'

'Had the van been there before? When they went in the shop?'

Vice-Chancellor Armworthy shook her head. 'It seems not. Our security staff spoke to the villagers. The van had been seen, parked further along the road. Apparently it drove up to the shop after the girls had gone in. We now presume that the girl's parents had sent someone to collect her.'

'From the village shop? Without a word to anyone? And in a Transit van?' Marcie's tone was scornful.

'We understood that there was some sort of family crisis,' said the Vice-Chancellor defensively.

'A crisis that involves waiting for the girl to come *out* of the school? A financial crisis perhaps, since I doubt that many of your parents normally drive Transits!'

Renee Armworthy flushed deeply, but didn't answer.

'When, exactly, did this happen?'

'It was the twelfth. A Friday. About three or four in the afternoon.'

Marcie thought about the dates. November twelfth was about three weeks after Ben's murder. Nearly two weeks after she'd confronted Vince Maddox with the flash card. It made sense that they would have waited to be sure that the investigation wasn't going in their direction.

And the transit had been white when she'd seen it in the drive at 34 Cyrus Street. They'd probably re-sprayed it after the kidnap.

Her unpleasant second encounter with Vince Maddox had been on the sixth of November. By the twelfth, they had probably decided that she'd been effectively scared off.

'What did you do then?'

'We searched for the van, of course. One of the villagers had noted the number – they do that, with unknown vehicles. Some of our security staff have certain contacts, and they tried to trace the number but without success.'

'It was false?'

'We couldn't be sure of that! It could have been taken down wrongly.'

'But you didn't call the police.'

'We contacted the parents first. The father. I understand the mother is often out of the country. He told us not to contact the police. On no account. Then he called us back, and informed us that it was alright. The girl's mother had withdrawn her from the school. He said she had decided to take her abroad with her. He apologised for the abruptness of the decision.'

'And paid the school fees for the rest of the year?' Marcie enquired.

The Vice-Chancellor was, once more, silent.

'But you took no further action.'

'What could we do? The parent had told us it was all in order. I agree it was unusual. Bizarre even. But we are dealing with people who have their own standards of behaviour.'

A polite way of saying that the rich can do whatever they like, Marcie thought. remembering just in time that she was supposed to be one of the rich.

'Very well,' she sighed. 'I'll pass this information on to Sir Brian. Of course, I will require some confirmation.'

Armworthy frowned. 'Confirmation? I'm not sure what you mean.'

'I will need to speak to the parents of the girl.'

The Vice-Chancellor shook her head. 'No, I'm sorry, but that's out of the question. We do not give out contact details of parents. But you have my word that the information is correct.'

Marcie gave her a long look. 'It's not that I doubt you, personally,' she said carefully. 'But the fact that I have had to take such lengths to get the full story does not – how can I put it? – it doesn't inspire confidence. I shall have to tell Sir Brian, and other interested parties, that the information cannot be confirmed.'

Marcie watched, not without sympathy, as the Vice-Chancellor contemplated the thought of the kidnap story spreading amongst St Celia's well-heeled and possibly paranoid clientele. A massive withdrawal of students was a distinct possibility. And even if the school survived it, the Vice-Chancellor herself would be on shaky ground, job-wise.

'I'm sure we can come to some arrangement?' She said eventually. 'Perhaps if I contacted the father myself – and asked him to call you?'

Marcie considered it. Having come so far, she didn't want to let it go now. But realistically, it was probably the best deal she'd get. From the Vice-Chancellor's point of view, giving out parents details would be almost as bad as the kidnap story.

'Very well,' she agreed, and wrote down her mobile number on an ornate St Celia's compliments slip. 'I hope to hear from him soon. Now – I think that's all we have to discuss. Thank you for your time.'

If her departure seemed a little abrupt, Vice-Chancellor Armworthy was only too happy to see her gone. For her part, Marcie was in a hurry to get away. She was well aware that the Vice-Chancellor, caught off guard by Marcie's apparent wealth of knowledge, had said much more than she would normally have. Given chance to reflect, she might become suspicious. Marcie half-expected security to stop her at the gate while her story was checked more carefully.

So it was with a sigh of relief that she left the grounds and turned the DB7 back north.

The euphoria of her success was short-lived. A sense of anti-climax crept over her as she drove. What had she actually achieved? Yes – she'd confirmed her suspicions that something had happened at St Celia's. She'd even confirmed that a white Transit van with false plates had been involved. But the trail went nowhere. She still couldn't prove a connexion with Maddox. She couldn't even confirm that there had been a kidnapping.

Even so she was absolutely certain that that was what had happened. The 'unorthodox withdrawal from school' theory was too bizarre to have any credence. She didn't think that Renee Armworthy believed it either. The woman was too intelligent to accept such an explanation. But the Vice-Chancellor wouldn't go any further with it without the parent's co-operation, and to be honest, Marcie didn't see what she could do either.

The father might or might not contact her. If he did, he would most probably confirm that his daughter was safe and well, whether or not it was true. No confirmed kidnapping meant no link to Ben's murder, and nothing she could pin on the Maddoxes. If she tried, she'd find herself in deep doodoo with Slippery Mick, at the very least.

To add to her growing depression, she felt weak and shaky. 'Low blood sugar,' she murmured to herself. Not surprising, since she'd had nothing to eat since breakfast apart from half a sandwich in 'The Green Man'.

The weather did nothing to lift her spirits. The sun had disappeared, and a steady drizzle began to fall from the low grey clouds. Seeing a lay-by ahead, she pulled in. A hunt through her bag produced half a tube of mints. She put a couple in her mouth, and reclined the seat, closing her eyes.

Perhaps, if Doug was talking to her again, she could discuss it with him? But she knew what he'd say. 'Drop it, Marcie.' And he was right. Time to drop the whole thing. She was sick of it anyhow. Look where it had got her. Arguing with her friends, falling out with her boss, lying to her husband, being threatened by Maddox...

'And sitting in the rain in a ridiculously expensive car, miles from home. With blonde hair,' she added out loud, and managed a tired chuckle. 'Lesson to you, girl.' She got out another two mints.

Her phone rang. She spat out the mints, grabbed it. 'Hello?'

A man's voice. Sharp, edgy, trace of some unidentifiable accent. 'Is that Jane Lawrence?'

'Er —yes.'

'St Celia's have given me this number. They asked me to call you. I understand that you are making enquiries about my daughter?'

CHAPTER 10

Suddenly, Marcie was alert and interested again, the tiredness and depression pushed out of the way.

'Yes. That's right,' she replied carefully, readjusting her Jane Lawrence persona. 'Who am I talking to?'

There was a pause. 'My name is Andreker.' The man sounded reluctant to part with the information. 'Tell me, what is the nature of your interest in my daughter?'

He sounded suspicious. But he probably had good reason to be.

'I am considering sending my daughter to the school. I also represent other parents with children at St Celia's. We had heard some disturbing rumours: apparently one of the students withdrew in somewhat unusual circumstances. St Celia's have informed me that the girl in question is, in fact, safe and well with her parents. I am trying to confirm if that is the case.'

'I see.' There was another long pause. 'Well, I can inform you that my daughter is indeed perfectly safe.'

The words were clear enough. But Marcie thought that there was something else in the tone. Disappointment, perhaps?

There was a moment of decision. She saw clearly the possibilities. She could accept the statement, finish the conversation, and go home. Tomorrow she'd destroy the Maddox file, forget the whole thing.

Or she could tell Andreker the truth. Tell him who she was. Go with her instincts. And risk her job, at the least, if she was wrong. If he put in a complaint.

She had already made her decision, even before she finished the thought.

'Mr Andreker, I have access to certain information which suggests otherwise.'

'What? What information? If you know anything about my daughter, Ms Lawrence...'

'Kelshaw. My name is Marcia Kelshaw. I work for the police.'

There was absolute silence at the other end of the line. Marcie, now fully committed, pressed on.

'I apologise for the deception. St. Celia's is not very forthcoming with information. However, we have established from them that a girl – your daughter, I presume – was driven away from the village near the school in a Transit van. This ties in with other information, which came to light during a separate enquiry. Information suggesting that criminal activity had taken place and a possible link to St Celia's.'

Marcie paused there, wondering how much she could, or should say. Andreker filled the silence.

'You are a police officer?'

'I'm with the Scenes Of Crime department.'

'Ah. Scenes Of Crime – that is forensics?'

'Yes.' Marcie didn't think it appropriate to launch into a detailed job description.

'What was this enquiry you mentioned?'

'I'm afraid that I'm not at liberty to release that information at present. But, Mr Andreker, you can confirm that something has happened to your daughter then I will have enough information to get some action taken.'

There was another long pause. Marcie could hear a muffled conversation in the background. Andreker had his hand over the mouthpiece, she thought.

'Mr Andreker? If you could just tell me, definitely, that your daughter has been kidnapped, that's all I will need. I'm sure we will be able to get her back for you.'

'Officer Kelshaw. I think we should meet. As soon as possible.'

That was unexpected – though perhaps it shouldn't have been. Marcie had been so focused on getting the confirmation that she wanted, she hadn't thought past this phone call. Still, she didn't like the idea.

'I don't think that's appropriate at the moment. And it won't be necessary. A verbal confirmation that a crime has taken place will suffice for now. Other officers will be in touch with you after that.'

'No. I must speak with you, in person.' Andreker sounded annoyed and impatient. He was not used to being argued with, Marcie thought. 'I have information you should know about. But not over the phone. There are things I must show you.'

That got Marcie's interest. A kidnap note, perhaps. If she had that – physical evidence, tangible proof, something directly from the kidnappers! Ideas whirled through her head. A note could be chemically treated for fingerprints, and any found might be matched against Vince Maddox's prints from her car. That would make it an ironclad case!

'Please, Officer Kelshaw. I would not ask if it was not important.'

There was sincerity in his voice, Marcie thought. Perhaps even desperation. A man trying to ask for help, who was unused to having to ask for anything.

'OK then. Where are you? If it's not too far, I'll come and see you now.'

'Good! Are you still at St Celia's?'

'No. Not far away from it, though.'

'Go on to the M25. Drive west, towards Heathrow. Then come off at the A404. Drive towards Amersham. After Amersham, take the A413. After about five miles, you'll see signs for a village called Greethill. Shortly afterwards, there's a public house on the left of the road – 'The Unicorn'. Stop there and wait in the car park. I will meet you. Do you have all that?'

'Yes, I think so,' Marcie answered, frantically scribbling notes in the back of her diary. 'But this may take some time.'

'It is important. What car will you be driving?'

'An Aston Martin DB7. Dark green.'

'Really?' There was some dry amusement in Andreker's voice. 'The police have a big budget for this operation!'

'It needed to be appropriate for St Celia's.'

'Of course. I look forward to meeting you.'

'Wait – just a moment...' but the line had gone dead. Andreker had said all he was going to say over the phone.

Among the gadgets fitted to the DB7 was a Satnav. Marcie didn't have one herself, but John did, of course, as he would never miss out on a new gadget. So, although she was more comfortable with a traditional map (such those as issued by the police) she knew how to use it, and after she had spent a few minutes fiddling with the buttons she eventually found the village of Greethill. Exactly where Andreker had said it was.

Meeting at a pub suggested that he didn't entirely trust her. Presumably he lived somewhere nearby. She used the Satnav to search the surrounding area, but there were any number of possible locations: villages, hamlets, isolated farms and other buildings, all within a few miles of Greethill.

She was wasting time. Putting it off because she still felt uneasy about it. But not so uneasy that she would change her mind. The chance to nail the case down and get Maddox arrested was too good to miss.

Marcie wondered whether or not to phone home. But what would she say? Better to get moving. If the M25 wasn't too jammed up, she could reach The Unicorn in a couple of hours, and if the meeting went well she could be back in Faringham tonight. If not, perhaps she could get a room at 'The Unicorn', or in the village. Just as long as she got the DB7 back to the garage by ten o'clock tomorrow. She couldn't afford the charges for an extra day!

Spirits rising, she started the engine. As an afterthought, she detached the two sticky mints from the leather upholstery and popped them in her mouth. She was hungrier than ever.

The M25 was bad, but not as bad as she'd feared. It crawled, but at least it moved, and by three o'clock she was on the A404 and making better time, in spite of the deteriorating weather. The drizzle had become a downpour, cascading down from dark, grumpy clouds and occasionally whipped up by a fitful northerly wind. Marcie drove doggedly through it with lights, heater and radio on, wondering why the ridiculous hire charges didn't include food. At least a sandwich.

Somewhere near Amersham, her phone beeped. She picked it off the seat and glanced at the screen. Text from John. She thumbed the buttons.

'Hi luv. Picked up kids, at McDonald's. Hope u r having as good a time as us!'

Marcie laughed. Trust John to take the easy option.

She thought about pulling over to reply – or maybe making a proper stop and getting something to eat as well. But then the signs for the A413 came up, and she decided to stick with it. She'd send a text and get something to eat from the Unicorn, which shouldn't be much further now. She fumbled out the last of her mints, and pressed on.

The sign for Greethill came up right on schedule. Even so, Marcie nearly missed The Unicorn. She had been expecting a brightly lit car-park, warm glows from the windows, a large welcoming sign, properly illuminated, with enticing hints of food and drink.

The sign was there, but not illuminated, and everything else was absent. If she hadn't had her headlights on she might have driven straight past.

Instead, she just had time to slam on the brakes and make a tyre-squealing turn into the car park. Thanking anyone listening that the traffic was light.

The car park was deserted. Driving up to the building, Marcie saw that the windows were boarded, the doors locked and chained. Her chances of a meal there looked remote. The Unicorn had served last orders some time ago, by the look of it.

She swore, several times. What was Andreker playing at? Had he changed his mind – or was this his idea of a joke?

Perhaps he'd left a message? Marcie drove as close as she could to the main doors, jumped out into the pouring rain and rain up to the meagre shelter of the doorway.

Nothing there. No notes, signs or messages, Just some very solid doors, locked and chained. She gave them an experimental shake. There was no significant movement.

The porch over the door was more decorative than useful, and wasn't giving her much shelter from the wind-driven rain. Cold water was already trickling down the back of her neck. Enough of this, Marcie thought. She'd text Andreker and give him ten minutes to arrive, then she was gone. She expressed her feelings by giving the door a vicious kick, and turned back to the DB7.

Another vehicle was sliding quietly to a stop next to the Aston Martin. Marcie caught her breath in surprise. It must have been parked out of sight round the back of the building.

She'd left her car engine running, and the headlights on. Squinting against the dazzle, she made out a large black saloon. A man was getting out of the front passenger door.

'Officer Kelshaw?'

'Mr Andreker?' She could make out a tall, heavily built man, dressed in dark clothing.

'Mr Andreker sends his apologies. He is unable to meet you personally. He's sent us to collect you – if you would get in the car, please?'

Marcie felt uneasy. 'How far away is Mr Andreker?'

'Just a few miles. It won't take long.' He beckoned to the back door of his car, a Lexus.

'You go ahead then. I'll follow in my car.'

'I'm afraid that's not very practical.' The answer came back very smoothly, very firm. 'It's a complicated route, and in this weather, you could easily miss us.'

'I'm sure I'll manage.'

'Please, Officer Kelshaw. This is the quickest way. You will be returned to your car as soon as you've finished your business with Mr Andreker.'

Marcie still couldn't make out his face, but he sounded calm and relaxed. Unthreatening.

'There are security implications as well,' he continued. 'You understand that Mr Andreker prefers not to reveal his location. Especially in the light of recent events.'

Marcie still felt uneasy, but also slightly foolish. It seemed reasonable that a man in Andreker's situation would be exceptionally careful about who he met and where. And he might be less open to sharing information if she didn't go along with his wishes.

'I'll need to get some things out of the car.' She said, walking towards it as she spoke.

'Of course.'

She slipped into the leather seat, reached over for her bag. It felt very safe and familiar in the DB7, which was ridiculous considering she'd only had it for the day. It occurred to her that this was her last chance to change her mind. The engine was running, all she had to do was shut the door, back out and drive away.

'Do you need any help?'

The voice was right at her side. Startled for the second time, Marcie whipped round, and found the man leaning in through the open door. In the courtesy light, she could see he had a round face, dark eyes and a trim little beard. He was smiling pleasantly, but he was casually holding on to the door, preventing her from closing it if she'd had that in mind.

'No. I'm fine, thank you – Mr.?'

'Davis. I'm Mr Andreker's assistant. If you're all ready?'

Marcie nodded. She switched off the Aston-Martin, climbed out, shut the door and thumbed the remote to lock it behind her.

Another man, presumably the driver (chauffeur?), was holding the rear door of the Lexus open for her. Inside was at least warm and dry, a thought she tried to hold onto as the shut behind her with a solid thunk.

There was a matching double-thunk as the front doors were shut. And an ominously solid click-clack, which sounded remarkably like doors locking.

'Don't over-react.' Marcie cautioned herself. 'Perfectly normal to lock car doors.'

The inside was all black leather and shiny chrome trim. The windows were so heavily tinted that she could see virtually nothing outside. An internal window screened off the front seats – that was tinted as well.

The car began to move off, very smoothly. Marcie sat back, put on the seat belt and wondered if she'd be able to track their progress by counting turns.

She felt them move from reverse, to forward, then a long slow turn towards the exit. A sharper turn out onto the main road, and they began to pick up speed. Marcie checked the time. It was twenty to four – though by all she could see, it could have been midnight. They'd turned left, she thought, away from Amersham and the

Greethill turn: if she had some idea how long they drove for, she might have a clue where they ended up.

One thing she could do, she decided, was to return John's text. She got her mobile out, started to compose a message, then noticed that the signal strength indicator was at zero. Frowning, she tried to dial out, and got 'No Network Coverage'.

Well, it happened.

They drove steadily on for another ten minutes. Assuming they'd been travelling at sixty, that would put them – where? Marcie tried to visualise the DB7's Satnav display, but without much success. Aylesbury was the next sizeable place – but she wasn't sure how much further that could be. And there were some smaller towns before then. Had she missed a turn?

At any rate, they should be out of the signal black spot by now. She checked her phone again.

There was still no signal. She tapped the screen in frustration. Surely the black spot couldn't extend this far. This would be a lousy time for her phone to die on her.

Unless – the car was shielded against signals?

She pressed the button to lower the window, and wasn't very surprised when nothing happened.

Marcie considered the option of banging on the partition to complain. It didn't seem likely to be very effective. She would just get more smooth and plausible excuses, while making her look silly and nervous. Which could be at least half right, but there was no point in advertising it.

Doug, she thought, would have said one hundred percent right. You could always rely on Doug for a helpful answer. She wished he was backing her up on this.

The car finally slowed, and turned off to the left. Marcie noted the time again: they'd been travelling for about fifteen minutes.

There was a sharp right turn, followed almost immediately by left. And after a few more minutes driving, a further series of turns. Marcie swore, as she began to lose track. The car was accelerating again, settling down for another long straight stretch, but she had no idea now which direction they might be heading in.

There were further turns. And a crunch of tyres on gravel. The car stopped. Ten past four, now. Marcie didn't have clue if they were back at the Unicorn, or fifty miles away.

The door opened. Davis peered in.

'We're here,' he announced, unnecessarily. 'If you'll follow me, Mr Andreker is waiting.' The tone of his voice implied that Mr Andreker did not like to wait.

Marcie climbed out. She was standing on a gravelled forecourt, brilliantly lit by floodlights, mounted high up on the building in front of her. Squinting against the glare, she could make out a large, sprawling building, its outlines picked out by black wood beams set into white plaster. Sort of a Tudor look, she thought.

She wasn't given time to dwell on the architecture. Davis was striding briskly towards the door, whilst the chauffeur hovered pointedly at her elbow. Marcie followed on with what she hoped was a confident tread.

Inside the building the Tudor theme was continued with enthusiasm. Solid looking furniture, low wooden beams and mullioned windows. Soft, warm lighting, in imitation lanterns and candelabra. But also some discreet yet efficient central heating, Marcie noted with appreciation.

They went up a staircase, and along a wood-panelled corridor, before Davis stopped to knock on a door. There was no answer that Marcie could hear, but he opened it anyway, and slipped smoothly inside, shutting it behind him.

Marcie looked at the closed door, and gave a puzzled glance at the chauffeur. He looked impassively at her.

'Should I go in?' she asked.

The chauffeur shook his head sharply. The strong silent type, Marcie decided.

They stood in uncomfortable silence for several minutes, then the door opened again and Davis looked out. He beckoned to her.

'If you please...'

It wasn't quite an order, but it was a stronger than an invitation.

Stepping through the door was like time travel. From vaguely Tudor to aggressively modern in one step.

The overwhelming impression was of light. Harsh white light from banks of halogen spots, gleaming on steel and glass furniture, highlighting bright abstract prints on the walls. The chairs were all light creamy leather, and one wall was dominated by a huge flat-screen TV, showing some news programme with the sound down.

Central to the room was a vast, curving glass-topped desk, holding two laptop PC's and a range of peripherals: squinting against the glare, Marcie could barely make out a figure rising from behind it.

'Officer Kelshaw?'

Shaking off a feeling of temporal culture shock, Marcie walked across the white carpet towards the desk. 'Mr Andreker?'

As her eyes adjusted, Marcie saw a slender man of medium height, with sharp features, dark eyes and sleek black hair. He had a neat little beard and moustache to match, and was wearing a light coloured suit, shirt and tie. He didn't come round the desk or offer to shake hands.

'Please, take a seat.' He indicated a comfortable looking chair in front of the desk. Sitting in it, Marcie found that it was as comfortable as it looked. Also a little low. Just enough to give Andreker a small height advantage as he resumed his seat.

'Old trick,' Marcie thought to herself, and sat back in as relaxed a posture as possible in order to demonstrate that she wasn't intimidated.

Rather more worrying was a movement in the corner of her eye. Davis and the chauffeur had followed her in and were standing silently at the back of the room.

'Would you like coffee? Or tea, perhaps? Something to eat?' Andreker enquired politely.

'I'm fine, thanks.' Meaning, 'I'm tired, thirsty and starving, but I'd rather get this over with as soon as possible.'

Andreker nodded. 'Thank you for coming to see me, Mrs Kelshaw. You are a mother yourself?' She nodded. 'Then you will understand my concern for my daughter.'

'Of course,' Marcie agreed. 'But with the information you can give me, I'm sure we'll get her back safely.'

'Good. Yes.' Andreker sat back, rubbing his hands together gently. 'You have some identification, I presume?'

'Yes, certainly.' Marcie fumbled in her bag, located her ID card, and pushed across the desk towards him.

'Faringham Police, Scenes Of Crime. Marcia Kelshaw.' Andreker read aloud. 'You picture hardly does you justice, Marcia,' he added with a smile.

'They rarely do,' Marcie replied, inwardly annoyed that he was taking liberties with her name. Only her parents ever called her Marcia.

He pushed the ID card back towards her. 'I must confess that I'm a little puzzled, Marcia. What is the connection between Faringham and my daughter's abduction from St Celia's?'

'I can't say too much at this stage, Mr Andreker.'

'But isn't it a little unusual for a Scenes Of Crime Officer to be conducting enquiries of this sort? And apparently carrying out a covert operation, using a false identity?'

'I'm involved in the enquiry. I discovered the link with St Celia's.'

Andreker's attention seemed to have wandered. He was glancing at one of his laptops.

'I see. So this is part of a wider police operation?'

'Yes, that's right.' The fact that this was the total opposite of the truth made Marcie feel suddenly very alone and vulnerable. She suppressed the feelings, telling herself that Andreker was only trying to establish that it was safe to trust her. 'We are very close to closing this, Mr Andreker. I only need you to confirm that your daughter was kidnapped and we can take action. And of course, any evidence you may have would be helpful. Did they send a ransom note?'

Still examining his laptop screen, Andreker shook his head. 'No. All communication has been by text messages. Somehow, they had access to my personal mobile number.'

Marcie frowned, disappointed. 'But you said you had something to show me?'

Andreker looked directly at her again. 'Yes. It was necessary to persuade you to come to meet me. I need to know exactly what has happened in Faringham that has brought you down here. I have to know everything.'

Marcie felt very cold. 'We've discussed this. I can't tell you everything. All I can say is that there is a possible link, and I believe that we may be able to find your daughter very quickly. If you could give me confirmation of what has happened – a written statement would be ideal, with details of the ransom demand.'

Andreker shook his head slowly. 'I'm afraid that that is not possible, Mrs Kelshaw. There are reasons why I prefer to avoid official involvement. But I do need the information you have. Surely as a parent, you can understand my feelings? Am I not entitled to know about my daughter? Where she is, who has her?'

Something about Andreker's words jarred on Marcie. Something about his tone. The worry, the concern seemed wrong. Forced, even.

She wondered how much Andreker really cared, but then dismissed the thought. Perhaps Andreker was one of those men who disliked expressing strong emotions. Perhaps he didn't have a good relationship with his daughter. None of that was any of her business.

She did her best to look sympathetic. 'I realise this is difficult for you, Mr Andreker. But the information I have is sensitive. There are connections to other crimes, not involving your daughter, and at the present stage I can't say more. But once we are able to take action on this, things will become clearer and all relevant information will be made available.'

Andreker gave her a searching look. 'Officer Kelshaw... the information would be given in confidence, and handled with discretion. No one else need know about this conversation.'

Marcie shook her head and began to answer, but Andreker held up a hand to stop her.

'I am a very wealthy man. I can promise you that your help in this matter would be suitably rewarded. *Generously* rewarded. My gratitude, Mrs Kelshaw, would be very tangible.'

Marcie was surprised to find that she wasn't shocked by Andreker's offer. And pleased that she wasn't even slightly tempted.

Of course, Ben would have said that she didn't need to be.

She shook her head. 'I understand that you're under some strain, so I'll forget that. But I must remind you that bribery is a criminal offence.'

Andreker sat looking at her, expressionless.

'I am no stranger to criminal offences, Mrs Kelshaw.'

Marcie met his gaze. 'That's irrelevant, just now. If you want your daughter back, Mr Andreker, I'll need your co-operation.'

He shook his head. 'I will get my daughter back, Mrs Kelshaw. And I will have *your* co-operation.'

He reached down into a desk drawer, and calmly produced a large shiny silver handgun, which he placed on the desk in front of him.

Marcie stared at it, dimly aware that her jaw was hanging open.

'Given the choice,' Andreker continued, 'I prefer more subtle methods. But the ransom deadline is close, and the possibility exists that my daughter could be moved. If, as I suspect, your information concerns her whereabouts, it would then become worthless. So I do not have time to be subtle. You have left me little choice.'

A calm and distant part of Marcie's mind was saying 'Slide-action large calibre semi-automatic pistol. Could be a Colt, or a foreign clone. Mac would know, he's done the course.'

What she actually said was 'But – but – you can't...'

Andreker spoke patiently. 'Of course I can.'

Mind reeling, Marcie tried to find a way to contradict this. 'People know where I am!'

He shook his head, smiling slightly. '*You* don't know where you are, Mrs Kelshaw. And as for other people – well, let's consider the possibilities, shall we?' He sat back, considering. 'Let me see... A colleague followed you here? No, that can't have happened. Mr Davis and Mr Jenkins, here, were behind you all the way from Amersham. (And thank you for driving such a distinctive car, it made their job much easier!) They would have known if someone else was also following you. Of course, they made very sure that they weren't followed from the Unicorn. Possibly your car is fitted with a tracker. But what of it? It's parked by a deserted building, many miles from here.'

'You yourself,' Andreker continued, 'could have a tracker on your person, or be carrying an active radio device of some sort. But in fact you are not. I have the means to check that.' He nodded towards the laptop that he'd been looking at earlier. 'You have a mobile phone, of course, but you have had no opportunity to use it since you left the

Unicorn. I assume that you discovered that my car is shielded against transmissions?

Frankly, Mrs Kelshaw, I doubt very much if you are part of a proper police operation. If you are, it's an extremely incompetent one. But that doesn't really make much difference, does it?'

Marcie noticed that she was shaking. Her voice was shaking as well. She couldn't help it. 'I'd be missed. If I don't make contact – if something happens to me....'

Andreker tapped the table lightly and frowned at her. 'My patience is starting to wear thin, Mrs Kelshaw. Must I spell everything out for you? It doesn't matter if you are missed. How am I involved? And suppose your body is discovered, hundreds of miles from here – perhaps the victim of a traffic accident? Perhaps the autopsy will show large quantities of alcohol? Or drugs even? Would you like your family to hear of it?'

Marcie could only shake her head.

'Of course not. Or – you could simply disappear. That might be the simplest thing. There are many ways to dispose of a body, Mrs Kelshaw. Your family and colleagues would never hear of you again. Oh, I suppose they might trace you to St Celia's – and perhaps even to me. But all I have to say is 'Yes, we spoke on the phone. I couldn't help her. My daughter is perfectly well. I never met this Kelshaw woman. So sorry I can't help you.'

He leaned forward abruptly, picked up the gun and pointed it directly at her face. 'Enough of this. Tell me all about it, Mrs Kelshaw. Don't leave anything out. And most definitely do not lie to me. I will check, of course.'

Marcie became aware that Davis and Jenkins had moved closer, and were standing close by on either side. She didn't look at them. She was too fascinated by the gun barrel pointing at her. By how large the muzzle seemed from this angle.

Starting with Ben's murder, she told Andreker everything.

She told him about the burnt-out Cavalier, the flash card, her meetings with Vince Maddox and the phone call from Jonathan Maddox. She told him about her surveillance of Cyrus Street, about the photos recovered from the flash card and how they had led her to St Celia's, and about her meeting with the Vice-Chancellor.

Dimly, she thought that she was telling him more than she needed to. That she didn't have to go into quite so much detail. But the gun that Andreker had now replaced on the desk – but was idly toying with as she spoke – convinced her not to hold anything back. She had no time to think about what she should or should not say. And she was too scared to try.

Andreker listened without interrupting, watching her intently, and scribbling notes on an electronic pad. When Marcie reached the point where he had called her, he raised a hand.

'I think I know the rest, thank you. And it is as I thought. You are pursuing this investigation on your own.'

Marcie nodded. Her throat felt dry from all that talking. She felt like crying.

'Rather foolish of you. But I am grateful for your stupidity! This information explains several things.' He looked at his pad, frowning slightly as he glanced over his notes.

Marcie was surprised to hear herself speak. 'What things?'

Andreker looked surprised as well. 'How persistent of you, Marcia. Your curiosity has got you into such trouble, yet you still ask questions?'

She really didn't like him using her name like that. In his mouth, it sounded like a taunt.

'Still, why not,' he continued, almost to himself. 'I owe you some information, I suppose. This Vincent Maddox you described. Unless I am mistaken, he once worked for me. As did his brother Jonathan, a more sophisticated sort of person altogether. They called themselves Harker then.'

'What did they do for you?' Marcie asked, hesitantly.

Andreker smiled. Not a nice smile, she thought.

'They made arrangements, let's say.'

'Arrangements?'

'Yes. For a price, they could arrange many things. For example, they could arrange for someone who disagreed with me to change their mind. Or they could arrange for people to pass on useful information. Or they could just arrange for them to disappear.'

'Thugs – murderers! You used people like that?'

'Oh, don't look so shocked, Marcia. 'People like that' are used all the time, by a great many other people. Even the most respectable, the 'pillars of the establishment'. Even the government! In fact, especially the government. All governments. Don't betray your naivety by showing surprise. Vincent and Jonathan have a certain reputation for efficiency. They specialised in doing local work for people whose main interests lay outside of this country.

'When I first began establishing my operations here, they were recommended to me, and I made use of them on several occasions. That was several years ago. Once I had my organisation in place, I had no further use for what you might call 'contract labour'.

Andreker waved a hand at Davis and Jenkins, implying that they now provided such services. 'However,' he continued, 'it seems that the brothers had learned more about me and my interests than I had realised. And they have kept that information up to date.'

'They knew about your daughter. And St Celia's.' Marcie put in.

'Exactly. And my contact number. More worryingly, they clearly have a lot of information about my business interests. They knew exactly how much I would be able to pay for my daughter, and how long it would take me to put the amount together.

'How much?'

'Two and a half million,' Andreker answered with, surprisingly, a note of pride. 'Sterling, that is. Not dollars.'

Andreker rather enjoyed letting her know how much he was worth, even if he was about to lose it, Marcie thought. She shook her head in astonishment. 'As much as that? You have two million five hundred thousand pounds you can just pay out?'

'Oh, I have much more than that,' Andreker assured her. 'Fortunately, the full extent of my resources are known only to me. Still, this affair has caused me enormous problems. Freeing up such a sum has set back some of my plans. But thanks to you, I should be able to minimise the damage.' He showed the most genuine smile Marcie had yet seen.

'How were you going to pay them?'

'Electronic transfer, to a numbered account. From which they would quickly be moved on, of course. Jonathan Harker – or Maddox – was quite good at such things.'

Pieces were falling into place. Even through her shock and fear, Marcie began putting them together.

'They targeted you because they knew all about you. Your daughter, your money, and the fact that you couldn't go to the police, being a criminal yourself.'

Andreker's eyes narrowed. 'Marcia, you are in no position to be using words like that. I am a businessman. I use whatever means necessary to achieve my ends, and in that I am no different from many others. Laws are made, changed or broken to suit the purposes of those in power. I see no reason to be bound by them! And 'criminals' are burglars and car thieves and muggers. Petty little people, scum. It is those who you should have concerned yourself with. But your naïve foolishness has involved you in larger affairs. You are out of your depth here – don't think you can pass judgement on me!' A faint flush had touched his cheeks.

Clearly, she had touched a nerve, The thought brought no satisfaction. Behind the smooth surface, Andreker was a very unpleasant and dangerous person, and she had just insulted him.

'I'm sorry,' she mumbled. 'I didn't mean to be rude.'

Andreker stared at her for a moment, then relaxed and smiled again. 'No offence taken, Marcia. Forgive me if I am a little touchy – it is a stressful time. The fact is, I would not go to the police in any case. I'm afraid I do not trust their competence in such matters.'

Marcie nodded, reflecting bitterly that she hadn't done anything to suggest otherwise.

'But I'm afraid we must finish our discussion now. I have much to do, many things to arrange, and quickly. The ransom money is due by the end of the week; therefore the time for action is now. Marcia, you will be my guest tonight. Tomorrow morning, we will travel up to Faringham, and you will show me 34 Cyrus Street.'

Marcie couldn't hide her shock. 'You're going there – yourself?'

'Not alone, of course. Mr Davis and Mr Jenkins will accompany us, and some other employees of mine. And yes, you must come as well, Marcia. It may be that you can be of further assistance.'

Andreker stood up. Marcie, aware of Davis and Jenkins nearby, thought it best to do the same, finding in the process that her legs had become surprisingly weak.

'Please excuse my impatience,' he added, putting the gun back in the drawer. 'You will appreciate the pressure I am under here, with so much money at stake.'

Not to mention a daughter, Marcie thought.

'But tomorrow we'll deal with it, and with the Maddoxes. Mr Davis will show you to your room, and will see to any needs you have. Oh – one thing before you go – your mobile phone?'

Marcie took it out of her bag and put it on the table without comment.

'Thank you. Have a good night, Marcia. And do bear in mind what I said earlier: I can be very generous to those who earn my gratitude. You may yet come out of this quite well off!'

Marcie nodded numbly, and followed Davis out of the room.

CHAPTER 11

They took her to a room further down the corridor, ushered her in, and left, shutting the door behind them. Marcie slumped into a chair and tried to stop shaking.

Her mind felt numb. Her thoughts were sluggish, unfocused. She was having trouble understanding what had happened. No – not understanding. The difficulty was in believing it. It was just too bizarre to be real.

'Get a grip, girl,' she murmured to herself. But she could not help replaying the moment when Andreker had produced the gun, and reality had flipped. In one fractional moment she had gone from being an investigator of crime to a victim of it.

She'd thought she was in control. Abruptly, she'd found herself to have no control at all.

After a while the shaking, and the desire to burst into tears, receded. She still felt fragile. Another shock would shatter her.

Without making a conscious decision, she got up and began walking around the room. Looking at things, touching them, confirming their reality.

At least she couldn't complain about her accommodation. It was more than comfortable. Luxurious in fact. Deep carpets, sumptuous decoration, elegant furniture. All much more in keeping with the Tudor theme than Andreker's office, but also lacking its useful additions. Such as a phone.

It was furnished as a sitting room. A doorway led into a similar sized bedroom, with a massive four-poster. Beyond that was a bathroom. The only exit from the suite was the door in the sitting room, which was, of course locked. She gave the handle a shake, testing it, and discovered that it was well made, solid, and quite effective as a prison door.

The casement windows were the same mullioned pattern that Marcie had seen from outside. Surprisingly, they weren't locked, just held shut with a simple latch. Marcie felt professionally offended by this lack of proper security, especially in view of the quality of the internal door locks. A house as wealthy as this should have proper protection against burglars.

Then again, remembering what Andreker kept in his office drawers, it was unlikely that burglars would bother him much. No doubt the word was out in the local underworld, just as it was in Faringham regarding 34 Cyrus Street.

She was staring out into the blackness beyond the window, when the door opened. She turned sharply, betraying her nervousness. No, the word was 'fear', she told herself grimly.

Davis came in, carrying a tray.

'Mr Andreker thought that you might like some dinner,' he said, putting the tray down on a table. 'I'm sure you'll enjoy it – the cook is excellent.'

'Thank you,' Marcie answered, wondering as she did so if she could make a break for it, through the door that Davis had left open.

Davis caught her glance, gave a little smile, and a slight shake of his head. She ignored him, sat down at the table and inspected the tray.

Some sort of meat pie, thick gravy – potatoes, veg. Conventional, but even allowing for the fact that she hadn't eaten properly all day, it did smell delicious. There was bread, butter, something solid looking in custard, and a pot of tea.

She barely noticed Davis leaving the room and locking the door behind him.

The cook, it seemed, was not overrated, and it was amazing what difference a good meal could make. Marcie eventually sat back from the cleared tray and reconsidered her situation. Of course, things hadn't improved at all. She was still in a lot of trouble. But now the initial shock had passed, she could face it. She was not going to fall apart after all.

She got up and went back to the window, opened it, and leaned out.

It was quite dark now. The rain had stopped, leaving the air feeling damp but fresh. In the dim light from her windows, and a few others, she could see a strip of gravel below her, then a lawn fading away into black shadow. There was a vague impression of trees and bushes. The room was on the first floor, the same level as Andreker's office, but apparently at the back of the house.

Which might make it easier to slip away, she thought. If she could get down to the ground. And surely that shouldn't be a problem? Perhaps the old trick with bed sheets?

She went into the bedroom. No sheets, but there was the duvet cover and a fitted mattress sheet. It might get her far enough down to be able to drop the rest of the way.

She shook her head, wondering. Surely it shouldn't be this easy? Did they think that she was too frightened to even try and escape? Or too stupid to see the need to try?

Opening the bedroom window, she looked down. It seemed do-able, if she could make the bedding into a rope. Or, looking along the wall, there was a drainpipe. Solid looking, cast iron, none of your cheap plastic rubbish. To a burglar, it would be as good as a ladder.

But to Marcie, it looked dangerous. Just out of reach, between the bedroom and bathroom windows. Perhaps a bit closer to the bathroom, but the only opening window there was a small transom. Getting into it would be a doddle for the hypothetical burglar, but a bit too tricky for Marcie.

So back to Plan A.

She began looking for somewhere to tie her 'rope'. The bed was solid and heavy enough, but something closer to the window would be better. No convenient radiator pipes. There was an upright chair. Too light to take her weight, but sturdy. Perhaps if she wedged it in the window frame?

Back to the window then, and as she was examining the frame, something moved out in the shadows on the lawn.

Marcie stared at the spot, frowning. If they had a guard out there, it would make things difficult. She would have to wait until they'd gone by – if she could see them at all.

Something else moved, in a different place. She strained her eyes. Shadow within shadow, something dark slinking through the darkness.

Something dark and low to the ground.

Of course. She thought, with a horrible sick feeling in her guts. Dogs.

A shape emerged from the blackness, loped towards the window. A large Rottweiler. It moved into the lit area, and seeing her looking out of the window, it sat down on the gravel and looked up with what Marcie thought was a hopeful expression.

'Oh, shit,' she said quietly.

Two more dogs appeared, sniffing along the gravel borders. Other shapes moved, further out.

Marcie had read somewhere that the Rottweiler's reputation for viciousness was underserved. She didn't feel inclined to test it out. Plan A was scrapped.

What really bothered her, she thought, was that they hadn't even warned her. Like they didn't expect her to try or didn't much care if she did. One possibility made her angry, the other chilled her. At any rate, it was clear now why Andreker had no concern over burglars. Anyone trying that would be dog meat before they could climb that convenient drainpipe.

She was about to turn away from the window, when her last thought suddenly took on a new significance. Climb the drainpipe? She'd been thinking about going down. But a burglar would go up, looking for an open window. An open window would take her back into the house, but she'd have some freedom of movement then. Perhaps to get to a phone. Or, better yet, a car!

She leaned out, studying the drainpipe. As far as she could tell in the gloom, it went right up to the roof, which wasn't very high at this point – just two storeys, in fact. There might be dormer windows above that. Had she seen any when she got out of the car? It was hard to remember with all that had happened since. And she had been dazzled by the lights. But in a house this size, dormer windows seemed likely.

All she needed to do was to get to the drainpipe.

Looking down – carefully not looking at the dogs – she could see one of the black timber frames running horizontally below her. In most Tudor-look houses that she had seen, the beams were flush with the walls: here they projected a few inches out.

She wondered about that. An architectural whim? Or a sign that it was genuine Tudor?

More to the point, it might be just wide enough to get a toehold.

She took a deep breath, and climbed up onto the window ledge. Sat there for a moment, thinking about it, planning what to do. Below, one of the dogs gave a little whine. Excited.

Turning round in the window was awkward, but she managed to find a position where she could reach down with one leg, feeling for the ledge.

'This is just a test,' she told herself. 'I'm not actually doing this yet. Just seeing if I can.'

Under her foot, the strip of timber felt even smaller than it had looked. Holding on very tightly to the window, she brought the other foot down as well. Both feet on now – toes, at least. Leaning forward, still gripping tightly, but she had her balance. Now, if she could move along...

She began to ease her left foot along the projection. Abruptly, it slipped off the timber, and as the other foot suddenly took more weight, it too went from under her. With a kind of breathless shriek, Marcie dropped. Not far. She was still holding on, elbows on the window ledge and a white-knuckle grip on the inner frame. Below her, the dogs began to snarl.

She hung there for a long moment, with her legs kicking helplessly in the air, before finding the toehold again and scrambling back over the window sill. She collapsed on the floor below gasping and shuddering. Back to safety.

Except, of course, it wasn't. She had to remind herself of that, before she managed to get back to her feet and look out of the window again. Half hoping that someone had heard her. That they'd rush in and lock the windows. Secure them shut, beyond any possibility of climbing out again.

Nothing happened. Nobody came. The dogs, disappointed, became bored and began to wander off. Probably not far, though. Certainly not far enough.

She had to think about this, Marcie told herself. The problem was that the outside surfaces were damp and slippery. Her shoes weren't designed for this, they were smooth soled. There was no friction, no grip.

So, simple solution. Take off the shoes, take off the socks, try again. Bare feet gave a much better grip. Well known fact.

The theory seemed good, the logic sound. None the less, it took Marcie several minutes to work up enough courage to act on it.

Finally, though, she climbed to her feet. Slipped off her shoes and socks, put them in her pockets. With an effort of will, she eased herself out of the window, and lowered a foot once more to the timber.

Discounting the sheer terror she felt, it was actually easier this time. She knew where the ledge was, and under her bare toes it felt rough. Cold and wet, but at least not slippery.

So, both feet then. Still holding the window frame firmly – so firmly that her knuckles were white – but standing on the ledge.

'Great,' she whispered. 'Well done, girl. Now, all you have to do is shuffle a few feet along to your left.'

Past the closed half of the window. Past a short section of brickwork. Two long paces, if she'd been standing on the ground.

The problem was, once she'd got past the open window, what was there to hold on to?

Tentatively, she reached up with one hand, above the closed window, and groped in the dark. The frame didn't fit flush to the wall, there was another narrow ledge at the top, a fingertip wide.

'People climb rocks with just finger and toe holds,' she told herself.

'*You've* been known to fall off ladders,' an unwelcome internal voice replied. She ignored it, and slid a foot a few inches left. Then the other one. And again. Walking the fingers of her left hand along the wood above, holding herself into the window with her right. Moving it carefully along the lower window frame, then up the side. Easing her toes along the ledge below.

Until her right arm was at full stretch.

She paused, staring through the closed window, back into the room she'd just left. Looking at the four-poster bed. She'd never slept in a four-poster. Wouldn't she be better off trying it now?

When she moved her right hand, there'd be nothing left to grip. She'd be balanced on fingertips and toes, poised over a long drop to the gravel.

And the dogs. A soft sound from below, a sound of claws on gravel, told her that her audience was back. A sudden vivid image came to her, springing out of a morbid section of her subconscious. She saw herself lying crippled on the ground, whilst the Rottweilers closed in, sniffing and baring their teeth.

'Oh, shit,' she sobbed. And, moving as swiftly and smoothly as she could, she let go, brought her hand up, caught hold of the ledge at the top of the window frame.

She waited for a moment. She'd held her balance, she was, somehow, still on the wall. But she wanted to stop. She wanted to go back. She didn't want to move.

Her muscles were starting to shake under the strain. She wasn't nearly fit enough for this sort of thing. She knew that it was only a matter of time, and not a long time, before her legs or arms gave way. She had to move.

Very carefully. Sliding one foot along, then a hand. Then the other foot, the other hand. There was a rhythm to it. All she had to do was keep the rhythm going. That was all.

Her left little finger slipped off the ledge, and wiggled desperately in empty space.

Marcie gave vent to a subdued shriek, a stifled mixture of frustration and fear. Her head was flat against the wall, staring left: she couldn't lean back, even a little bit, to get a better perspective, to look for handholds. But she could see the drainpipe, just a few feet away – a solid dark line in the gloom. So close. Just out of reach. Perhaps it was time to give up. To go back, while she still could. She didn't have the courage to go any further.

But if she went back, all that she would have left would be waiting, helpless, for whatever Andreker had planned for her. She didn't have the courage for that, either.

And the drainpipe was so close.

Her left hand eased its way off the ledge, slowly abandoning the precarious security of the window frame to creep, terrified, out into the unknown.

Working its way across the flat, open, white plaster that covered the brickwork, searching for a new home.

Some crumbling plaster, a crack in the brickwork beneath. Anything that could take a finger hold for just a few moments. Surely an old house like this would have plenty such?

But the plaster was smooth and unbroken, the brickwork was solid. Andreker kept the place up well.

It was so dark beyond the window that Marcie could barely see her hand. A pale shadow on white plaster in the gloom. She wondered if the drainpipe was as close as she'd thought. In the darkness, with her awkward perspective, she could be mistaken.

She had a much better idea of how far down it was. She didn't need to look, she could hear the dogs moving round below her, with the occasional excited whine.

Her arm was near full stretch. Her grip couldn't last much longer.

It was too late to go back now, though. She wouldn't make back to the window, back to the room. But she couldn't go any further, couldn't even make a lunge for the pipe from this angle. Her hand slid another inch, reaching as far as it would go.

At one time, there had been another pipe on the wall. Perhaps part of the plumbing. When it had been removed, the supporting brackets had mostly been cut off flush with the wall and plastered over. Except one, which a careless workman had overlooked. Or perhaps just not bothered with, thinking that no one would notice a few inches of metal in the wall, twenty feet or so above the ground.

And nobody had. Not until Marcie's questing fingers had chanced on it.

She let out a gasp of incredulity, almost of wonder, as her hand clamped tightly onto the metal. For a weird moment she was amazed at the firmness, the solidity of it. It seemed too good to be true, it was like experiencing a miracle.

Miracles happen. Marcie believed it now.

She was moving again, back in the rhythm, toes sliding steadily, an inch or two at a time. Right hand following. Until it, too, reached the end of the window ledge.

Resisting the urge to grab, Marcie continued to move, working her way along the wall with just one hand keeping her in. But the grip was firm, and under her feet the ledge had widened. Not just her toes but the balls of her feet were supported now, which made her balance a little surer.

Standing on the ledge, the bracket was about neck height to Marcie. She had to lean out, ever so slightly, to get past it: but then she could reach it with her right hand, carefully changing grip and moving her left hand again, fingers searching for the drainpipe. Finding it, round and solid, and got a grip. A foot on the other side, and then her right hand again. And she was standing, at the drainpipe, holding on with both hands.

The wave of relief she felt was incredible in its intensity. It was also dangerously premature, as she reminded herself.

'Not over yet, girl,' she whispered. 'Straight up now. Not far.'

She desperately needed to rest. Her muscles were flooded with lactic acid, and screaming for relief. But, although the drainpipe was a more secure hold, there was nowhere she could rest without holding on. There was only up.

Or down, but she wasn't thinking about that.

Searching by touch, Marcie found a supporting bracket just above her head. Setting her grip, and ignoring her pain, she began to climb on sheer will power and desperation.

It got harder when she had to move her grip up, hands behind the pipe, jamming her feet in the gap between pipe and wall. Gasping for every breath, now.

Easier when she managed to get a foot on the bracket, and found another higher up. Just above it, the drainpipe opened out into a sort of bucket shape. And that was hardest of all, pulling herself past the overhang. There was no strength in her arms at all, but her feet managed to find some purchase and pushed a little more, until she could get her elbows over the edge, and then swung a knee up.

She needed something to grab hold of, for that last effort of getting over the lip, but for a panicky moment she found nothing but slick, wet tiles. Then she caught hold of something, just a little higher than the guttering, but firm.

With the last of her strength Marcie half pulled, half rolled herself up, past the guttering and over the edge.

For a long time she could only lie, totally surrendered to the utter luxury of having a firm, flat surface underneath her. Of not having to hold on. Listening to the dogs expressing disappointment before wandering off in search of better amusement.

Life surely couldn't get better than this.

Eventually, however, she became aware that the trembling in her limbs wasn't only exhaustion. It was very cold, she was wet, and she wasn't dressed for climbing round on roofs. She had to get moving, and soon.

She was also beginning to wonder just what this flat surface was. It obviously hadn't been put there for the succour of stray climbers. It was metal, with roughened patches to provide grip, and about a foot wide. It ran along the edge of the roof, just above the tiles – how far it went was impossible to see in the darkness. Its purpose wasn't clear. Perhaps maintenance access? Or did Andreker have guards patrolling up here?

That was a worrying thought. But there were none visible just now. And whatever it's reason for existence, there must be some way to reach it from the house.

Or to reach the house from it.

Marcie's feet were ice cold. She slipped her shoes and socks back on, but then – not trusting herself to stand up – she began to crawl.

There was only a faint and intermittent breeze blowing, which was fortunate. A wind chill factor now could be lethal. As it was, the metal plates seemed to burn the flesh of her hands, leaching the last warmth from them. How cold would it have to be, she wondered, before her skin began to stick? She'd read that it happened in the Arctic. Did it ever happen in England?

The walkway passed just below a dormer window. She glanced up, trying to see if it was open, but could make out no details in the darkness. She might stand up and try it – but the effort seemed too much. Not with the hope of a door ahead. She crawled on.

It ended abruptly. She saw the end only just before she reached it, the dark grey of the metal making a barely visible line against utter blackness beyond.

It seemed a strange place for it to finish. She lay down, felt around with her hands.

Ahead, she felt only slick wet tiles. To the right, empty air. But to the left, lower down, more metal. A step. Steps, in fact, leading down and inward. Into the house, she hoped. Edging carefully round, she went down the backwards.

Roofs rose above her on both sides. She was in a valley between two sections. The steps ended. Marcie turned round and began crawling forwards again.

It was pitch black now, without even the minimal light scatter from windows below. A few stars twinkled far above, powerless to help. She groped her way on. At least it seemed to be distinctly warmer here. Perhaps there was an active chimney or a hot air vent somewhere nearby. Whatever, Marcie was grateful.

The walkway came to an abrupt end. Marcie reached in front of her, and felt a vertical sheet of – wood? Hard to tell, in the dark. It wasn't as cold as metal: smooth, but with imperfections. Bumps and rough patches. Varnished or painted wood, she thought. Or, in other words, a door. Unfortunately, a closed door, with no handle that she could find. Not even a lock.

She found a vertical crack on her right, traced it round, marking out the door's extent. Brickwork extended either side of it. Getting her fingernails round the edge, she tried a little tug, but it was solid. She wasn't at all surprised to find that pushing didn't work any better.

Of course it was locked. Or bolted. From the inside.

She slumped down, sitting with her back to the door. At least it was warm here, almost comfortable in fact. She could stay here for a while, until... what? Until someone opened the door and discovered her propped up against it? Until they missed her and came looking?

It wasn't time to give up yet, she decided. Not while there were some windows she could try. And there was the other end of the walkway to consider. Nothing said that there had to be just one door.

She stayed a little longer, none the less, letting the warmth work its way into her bones and stop the shivering. Then she hoisted herself to her feet and went back the way she'd come, walking this time. Partly because she needed to try those windows, and partly just to prove to herself that she could.

The dormer window she had passed was a disappointment, being solidly locked. In theory, of course, she could smash the glass, but there were problems with doing that – not only the noise, but also a good chance of cutting herself, perhaps seriously. She'd leave that option until she was really desperate. And there were other windows further along, past the drainpipe she'd climbed. She moved on.

In fact, there were three windows along the walkway. Unfortunately, they were all as secure as the first. Not helpful at all. But the walkway continued, and now took a sharp right angle turn. There were more steps, this time going up, and Marcie found herself climbing towards the peak of the roof.

There was something strange about it, though. Pausing to peer upwards, she tried to distinguish shadow from dark sky and solid black. Some kind of structure seemed to have been erected on the highest part of the house.

Cautiously, she continued to climb. Shapes became visible, and rows of red and green LED's, some steady, some blinking. As she reached the top, they provided enough light for her to make out a broad platform, built over the peak of the roof. On it were mounted several large satellite dishes, a cluster of assorted aerials, and some box-like shapes with the LEDs glowing or flickering along their sides.

The mystery of the walkway was solved. It provided maintenance access for what was apparently a powerful communications array. After seeing Andreker's office, Marcie wasn't surprised. The man was a gadget freak. With this set up he could probably talk to Mars.

Unfortunately, this didn't help Marcie in the slightest. No doubt a real undercover cop would be able to fiddle with the wires and send an SOS or something. But she lacked the technical expertise for that sort of trick, and the walkway lead nowhere else.

She slumped down on one of the boxes, and considered her options. The only possibility seemed to be the dormer windows. She would have to try and break one and hope that it wasn't alarmed.

For the moment, though, sitting felt good, though the cold was more intense than ever. She would have to move soon. When she'd given her legs a respite.

It was very quiet. Peaceful, even. The stars were bright and clear now that the last of the clouds had moved on. She felt exhausted. She had to move soon. She didn't want to move.

In the distance, she could hear cars. A road perhaps. She wondered how far it was. Sound could travel a long way on a still night like this. In any case, however close it might be, the dogs were closer.

The vehicle noise was louder now. She forced herself to her feet, and moved towards the front of the house. Unlike the walkway, the platform had a safety rail round the edge: she leaned against it and strained her eyes into the darkness.

There were headlights in the distance. Flickering and fading as the vehicles moved through trees. Coming up the drive towards the house.

Below her, the floodlights suddenly came on. Marcie crouched instinctively, then slowly stood up again. No one would be looking up here, and if they did, they wouldn't see anything past the glare of the lights.

She could now see the gravelled forecourt and the drive beyond. Down which came two cars – Andreker's black Lexus and her own DB7.

Marcie watched them approach with strong emotions. She felt almost homesick for the Aston Martin. If she'd only had the sense to stay in it, she'd be back in Faringham by now.

The vehicles disappeared from view as they reached the forecourt and parked close to the front of the house. There were voices: the engines stopped, and she could hear Andreker speaking.

'.... no tracker fitted?'

'No sir.' It sounded like Davis. 'And nobody watching it.'

'Good. Anything of interest inside?'

'The hire documents. She paid cash and used the false name.'

'Excellent!' Andreker sounded pleased. 'That makes things much simpler. Have one of the men drive it back to Faringham tonight. Get it back to the hire company before they open and drop the keys through the letter box. It should wrap that side of things up quite neatly, with no connection to a missing Scenes of Crime Officer.'

Marcie had thought she was cold before. But that had just been her body.

'I'll do it myself.' Davis was saying. 'No mistakes. When I've sorted the car, I'll find this Cyrus Street and do a recce.'

'Good. Call me when you've done that. We'll be leaving early – I want to be in place by eight a.m.'

'And the woman?'

'We'll bring her along. I have a use for her. We can make permanent arrangements afterwards.'

'She might be trouble.'

'I doubt it.' Andreker replied easily. 'I've convinced her that she'll get a reward for helping us. And she's also terrified! In between the carrot and the stick – and her own stupidity – she'll do as she's told, for as long as it suits me.'

Marcie almost swore out loud. Andreker's smug arrogance triggered a wave of fury that drove fear out of her head. 'You treacherous, lying, little – *bastard*!' she hissed. She felt a strong urge to throw something down at him. It would be a stupid thing to do of course, but oh so satisfying! She ducked under the railing, leaned out and looked down. Perhaps a loose tile might happen to fall on his head?

Fortunately, perhaps, there were no loose tiles in evidence, and Andreker's head was still not visible.

He was speaking again. '...see if she's asleep yet. When she is, go through her bag and pockets. I want any paperwork, anything that could identify her or link her with St Celia's...' the voices faded, and a door slammed as they went inside.

They were coming to look for her. To see if she was asleep. They'd find her gone.

Before the lights went out, Marcie had seen something below her. Another dormer window, projecting out of the roof. The platform seemed to extend further out on this side of the house. What it must look like in daylight was nobody's business, she thought. Clearly, Andreker had little concern for the aesthetics of his home. But the overhang had enabled her to see the top frame of an open window.

Without wasting another moment thinking about it, she turned round and slid feet first off the platform.

CHAPTER 12

It was further down than she'd thought.

She lowered herself carefully until she was dangling at full stretch from the platform, and still couldn't feel anything under her feet. Fortunately, her knee bumped against something. With her night vision slowly returning, she could make out that it was a support stanchion. Wrapping a leg round it, she transferred her grip, and descended.

It was only a few inches further to the roof, and from there a relatively simple matter for Marcie to work her way down the slope and round to the open dormer window.

Under normal circumstances, scrambling over a wet roof, clinging tightly to stanchions and window frames – all in near freezing cold darkness – would have been a nightmare. Now, however, having something firm to cling to was sheer luxury. It even made up for the slickness of the tiles, all the worse since she was still wearing her shoes. 'Amazing how experience can alter your perspective.' she muttered to herself.

Peering in through the window, she could make out nothing of the room itself. But directly opposite a door was faintly outlined by light beyond it. Hopefully, a way out.

She listened.

There was no sound in the room, or from beyond it. No clock ticking, no TV or radio. Most importantly, no talking. Except the faintest of noises. So faint that she might have imagined it. A gentle, rhythmic, movement of air. Like someone breathing.

Marcie held her own breath, strained her ears. Had she heard it?

She couldn't be sure. But it didn't make any difference. She couldn't go back now.

Feeling below the window, Marcie found a flat surface just under the sill. A table or desk. She explored it with her fingertips, moving very slowly. Something made of cloth – clothing, perhaps. A desk lamp, a cigarette lighter and a bowl of gritty powder, which her nose identified as cigarette ash.

That might explain why the window was open in the middle of a cold night. The occupant liked to stand there for a smoke. Perhaps they didn't want the smell to permeate the room. She could imagine Andreker having a pretty strict no-smoking policy.

She carefully moved items out of her way, clearing a space, then got a good grip on the frame and swung a leg inside.

At that moment, a gentle snore confirmed that she had heard breathing before.

She froze, half in and half out of the window, with one hand over her mouth to physically restrain the squeal that threatened to burst out.

The snore, once begun, continued, settling to a steady rhythm. Marcie relaxed slightly, and lowered her hand.

Though not a snorer herself, she was still something of an expert, as John had a considerable repertoire. Over many broken nights in the early years of their marriage she had categorised them. There was, for example, the loud and rough number one (inebriated), which resulted from a drink or two over the top, or the light and fluttery number three, which meant 'I'm getting round to waking up, but don't rush me'. This, however, rather resembled John's powerful and resonant number two, which indicated that he was settling in for a long haul.

If the occupant was anything like John, then it would be safe to enter in marching boots, banging a drum, but Marcie saw no need to test it to that degree.

She moved as quietly as possible, climbing on to the table and down to the floor. Then, on tip toe over to the door. She fumbled for the handle, which creaked alarmingly as she turned it. The snores never faltered. She eased the door open.

The corridor light shone on the bed, revealing a beefy young man with a cherubic curl of blonde hair over his forehead.

'Sweet dreams!' Marcie whispered, and slipped out into the corridor beyond. A quick glance either way showed her that it was deserted.

Up here on the second floor there was little attempt to maintain the Tudor look. The walls were painted plaster, without decoration, the floor was tile carpeted, and the lighting fluorescent strips. Obviously this was where Andreker kept the hired help.

At least it was warm. Almost uncomfortably so to Marcie, after spending so long out on the roof. She stood still for a moment or two, luxuriating in the heat, and trying to decide her next move.

They'd be searching for her soon, she reflected – if they hadn't already started. With luck, they'd begin outside – looking for anything the dogs might have left – but she had to assume that sooner or later they'd search the house. She didn't know how much time she had, but probably not much. She just hoped it would be enough.

She wondered whereabouts she was in the house. She must be on the opposite side to her room. Not that it mattered. The first thing had to be finding a way down.

Choosing a direction, which she thought led towards the centre of the building, she started cautiously along the corridor.

For no obvious reason, the corridor took several right-angle bends and included some random steps up and down. Apart from making further assaults on Marcie's shaky sense of direction, this also served to increase her stress levels, since she couldn't see what lay beyond the corners. She approached each one with a rising tension that became nearly unbearable, half expecting Andreker or one of his men to suddenly step out in front of her.

On the other hand, she reminded herself, if it weren't for the eccentric architecture she would be seen as soon as someone else entered the corridor. At least this way she might hear someone coming.

'And do what?' she wondered. She would have to try and duck into one of the doors she passed, hoping that they were both unlocked and unoccupied.

After several turns, she came across a flight of stairs on her right. Unfortunately, they went up, not down. A brief investigation showed that they led to a short landing and a solid door, firmly secured with a Yale lock on the inside.

This, Marcie decided, was probably the way out to the comms. platform. The legitimate way. Which gave her a better idea of where she was, but didn't help in finding the way down.

She leant against the door, and shut her eyes, struggling to create a mental map of the house. As far as she could make out, she had come most of the way along the length of it on the roof. Which meant she was almost all the way back again. She must have passed over her room, and the stairway from the front door to the first floor had been near the centre of the house. She couldn't recall seeing another flight of steps going further up from there, but she might well have missed it. Did that mean that she'd also missed the way down? She didn't see how, unless it was behind a door.

Not a pleasant thought, that. It would mean going back and trying every door until she found the right one. Her mouth went dry as she thought of the risks involved with that.

Of course, it could be that the stairs down would be at the end of the corridor, rather than near the middle. Or they could be somewhere completely random, which would fit with the way the corridor ran.

Marcie started back down the short flight from the walkway door. Just as she did so, a door was flung open somewhere nearby, and footsteps pounded along the corridor below.

A dark figure rushed past the bottom of the stairs. Too fast to recognize. Too fast, she hoped, to have looked up and seen her. Perhaps. She jumped back on to the landing and lay flat on the floor.

Below, there was loud knocking, doors being thrown open, and voices. Shouts. Questions, angry complaints – people being woken up. Straining her ears, Marcie could make out a few words.

'Everyone up! Search the grounds! Hurry! Mr Andreker wants...'

Steps coming back towards her. More doors were opening in the other direction, more people coming. She wondered how many Andreker had. It sounded like an army.

Snatches of conversation came up the stairway as people passed below.

'But the dogs!' 'What's going on?' 'Woman's escaped....'

Doors slammed. The noises faded. A straggler rushed by, swearing. Marcie listened as his footsteps went past, paused, clattered down some steps. Another door crashed shut, and the footsteps became muffled. Then silence.

When she was quite sure that everyone had gone, she got shakily to her feet and went warily back down the stairs, listening intently as she did. Then back down the corridor, this time trying the doors. At least she now knew that there was no one else up here. Because they were all out looking for her. It should have been funny, really.

The first door was an empty bedroom. The second was a broom cupboard. The third opened to a flight of stairs, leading down.

Treading as lightly as possible, Marcie followed them.

There was another door at the bottom, which perhaps explained why she hadn't noticed the staircase earlier. It had been left slightly ajar. She paused, listened. Hearing nothing, she eased it open and peered through.

She was back in the Tudor area, in the corridor that led to Andreker's office. Progress at last! The main staircase should be just along there....

A sudden flood of light spilled from an opening door a little way down the corridor. Marcie slipped back into the stairway, pulling the door almost shut.

Andreker's voice, came closer. 'Well search again then! I don't believe she could have got out of the grounds. Perhaps she's up a tree?'

'Yes sir, we'll keep looking.' Davis's voice. 'But it occurred to me that, if she saw the dogs, she might have tried to get back inside. Or perhaps she was planning that anyway, to get to a phone. Or a car.'

The two men paused, out in the corridor, close to the door.

'How could she have got back inside the house again?'

'I'm not sure. But if she made her break when the cars were at the front the dogs would have been distracted to that side of the house. There may have been a door or window open, and she *is* Scenes of Crime. Presumable she knows something about forcing locks.'

Andreker swore softly. Not in English, but the tone was clear enough. 'I doubt if she could have forced these locks without tools.'

'I'll have the windows checked. The phone system is already locked against outgoing calls. The garage should be secure, but I'll make sure.'

'Do that.' Andreker agreed. 'And I want all mobiles accounted for as well.'

'There's not a lot she could do if she got one.' Davis said. 'She can't tell anyone where she is, and they can't trace a mobile call as accurately as a landline.'

'They can find which cell received the call, and that would put them closer than I like, especially if she got out a description. No, I don't want any loose ends. If she manages to make a call we'll have to finish her immediately, and I don't want to do that while I still have some use for her. Get the mobiles sorted now. I'll check the garage myself, and go round the windows. If there is any...'

Andreker's voice faded as they moved on down the corridor. Marcie sat on the bottom step, trying not to panic at the casual way Andreker talked about murdering her.

'No *time* for this!' she whispered through clenched teeth. '*Move, girl!*'

Out of the door into the corridor. Pause to listen. Andreker's office was just over there, brilliant light still pouring from the door he'd left open. The stairs – that way.

That was the way out, but the grounds were now full of men searching for her, as well as dogs. The garage was secure, and Andreker was making sure of it. There would be no car.

She wasn't going to get out. And not getting out meant that, eventually, she'd be re-captured. She couldn't stay ahead of them forever.

Think! She told herself. If she couldn't get out, she had to get a message out.

The landlines were already locked down. There might be a few mobiles around, perhaps in people's rooms? But they'd be coming back to secure them.

She thought of all the aerials she's seen on the roof. There must be something she could use. E-mail? Or would Andreker have one of those satellite phones? Probably.

No time to debate it. The corridor was empty now, and so was Andreker's office. Time to move.

Marcie ran the short distance to the office. The door was still ajar. She pushed it open and walked in.

It was just as she remembered it – light and bright. So much that it hurt her eyes again. The big TV was now displaying several different pictures simultaneously. After a few moments Marcie realised it was showing different views of the house, the grounds, and (presumably) the perimeter. The pictures changed at regular intervals as some automatic programme switched between cameras.

Every now and then she saw groups of men with torches. Searching the bushes, looking up trees, being very thorough. The dogs were out as well – on leashes, but joining in avidly.

It confirmed her gut-instinct. Escape was no longer an option. And once they were convinced that she wasn't out there, and began searching the house, her re-capture would be swift.

She went to the desk. Both laptops were still there, both switched on and running screensavers. She tapped keys, and both came up with a password request.

OK, no e-mails.

She cleared the request boxes, got back the screen-savers. There was a phone on the desk, of course. Something sleek and stylish in chrome, with a multitude of functions. She picked it up and listened. No dialling tone. Tried a few buttons, searching for an outside line, and eventually heard a strange warbling note. Puzzled, she listened for moment until the thought occurred that it might be the ring tone for an internal connection. She slammed the receiver down hurriedly, before it could be answered.

The landline phones were locked out, as Davis had promised. What about mobiles? Andreker would have his with him, probably never moved without it. But gadget freaks usually had more than one. She began trying the drawers.

What does a criminal keep in his desk? Apart from a gun, of course. She checked that drawer first. Not surprisingly, it was gone. The rest had a few pads of blank paper, some pens, several notebooks, written in a foreign language. Surprisingly, one drawer yielded a large bag of sweets.

Behind it were various electronic gadgets – executive toys. And two mobile phones. One of them was Marcie's.

She let out a gasp of relief, and snatched it up. She switched it on, waited impatiently while it went through its start-up sequence, then began to dial 999.

And paused. Thumb over the green button. Remembering what Andreker had said to Davis.

'If she manages to make a call we'll have to finish her immediately.'

If the police turned up at the gates, he would know she'd made a call.

They'd take it seriously, if she called in with story of kidnapping and guns – they'd have to respond. But it would take time. Time to get officers into the area, to get Armed Response Vehicles on scene. And it would take time to track the call, to identify the cell, to cross check that with her patchy description of the house.

She didn't know how much time. And they'd want her to stay on the line, keep talking. They'd need local police, for knowledge of the area. How many coppers would be covering a rural area like this, at this time of night? Police out here were spread pretty thin.

They'd want to check back with Faringham Police, to confirm her identity. Command would have to be informed.

Could she stay out of Andreker's reach while all that happened?

Could she gamble her life on it?

It would mean her life. Marcie had no doubts at all on that. If Andreker had her when the police turned up at the gate, she'd be dead before they reached the house.

And what would happen then? Andreker would be at his most charming, most sincere.

'Yes, officer, I spoke to the lady on the phone earlier. She had some idea that my daughter had been kidnapped, if you can believe that! I assured her that my daughter was safe and well and on holiday with her mother. No, she didn't come here, officer – but please feel free to look around.'

They wouldn't find anything. They would look properly, of course, and no doubt Andreker would be seriously inconvenienced. But he would be adept at hiding bodies. They wouldn't find her. No one would. Ever.

She cancelled the call, and stared numbly at the phone.

'Out of your depth'. Andreker had said to her. And he was right, she was. Out of her depth and drowning.

'Stupid little bitch,' Vince Maddox had called her. And he was right as well. She had stupidly got herself into this situation. Stupidly ignored advice. Stupidly pressed on, thinking herself so clever.

And she knew with utter certainty, that she couldn't afford one more mistake. Because the next stupid thing she did would kill her.

She had only one chance, if that. She had to use the mobile while she still could. Who could she call?

She wanted to call John. She desperately wanted to call him, to hear him. But that would be stupid. Because there was nothing that John could do. She'd have to explain it all to him, and then he'd be crazy with worry, but wouldn't be able to do anything. Except call the police, and she'd already worked out where that would lead.

Calling anybody else would have the same effect. She couldn't get help because she didn't know where she was. No-one could reach her before Andreker did.

Desperately, she began flicking through the stored numbers, searching for inspiration.

John's work number. Rory's school. Doctor. Childminder. SOCO office – no one there now. Doug's mobile. She wished she could call Doug, at least he'd understand what was going on, but she *still couldn't tell him where she was!*

And in any case, it was his work mobile number. He didn't take it home, except when he was on call. It'd be in the office. He had this routine. She'd seen him do it so many times. Last thing before leaving, he'd scroll through the recently used numbers, delete the ones he wouldn't need again, put it on charge.

He never used the voice-mail function. She could send him a text, but he wouldn't get it until morning, when he came in and switched it on. By morning, if she wasn't dead, Andreker would have her on her way to Cyrus Street.

Movement on the big screen caught her eye. One section had cycled to a view of the main house entrance. Figures were gathering there. She recognised Andreker. And Davis – but others were arriving. The search teams were coming in.

By now they must be all but certain she wasn't out there. So they'd start searching inside.

She had to make the call now. Call someone – anyone!

And tell them what?

It exploded in her mind. A revelation, bursting out of her subconscious with such completeness, such clarity, that she actually gasped with the shock of it.

Tell them where she would *be!*

She didn't know where she was now – but she knew where she would be tomorrow morning! What had Andreker said? He wanted to be there by eight a.m.? Doug was on an early shift tomorrow. He'd be in by seven. If he checked his phone soon enough, there'd be time.

Even as she formulated the thought, her fingers were moving, tapping in the text message.

The main entrance came up on the screen again. More people there now. Andreker was turning towards the door, climbing the steps.

She finished the message. The bare minimum. All she had time for. Pressed 'send'.

Message sent.

She started to switch off, swore, and hastily deleted the message. Just in case. Switched the phone off, and dumped it back in the drawer. A quick check – there couldn't be any sign that she'd been there. She hastily banged a drawer shut than ran for the door.

Listening, she heard voices, muffled, down the stairs. She risked a glance round the door – clear – ran for the stairway up. Shut the door behind her, and went up as quickly as she could.

She paused at the top. What was her plan?

No point in trying to get back to her bedroom, obviously. Even if she could face that route again. But to be caught in the corridor would be as good as jumping off the roof, survival wise.

The roof! That was the only place. They might not even look up there – and if they did, then perhaps she could convince them that she'd got no further!

Which would be easier if they didn't find a window open.

Running now, full tilt along the twisting corridor that she'd crept along just a little while before. And suddenly realising that she'd didn't know which door she'd come out of! Which was Curly's room?

She started slamming doors open, hoping that no one had ignored the call-out. Safe enough, no one was going to ignore Andreker!

Door after door. Bedroom after bedroom. None with open windows. She came to the end of the corridor, a communal bathroom. She'd missed it somehow!

Near panic, she ran back again, wildly bursting in the doors, looking for open window, an ashtray... she was nearly back to the stairs now. Had she gone the wrong way down the corridor?

It came to her with a dizzying burst of relief. Curly had shut his own window, and hidden his ashtray, before he came out. If he was a secret smoker, he'd take precautions. Probably sucked a peppermint as well.

Pausing to catch her breath, she heard movement below. Voices. Coming up? She didn't wait to find out. She ran for the short flight leading to the walkway.

The Yale lock opened easily, the door itself less so. It was stiff, not often used. Throwing her weight behind it, she forced it to move.

The cold hit her as she stepped through. She lingered by the door. After all the effort she'd expended to get inside, shutting herself out again was heartbreaking.

Getting caught inside would be a lot worse.

There were definitely voices below. She heaved on the door, swinging it shut. Catching it at the last moment, to stop it slamming. Then gently pushing it the last little bit, till she heard the lock click shut.

She leant against the door, listening. No sound came through the thick wood, even when she put her ear to it.

This had been the warmest place on the roof before. Perhaps it still was, but coming out of the house, it felt below freezing. Already she could feel herself starting to shiver.

Wrapping her arms around herself, Marcie sank down on to the walkway with her back to the door. Perhaps it would be warmer down here. Was that hot air vent still operating?

Looking up, the stars were brilliantly clear. Frost tonight, for certain. How cold did it have to get to kill you? Ironic, if Andreker's men didn't find her and she died of hypothermia, here on the roof.

Perhaps she should do something about that? Go to the edge of the roof and attract attention?

She couldn't decide if that would be a good idea or not. She didn't want to move. Cold as it was, it'd be colder out near the edge. And now that she had stopped running, stopped moving, exhaustion was threatening to overcome her. Moving anywhere would be such an effort, she had to be sure it was the right thing to do.

She was still thinking about it when the door suddenly groaned open, flinging her forwards. A voice swore and light shone in her eyes as she began to sit up.

'So here you are!' said a man's voice from behind the light. He sounded surprised but glad to see her, like he'd just won a game of 'hide and seek'. 'Dog's didn't get you after all!' He turned and shouted down the stairs. 'Got her, lads! She's up here! Someone tell Mr Andreker!'

Feet, pounding up the stairway. Marcie started to get to her feet. Before she could, she'd been grabbed by both arms and hauled roughly upright.

'Come on, you!' She was hustled back inside.

Down the stairs. Corridor, stairs, corridor. Warmer, at least, she told herself, trying to overlook how terrifying it was to be so helpless.

At the top of the main staircase, they met Andreker and Davis.

Andreker's face was expressionless. He looked her over clinically. 'Where was she?' he asked one of the men holding her.

'Comms platform walkway, sir. Just outside the door.'

'Could she have been inside?' Marcie tensed, waiting for the answer, then forced herself to relax. Hoped it hadn't been noticed.

'No sir. Door was secure.'

Andreker glanced at Davis. 'Anywhere else she could have got into the house from the walkway?'

Davis was studying her closely. 'There are a few windows that open on to it, but we've checked them. They're shut and locked, haven't been opened for ages. She'd have had to smash the glass to get in.'

'Check them again,' Andreker said tersely. 'Make sure that there's no sign of forced entry. And take her down to the wine cellar. Search her. Properly.' He still hadn't addressed a single word to her. As the men hustled her off, he was walking swiftly towards his office.

Whatever his other indulgences, Andreker wasn't a wine buff. The cellar, when they reached it, was full of dust and wine racks but empty of wine. Not big. Smaller than her kitchen. Wooden floor, wooden walls, one of brick. The outside wall, she thought. Some broken furniture in the corner. Three wine racks, each capable of holding maybe a hundred bottles.

Marcie concentrated on the racks, tried to count the spaces, while they searched her. It was rough, intimate and humiliating. And frightening. Her sense of helplessness increased. She had a sickening sense of confronting a harsh reality that she'd been aware of, but not really understood before. Anything could be done to her here, anything at all, and she could do nothing about it. Nothing.

She counted spaces to keep it at a manageable distance, to keep from screaming or begging.

The men were impersonal and efficient. After they finished, they let her sort her clothing out. She wanted to sit down, but that would emphasise her vulnerability. So she stayed standing. Not that it made much difference.

Andreker came in. 'Well?' he asked.

One of the men nodded towards a rickety table. 'That's all she had on her, sir.'

Andreker glanced at the small collection. Watch, handkerchief, a pen, some crumpled receipts. Marcie didn't keep much in her pockets. That was what her bag was for.

Davis came in. 'Windows all secure, sir. She hasn't been inside.'

Andreker nodded. And turned his attention to Marcie. He was still expressionless, but there was something in his eyes which made her want to shrink back.

'What, exactly, did you think you were doing?'

'I – I was frightened.' No need to try to put a quaver in her voice. 'I wanted to get to a road – to find a telephone box – but the dogs were there, and I couldn't get back to my room – I had to go up. I nearly fell. I'm sorry.' She hadn't intended that last bit. It just slipped out.

Andreker nodded. He looked almost understanding. 'Of course you are. Of course. I must say you have surprised me, though. I didn't expect you to be so enterprising. Or so stupid.'

Marcie stared dumbly at him. He stepped forward. Put his cheek gently against hers and whispered, so close to her ear that she could feel his warm breath.

'I – don't – like – surprises.'

He stepped back, and jerked his head towards the wall.

'Wait...' she began, but her arms were grabbed, she was dragged backwards and slammed against the woodwork. Her vision blurred as the back of her head bounced off it.

Andreker stood right in front of her. His shiny silver pistol was in his hand. He held it in front of her, and cocked the hammer.

'When you came to me with your information,' he said conversationally, 'I had some gratitude to you. I also felt that you might be of some use in getting my daughter back.'

He levelled the gun, pointed it at her face. She stared, unable to look anywhere but at the muzzle.

'My gratitude, and indeed my patience, is now exhausted.' Andreker continued calmly. He extended his arm, pushed the muzzle against her forehead.

Marcie heard herself give a strangled little sob. She was pushing her head back against the wall, as far as it would go, but the gun barrel was a cold, deadly circle on her forehead, grinding into her skull as Andreker leaned a little closer.

'So the only question that remains, Marcia, is this: are you going to be of any use to me?'

She couldn't answer. Her whole body was shuddering, only the men's grip on her arms was keeping her upright.

'Well?' Andreker raised an eyebrow. Suddenly his voice changed to a snarl. 'Damn you, woman – answer me! Are you going to be useful?'

'Yes!' she shrieked. 'Yes! Anything! Please!'

A distant part of her heard the shrieking, and was disappointed. But that was a long way away. Andreker and his gun were much closer.

'Good.' Andreker's voice was calm again. 'Much better. Just see that you are. Because if you cause me any more trouble...'

His hand twitched, flicking the gun to one side. There was a massive explosion in her right ear, a searing pain in the side of her head.

The gun flicked the other way, the smoking muzzle inches from her eyes. Another thunderous explosion, a burning pain on her left ear.

Her head was ringing, her mind was overwhelmed with noise and pain and terror. Dimly she was aware of Andreker turning away, walking towards the door. If he said anything else, she didn't hear it. Couldn't hear it. She could hear screaming. It sounded a long way away, but she knew it was her, she could feel rawness in her throat as she screamed and screamed, hardly able to take breath.

Davis was walking away as well. The two men let go of her, and followed. She slumped, collapsing down the wall. The door slammed shut, the light went out.

She sat huddled in the darkness, listening to herself scream. It stopped after a while, died away into sobs, but they went on for a long time.

CHAPTER 13

There were no windows in the wine cellar. They hadn't given Marcie her watch back. She had no idea how long she lay in the darkness. Perhaps she fell asleep. When the door opened and light filled the room it seemed like waking up.

It seemed like waking up into a nightmare. Her first thought was that Andreker was coming back to finish the job, and she pushed herself back against the wall, shuddering and sweating. Part of her, hearing the pathetic little whimpering sound she was making, was ashamed. But it wasn't something she could control. She couldn't even try.

It wasn't Andreker.

Two of his men came instead. Not ones they had seen before. They pulled her to her feet, and hustled her out of the door. Through the corridors, up the stairs. She thought they were going to Andreker's office, and began to tremble again. But the door was closed, and they went by without pausing.

They took her back to her old room. It was still dark outside. A breakfast was laid out on the table.

'You've got half an hour,' one of the men said. 'We'll be back for you. Be ready.'

Marcie ignored the breakfast. Instead, as soon as the men had left, she went into the bathroom.

Looking in the mirror, she saw a stranger. It wasn't the blotchy, tear-streaked face, or the bedraggled blonde hair. It wasn't even the still painful burns on the side of her head and her ears.

What had changed was something in her eyes. There was a desperation, a despair, that she'd never seen in anyone.

The face could be washed, the hair combed. The burns would heal. The new silk blouse, the smart suit – ruined, but they could be replaced.

The real difference was in the person that she was. That had changed irrevocably. Andreker had deliberately missed, but the old Marcie Kelshaw was dead and gone forever. She wasn't sure who she would be now.

She was dressed when the men returned. They escorted her outside without a word.

The black Lexus was parked on the gravel, Jenkins standing by the door. Her DB7 was gone, instead there was a Galaxy, with the same heavily tinted windows, and the doors already open. Waiting for her.

They put her in the back, and got in themselves. There were two others already there, one of them the driver. Hard looking men, dressed in nondescript dark clothing. They loaded sports bags into the spare seats, and settled in, swapping jokes, talking sport and women as the Galaxy started up and headed down the drive.

They ignored Marcie. She sat numbly in her seat, and ignored them.

She couldn't see much through the tinted glass. She could have leant over and looked out of the windscreen, but that might attract attention to her. She didn't want that. She wanted to be ignored and forgotten about. So she sat and stared at her hands, and thought about home.

She thought about John, and Rory and Kady. She thought about their last holiday together. Just before all this had started. She concentrated on remembering every day in detail. Every word spoken. Every expression on the children's faces.

She didn't think about Andreker. She didn't think about the Maddoxes, or the fact that she was being taken back to Cyrus Street. She didn't even think about her text to Doug, or what he might do when he got it. To think about that might lead to hope. And hope would need courage. She had very little courage left, if any. She couldn't afford to spend it on hoping.

She had worked her way deep into the past, going back through holidays, Christmases and other happy events, when a loud argument in the front of the Galaxy brought her unwillingly back. The driver had apparently lost sight of the Lexus which they were following, and was cursing the man next to him for not keeping track. He cursed back. Both had a fine command of profanity, and the other two joined in with their own opinions, colourfully expressed.

Marcie took advantage of the situation to take a look forwards. It was getting light, and the streets were familiar.

The argument resolved, and their location identified, the Galaxy continued on its way, passing within a few streets of Ash Ridge Police Station. It must be past seven, she thought. Her shift would be in the office, getting their jobs, making coffee, chatting. Perhaps wondering where she was?

Doug would be getting out his work phone, switching it on, checking the charge. Would he notice her message? Surely he'd notice that there was a message?

Unless he was late in.

Or something happened and he had to take the day off.

Or...

There were so many things that could go wrong. An almost unbearably hard knot of tension developed in her guts.

She watched as they threaded their way through the morning rush hour traffic. Getting stuck for a few minutes in Central, veering off through Richardswood, before entering Old Northdale.

They finally pulled up on a side road not far from Cyrus Street. She dredged the name up from her memory. Thurlingham. Thurlingham Road. She'd been to a burglary along here last summer. Cyrus Street was just round that corner ahead.

The side door slid open and Andreker climbed in. Involuntarily, Marcie flinched back at the sight of him. He saw it, and smiled.

Which triggered a little burst of anger inside her. Deep down, beneath the blanket of fear that covered every other thought and emotion, but strong enough to help her stay in control. She nurtured the anger carefully, fed it, and drew on it. She couldn't help huddling back in her seat as he sat down next to her, but she managed not to cry, not to beg.

'Had a good journey, I hope?' Andreker said brightly. 'I take it you know where you are?'

Marcie nodded.

'Good. Well, now, Marcia. It's time for you to be useful.'

Not trusting herself to speak, she nodded again.

'You'll be glad to know that Mr Davis has very kindly returned your car for you. So no loose ends there!' He smiled broadly.

Marcie understood the hidden message. No one would be looking for the car, or making enquiries about what had happened to it. And if anyone was looking for her, there would be no trail to follow.

In other words, she had no choice but to be useful.

'What do you want me to do?' she asked. Her voice sounded flat and tired. But Andreker seemed unconcerned by her lack of enthusiasm.

'Mr Davis has also had a look round the area. As you informed us, the Maddoxes have put some impressive security in place. The gate, he assures me, cannot be easily forced or broken down, and it is well covered by CCTV. The surrounding walls are quite high and further protected by wire, probably alarmed and possibly electrified.'

'You can't get in,' Marcie said quietly. She thought she knew where this was going.

'Not easily, no. But this is where you can be useful!' Andreker sounded very pleased with himself. He was, Marcie thought, congratulating himself on his forethought in keeping her alive.

Andreker continued. 'Mr Davis assures me that, because of the way the street curves, we can get men within fifteen metres of the gate without being seen.' He frowned, thinking. 'Let me see – that would be about fifty feet?'

'I understand metres.'

'Of course! So, the point is, we will be very close behind you when you go up to the gate.'

Marcie closed her eyes. It was what she'd been expecting, and fearing. 'You want me to go up to the gate?'

Andreker spread out his hands, as if in surprise at the question. 'Yes, of course! Go to the gate, press the bell or buzzer or whatever they have. Announce yourself on the intercom. When they open the gate, wait for a few moments. Allow it to be fully opened before you enter. Then walk slowly up to the door. You said it was thirty or forty feet from the gate?'

Marcie struggled to remember the brief glimpse she'd had that first time she'd come to Cyrus Street. 'About that. Less than forty, I think.'

'So, not much more than ten metres. I assure you, Marcia, that my men and I will have caught up with you by then. The Maddoxes will not have time to close the gate, and from what you told me, there can be no more than four men there.' He indicated the other occupants of the vehicle. 'As you see, we have them outnumbered, and the advantage of surprise. I'm sure they will not give us much trouble, and I will have my daughter back.'

Andreker leaned forward and patted her hand. 'After that, Marcia, you will be free to go, with my thanks. And all our past little disagreements will be forgotten.'

Marcie couldn't look at him. Not without giving away the fact that she knew he was lying.

'I don't think the Maddoxes will give up so easily. They'll be armed, you know.'

Andreker raised his eyebrows. 'Will they? Oh dear! But look....' he reached over to one of the sports bags, and unzipped it. Reaching in, he produced – with a definite flourish – a sub-machine gun.

Marcie was surprised how small it was. Not much bigger than a pistol, square and chunky. It looked vaguely familiar from that firearms course – not an Uzi, a MAC-10 or something like that.

Andreker pulled out a magazine longer than the weapon itself, slotted it into place. 'As you see, Marcia, I think we should have the upper hand there as well.' Andreker smiled, and cocked the weapon. It made a solid, well-oiled sound.

Marcie looked away from the gun, thinking desperately. She did not share Andreker's easy confidence in his plan. From what she remembered of Vince Maddox, he was not the sort to simply give in to the logic of superior numbers and weaponry.

And, whatever happened, she would be right out in front.

'I think you've forgotten something.'

Andreker looked amazed. 'Really? What could that be, Marcia?'

'There's no reason why the Maddoxes should let me in. No reason for them to open the gate. They know I'm Scenes of Crime. They wouldn't want me getting a look inside! They'll just tell me to get lost.'

Andreker was smiling and nodding gently. 'Oh, yes, I'm glad you mentioned that. Something I forgot to tell you – you're expected!'

'What? What do you mean?'

He held up a mobile phone. Hers. For a terrible moment, she thought he was going to tell her he knew about her text to Doug.

'I borrowed it last night. Just for a short text.' He sat back, relaxed and happy, enjoying his own cleverness. 'Fortunately, I still have contact numbers for the Harkers, as I knew them, and they are still active. So I sent them a message – in your name, of course – to the effect that the missing flash card and photographs (including those of St Celia's) could be returned to them. For a price. And I told them you would visit them to transact business early this morning.' He glanced at his watch. 'In fact, you're running a little late for your appointment, Marcia, so if you're quite clear about things…?' He gestured towards the door.

Marcie felt the growth of something freezing and deadly in her gut. 'You told them – you told the Maddoxes *that!* You told them that I had the card?'

She glanced up and finally met Andreker's eyes. Amused, self-satisfied, manipulative.

'They'll be suspicious. They won't believe me.'

Andreker nodded. 'Yes, suspicious, I'm sure. But they will believe it. They believe in greed and stupidity. They deal in it regularly, as I do.'

'But how would I get their mobile number to text them?'

'I'm sure that's something else they will be anxious to ask you about. But we do need to be getting on.'

'If they think I've got the card they'll kill me.' She said quietly.

'Of *course* they will.' Andreker sighed, exasperated at being told the obvious. 'If they get the chance. So *your* only chance is to do exactly as you've been told.' He leaned very close to her, and almost whispered in her ear. 'Don't screw up, Marcia. If you do, you'll have both me and the Maddoxes to deal with.' He pulled back and got out of the Galaxy.

He turned back to her from the door. 'Now, please.'

Marcie got slowly to her feet, and climbed out of the vehicle. Grey early morning in late November. A cold, damp breeze blowing. She shivered as she left the warmth.

Behind her in the Galaxy a series of metallic snicks and clacks sounded as Andreker's soldiers readied their weapons.

The Lexus was parked just in front. Davis and Jenkins, were standing by it, both with sports bags slung over their shoulders.

Davis gave her an affable nod, 'Just down there and turn right,' he told her.

'I know,' she answered, and began walking.

She could feel the pavement beneath her, but it seemed remote – a million miles away. It was hard to believe where she was or what she was doing. There was a strong temptation to dismiss it all from her mind, slip back into the comforting reality of her memories.

'Get a grip,' she muttered desperately. *'Focus!'*

She reached the corner, and turned down Cyrus Street.

It looked just as she had remembered it, the old red-brick houses with their architectural idiosyncrasies, huddled away, introverted, behind the trees and bushes and walls. Especially walls. She could see the walls of number 34, but the gate was hidden by the curve of the street. Just as Davis had reported.

She walked on.

Had Doug got her text?

She'd been trying not to think about it, but there was no more avoiding the question. Somewhere at the back of her mind she'd imagined that Doug would have passed the message on, that police officers would have the street under observation, and that as soon as she'd appeared, they'd be rushing out from cover. Coming to her rescue.

There were no police cars visible – but of course, there wouldn't be. It would have to be a plain clothes operation. CID would run it, with Armed Response Vehicles in support.

Realistically though, would Doug have had time to set that up? He couldn't have got the text more than an hour ago, if that. Not enough time to mount a major operation, but surely time for him to inform the Control Room, time to get some backup in place.

Surely he would have come to check it out himself. Surely he trusted her enough to do that much?

She wished she knew what time it was. Were they early? Or late. Could he have been there already – seen nothing, gone again?

There were no vehicles parked up at this end of the street, but as she came round the curve she could make out a van half-way down on the other side. Her heart leapt – but sank again. It wasn't a SOCO van, but an unmarked grey vehicle. Some workman, a plumber or chippy doing a job in one of the houses.

Doug wouldn't be daft enough to come in a marked van, anyway. He'd use one of the unmarked cars.

There were cars, down at the far end of the street. She was fully round the curve now, nearly at the gate of number 34. She could see the cameras mounted above it.

She heard the little whirring noise as one of them swivelled to focus on her.

She didn't recognise any of the cars.

The desire to panic began to grow. She pushed it down, desperately. Doug wouldn't let her down! Not Doug. He'd get here. He was probably getting things moving, calling in favours, getting coppers to go with him. She'd have to stall, keep it going for a few minutes. He'd get here.

She walked more slowly.

It was very quiet on Cyrus Street today. There was a distant noise of traffic. Faint sounds from behind her. Andreker and his men. She didn't dare to look back. Didn't have to.

She was almost at the gate.

Surely this hush was unnatural? Could it mean that they were already here – the Obs. Teams, the Armed Response, whatever – hiding in the neighbours gardens, telling the occupants in whispers to, *'Keep it down!'*?

That could be it! They'd be waiting for things to happen. Waiting for the Maddoxes to open the gate. It made sense, she decided, to hold on until the last moment, make sure everyone was in the bag.

Doug must have lit a fire under them to put it in place so fast. She was going to owe him, big-time, for this.

The gate was there. She stopped, next to the intercom, the button. She was still thinking about Doug, imagining what his reaction would have been when he read her text. The first thing he would have done was...

Marcie's finger was already reaching out to press the buzzer, when she realised what Doug would have done first. The shock froze her. Stopped her short. Nearly stopped her heart.

The first thing Doug would have done would have been to phone her. To try and talk to her.

He would have tried the mobile first. But that was switched off. So he'd try her home number.

And John would have answered. And he would have covered for her. That's what he'd promised. *'I'll cover for you, work wise,'* he'd said. So he'd have some excuse ready. 'She's a bit poorly this morning – staying in bed. She'll probably be in tomorrow.'

And Doug would say thank you, and shake his head, and tell the rest of the office that Marcie was off sick – probably self-inflicted, a touch of alcohol poisoning, to judge from the weird text that she'd sent! And they'd all have a laugh about it, and take their jobs and go out, and no one would come anywhere near Cyrus Street at all.

She was on her own, Marcie realised. Completely on her own. She'd made her last stupid mistake, and now she'd pay for it, and there was nothing else she could do.

Her face was wet with tears. The intercom button was just in front of her. So she pressed it, because she didn't have any more choices.

'Kelshaw.' The answer was immediate. She had been expected. And recognized, on the CCTV. Even through the tinny crackle of the intercom, Marcie could recognize Jonathan Maddox's cultured tones. 'You'd better have it with you.'

Not wasting any breath on politeness, Marcie thought tiredly. 'Of course,' she said into the microphone. Anything to get her inside.

There was a buzzing noise, and the gates began to swing open.

She'd only had a brief glimpse inside, that time before, when she'd first met Vince Maddox. Things looked much the same, though. The same stretch of weedy gravel. The Transit, parked on the left. Blue now, of course. The silver Mercedes on the right. Beyond them, the house. Three storeys of dull red brick. Dark, flaking paintwork on sash windows, all obscured by dirty curtains. A wide arched porch directly facing the gate, set over a double door. Elegant once, perhaps, but now showing neglect. Dusty glass panes, discoloured brass, worn wood with peeling varnish.

The gates stopped with a muffled clang, as they hit their stops. Fully opened. As if it were a cue, the double doors also opened, and out stepped the Maddoxes.

She recognized Vince, of course. All too well. Thick black hair and beard, leaning forward aggressively, eyes glaring. She could see that, even at this distance. Wearing the same dark, padded coat she'd seen him in before. Hands deep in the pockets.

So that had to be Jonathan next to him. Taller, smarter. Dark hair better cut, and no beard. But with a strong resemblance to his brother. Not just in looks. There was something about the way he stood, the way he stared at her, that suggested the same deep anger. Better controlled, perhaps, but just as dangerous.

Both of them, she thought, looked pleased to see her, in a pissed-off sort of way. Like they were looking forward to being very angry.

Jonathan Maddox raised a hand and imperiously beckoned her forward.

Having no choice in the matter, she reluctantly began to walk towards them.

She knew the exact moment that Andreker and his men appeared behind her. She saw it in the altered expressions on the brother's faces. Anger to shock to fury in a heartbeat. And not looking at her anymore, but past her, to where she could hear running feet.

Then she felt Andreker's hand on her shoulder, and his shiny silver pistol pushed past the ear it had burned the previous night. At least it wasn't pointed at her now.

'STAND STILL! BOTH OF YOU!' Andreker was shouting. 'DON'T MOVE!'

His men were coming up behind, fanning out. From the corner of her eye, Marcie saw Davis on her left, moving past her, sub-machine gun at the ready.

'*They don't have to move,*' she thought. Looking at Vince Maddox. Looking at his hand in his pocket. '*He's already ready for you. He's paranoid. He's always rea*dy.'

Looking at the tension in the muscles of his face, and reading the future in them.

Davis saw it as well. 'Get your hands...' he started.

There was a bang. Not all that loud. Muffled perhaps. And a cloud of white lining exploding from Vince's pocket.

Simultaneously, Davis's head snapped back, a fine red mist appearing round it.

For Marcie, time froze.

A fraction of a second, stretched almost to infinity, every detail of the scene recorded on her mind with vivid clarity.

White cloud, coming from Vince, red mist from Davis, suspended in mid-air. Davis sagging backwards, dead without the time to know it. Vince, snarling something. Jonathan, half turned towards the door.

A weak sunbeam, slipping through the clouds to brighten the dull windows.

Then Andreker's gun roared in her ear, and time started again with a rush.

There was shouting, everybody was shouting, and Andreker was blazing away, deafening her again, so she could barely hear the rattling of the machine guns. But she saw the doorway disintegrating into splinters of wood and glass. Jonathan Maddox, diving back inside, Vince Maddox, falling back in, roaring with fury and still shooting, although his coat was shredding under the impact of the bullets.

Andreker still had her shoulder, was rushing forward, pushing her ahead of him. His shield. She ran, half propelled, half trying to get away from him. She tripped over the front step, flying forwards, tearing out of his grasp and landing on the floor, just inside the hallway. Hands flat down to take the impact, in a mess of broken glass, but she didn't have time to feel anything – kept moving, kept down, scuttling forward on hands and knees, driven by a desperate instinct to *get away*.

Dark inside. Glimpses. Open door on the right, someone going away. Stairs ahead, a figure running down, pointing a gun. Long barrel, rifle or shotgun....

Vince Maddox, on the floor to her left. Blood over his face, blood everywhere, but somehow still moving, still shooting even.

She was past them, somehow. Half running, half crawling over black and white tiles, heading down a passage, away from the shouting and shooting. Past the stairs – a door off to the right, under the stairs. Something struck a tile near her hand, whined away ahead of her, and she leapt for the door, desperate to get out of the line of fire, to find a hiding place. Pulled it open and dived in, with something thudding against it as she did.

Brighter lights. Stairs, bare concrete, going down.

Marcie paused, crouching. Wondering if anyone had seen her go through the door – if they'd follow her. Thinking of that, she reached out to the door handle, to pull it shut behind her.

As she touched it, there was a thunderous explosion. The door slammed into her, sending her sprawling backwards, bouncing off the wall, unable to get her balance and falling towards the stairs.

Her head smacked into the concrete, and a sickening wave of pain turned the world fuzzy and remote.

Doug

I was in work early that morning. I wanted a quiet talk with Marcie before things got busy. I hadn't handled our last conversation at all well, and not only did I feel bad about that, but I was worried about what she might do next. My conversation with Slippery Mick was lurking at the back of my mind, and while I didn't want to do his dirty work for him, I didn't want Marcie getting into more trouble either. Best, I thought, to try and sort things out, find out what she was up to, and work with her a bit.

I was glad to see her Focus already in the car park, but she wasn't in the office. I had a search round the station. SOC store, canteen, parade room, front desk – no sign. The Seniors' Office was still locked up, neither Mick nor Jim were in this morning. The only other possible place was the ladies' loo, which I wasn't going to investigate.

Back at the office, the rest of the shift were wandering in. I got on with sorting some jobs out, still expecting her to turn up at any moment.

With my usual routine disturbed, it was nearly twenty past seven when I turned my mobile on – and got her text.

'Help 34cyrus st0800. Dngr'

Worst fears realised. Marcie had got herself into really deep shit. And head-first, by the look of it.

'Anyone seen Marcie this morning?' I asked the office in general.

There was a chorus of 'No's' and shaking heads. 'Her car's in the car park.' Ali volunteered.

'It was there all day yesterday,' Sanjay put in. 'I thought she was off?'

Memory clicked in, of words exchanged in anger. 'She was going to Saint Celia's,' I said. Puzzled expressions all round. 'It's a long story. But I think she's got herself in trouble.' I passed the mobile round the room.

When I got it back, I called Marcie's number.

'Her phone is switched off,' I explained to the expectant faces. 'Anyone got her home number handy?' Sanjay began digging round in the filing cabinet.

'I shouldn't be too worried,' said Mac, looking worried. 'I'll tell you what's happened. She had a bit of a party last night, and got bladdered. Probably planned to, that's why she left her car here. Sometime between the 'merry' stage and the 'sleepy' stage, she thought it'd be fun to wind you up with that text. Right now, she's sleeping it off, and when she wakes up she won't remember anything about it.'

I nodded, wanting to believe Mac's explanation.

Sanjay found the number. I dialled and waited. Work in the office had come to a standstill, as the rest of the shift watched.

After six rings, the answering machine cut in. 'Marcie?' I said. 'Are you there – can you pick up?' No answer. 'OK – Marcie, it's Doug. I need you to call the office A.S.A.P. Oh, and John – if Marcie's at home, or if you know where she is, please get in touch. Or get her to. Thanks.'

I hung up and looked around the office. 'Someone should be there to answer. At this time of day they should be getting the kids ready for school, even if Marcie's taking an extra day off.'

'Perhaps they've already left?' Ali suggested.

'Perhaps.' I shook my head. 'I don't know. I think I ought to check it out. Go over to Cyrus Street. Just to be on the safe side.'

The others nodded agreement. Sanjay offered me some keys. 'Take one of the Fiestas. A marked van would be a bit obvious.'

'They've already clocked the Fiestas,' Mac pointed out. 'I've got a better idea. We've got an unmarked Fiat on loan – demo vehicle, the department's thinking of getting some. I'm supposed to be evaluating it this week. I don't suppose it'll matter if you take it today.' He tossed me a set of keys. 'Grey van, down in the car park. Please don't break it!'

I left the others to sort out the jobs between them, and left in a hurry. It was twenty to eight. I didn't waste any time familiarising myself with the Fiat, just jumped in and drove. The clutch was a bit light, and I stalled twice getting out of the yard, but after that I had my foot down. I made it to Cyrus Street in fifteen minutes – good going for that time of day. I pulled up just in sight of number 34, a few minutes short of eight.

No sign of Marcie. No sign of anything. Cyrus Street looked like it was the quietest place in Faringham. Nothing happening at all.

I sat for a few minutes, recovering from my mad dash across town, and thought about it.

If it was a joke, then it was the most successful wind-up in the department's history. I hoped it was, but I didn't really believe it. It wasn't something Marcie would do, no matter how pissed.

But getting herself into some seriously deep shit – that sounded like Marcie.

I got out my mobile, tried both her numbers again. Same results.

Nearly ten past eight, and still nothing happening on Cyrus Street. The only movement was the CCTV cameras above the gate to number 34. They were twitchy, moving around a lot, scanning the street.

Normal security, or were they expecting something to happen?

I felt unpleasantly conspicuous, sitting in the van with the cameras glancing in my direction. Could they see inside the cab? I slid down in the seat, and immediately sat up again, feeling foolish. If I was visible to the cameras, trying to hide would even more suspicious than just sitting there.

Unlike the normal SOCO vans, the Fiat had no bulkhead between the cab and cargo sections. I waited until the cameras were looking away, then climbed into the back, and sat down on an equipment box.

I had no idea if it would make any difference, but I felt less exposed.

I re-read the text, checked the time. Quarter past. How long should I hang round here? I couldn't stay all day. There were jobs to get to. But if Marcie was in trouble...

I'd give her till half-past. Or perhaps a bit longer. But no more than an hour. At the most.

A woman came into view round the bend at the top of the street. Not Marcie. This was a dishevelled blonde. Looked like she'd been through a hedge backwards, I thought.

Another look. Was it Marcie?

It wasn't the blonde hair that threw me. I remembered, now, she'd arranged that with Ali. It was her whole appearance – and the way she walked – slumped, tired, hopeless. Like every step was barely worth the trouble. Not like Marcie, not at all.

She stopped at number 34.

It was Marcie. I could see her more clearly now. Marcie, looking like she'd suffered something traumatic, and was still not through it. Marcie, in deep trouble.

I started to clamber over the seats, to get out of the van. Then I saw the line of men following her down the street. Big lads, dressed in black, and walking in a line close to the wall. Staying out of the CCTV's line of sight, I realised. It didn't need a trained observer to think that there was something a bit dodgy about the way they all kept a hand inside their sports bags.

Just what was going on? Whatever it was, Marcie was in even more trouble than I'd realised.

The gates to number 34 began to swing open.

It was definitely wrong, all wrong, and whatever was happening here I needed help.

'X-ray Mike...' *I paused. I hadn't asked Mac what the call sign for this van was. No matter, I'd use my normal one.* 'X-ray Mike Four Six to control.'

'X-ray Mike Four Six, stand by unless urgent.' *I'd been vaguely aware of some heavy radio traffic going on – coppers over in Longmile dealing with a multiple RTA – but I was sure this took precedence. I hoped it did, or I was going to be in deep shit.*

'X-ray Mike Four Six to Control, this is urgent!' I snapped. 'I'm on Cyrus Street. There's another SOCO here, entering Number 34 under duress! Back-up requested.'

There was a stunned pause. The gate finished opening, and Marcie walked in. The line of men rushed forward, following her through the gate, and pulling out – shit! Were those submachine guns? I'd only caught a glimpse.

Control was back on. 'X-ray Mike Four Six, copy that – All units, officers required urgently, 34 Cyrus Street, Scenes Of Crime Officer in trouble!'

I was out of the van now, running up the street. On the radio, a chorus of Police officers were calling in, reporting availability and ETA to Cyrus Street.

From inside the open gate, there was a shot. And others. Loud noises, shouts.

I skidded to a stop, just short of the gate. 'X-ray Mike Four Six – shots fired! Gunshots at 34 Cyrus Street!'

Another voice came on air, the Control Room Inspector taking charge.

'All units – gunshots reported at 34 Cyrus Street. Do not, repeat do not enter the street. Officers on scene establish a cordon at the street entrances. Armed Response Vehicles are State Five. X-ray Mike Four Six – Do NOT approach the premises. Repeat, stay clear! Acknowledge!'

Too late. I was already running, up to the gates now, stopping to peer round them.

I got a brief glimpse of a group of men, charging into a doorway.

Then the scene disintegrated into flame. A thunderous noise filled my ears and I was flung backwards into the road.

CHAPTER 14

Marcie never completely lost consciousness, but when the blinding agony in her head had subsided a little, she was at the bottom of the stairs, with no recollection of how she'd arrived there.

She tried to get up, but couldn't find the strength. Instead she slumped weakly onto the bottom step, and peered fuzzily round her.

The stairs ended, unsurprisingly, in a cellar. Bare concrete floor, whitewashed brick walls, all painfully bright under fluorescent strips. Along the far wall was a bare plywood partition, not quite reaching the ceiling, and inset with four plain doors of the same plywood. They were all bolted shut on Marcie's side.

A small CCTV camera was fixed to the top of the partition, above each door, looking down on the far side. Mounted on the cellar wall to Marcie's right was a corresponding bank of monitors. She squinted a bit, but couldn't make out what they showed. They were small screens, and her vision was blurred.

Making a huge effort, Marcie pulled herself to her feet. Leaning on the wall, she managed a few shaky steps towards the monitors. Below them was a trestle table, partially covered with boxes of various kinds and a stack of disposable plates. Still half supported by the wall, she made her way closer.

Her progress came to an end when she reached a small alcove, set into the wall under the stairs. She didn't feel quite ready for unaided movement just yet. Instead she leant on the wall and studied the monitors.

Each had a colour picture of a small room, all identically furnished with a camp bed and a bucket. Three of the rooms had occupants.

The pain in Marcie's head had subsided to the grandmother of all headaches. Squinting from the pain, she struggled to make out details.

The empty room was furthest left on the monitors. In the next one was a small figure curled up on the camp bed. A little boy, she thought, no more than seven or eight years old.

The monitor next to him showed a young girl. She was sprawled on her back, and Marcie could see her better. Long blonde hair, wearing some sort of pink jogging suit. She looked about ten years old. Fast asleep, or at least not moving. Asleep, Marcie hoped, though how could she have slept through that explosion?

The final monitor showed an older girl, in her teens perhaps. Face away from the camera. Marcie couldn't see much more than dark hair.

And a grubby but still distinctive school uniform.

'St Celia's missing student.' Marcie muttered to herself. 'Miss Andreker, I presume.'

She had been right. She had been right all along. She had been right about everything.

The knowledge wasn't especially thrilling. She was far too exhausted for any such strong emotion. But at least there had been a point to all this, however badly she'd bollocksed it up.

The empty fourth cell suggested that the Maddoxes had made plans for another kidnapping, not yet carried out. The alternative was that they'd already disposed of one child, which she didn't want to contemplate.

With an effort, Marcie peeled herself away from the wall, and staggered the remaining distance to the table. There was a plastic garden chair. She collapsed into it.

Among the boxes on the table was a crate of mineral water, and some opened bottles. She twisted the top off one of the bottles, took a sip and coughed. Her mouth was dust dry, her throat parched. Feeling the liquid on them was a shock. Recovering, she drank some more, then poured the rest of the bottle over her head.

It did help. Sort of. The headache had receded sufficiently for her to be aware of other aches and pains. Her hands, were throbbing and covered in blood. There was a vague recollection of crawling over broken glass. Passing Vince Maddox, shot to bits but still firing back. He must be dead by now. What about the others? What about Andreker? That explosion – had that been something the Maddoxes had set off, or had it been part of Andreker's arsenal?

Marcie opened another bottle of water, drank some, poured the rest over her hands.

Most of the other boxes on the table were disposable cups, plates and cutlery, but some had a medical look to them. The name of a drug company was stencilled on the side, along with a batch number and the product name. Morphine Elixir. And a warning notice – Controlled Drug.

One box was opened. Marcie reached in and pulled out a small brown glass bottle.

'So that's the drug connection,' she said to herself. 'Right again, Marcie.' Perhaps she could allow herself a small moment of mild satisfaction. The Maddoxes were definitely linked to Ben's murder. She would have done, if she'd hurt less, and if she had any idea what to do next.

Finding a phone and calling for help seemed the obvious thing, but that would mean going back up the stairs. And she had no idea what was happening up there, if anyone was left alive, if anyone was still shooting. Staying put and waiting for help was more attractive. Surely that explosion must have got somebody's attention?

In the meantime, she ought to check on the kidnap victims. The morphine probably explained why they had slept through the noise, but she wanted to be sure. She'd stand up, and go over to the plywood cells. In a moment or two. When she felt ready for a long journey.

Up at the top of the stairs, the door swung open. She heard the hinges squeak. And squeak again, before it slammed shut.

There were footsteps on the concrete stairs. Slow, rather unsteady footprints.

Maddox, coming to check on the kidnapped children? Andreker, looking for his daughter? Either way, Marcie didn't want them to find her, and the sound triggered enough adrenaline to get her moving. As quietly as she could, she stood up, and backed carefully into the alcove below the stairs.

The footsteps paused at the bottom of the stairs. Then moved out into the room.

Marcie saw black shoes and trousers, then a black jacket. She knew before she saw his face that Jonathan Maddox had survived the carnage above.

Only just, though. He didn't look good. Face and clothing covered in dust and blood, left arm dangling limply, walking as though each step was an individual effort. All in all, he looked like Marcie felt.

However, his right arm seemed to be in working order, since he was using it to carry a large handgun. Silver, like Andreker's.

She held her breath as he continued across the room. Heading for the cells. For the kidnap victims. The children.

Would he really do it? Shoot kids in cold blood? Just out of revenge for the failure of his plans?

It was incomprehensible. But she'd seen the madness in Vince Maddox. She thought she'd seen it in Jonathan as well. It was all too possible.

Marcie didn't think about doing something or not. She was still wrestling with the horror of the situation, still trying to deny that it could really happen. But while she was thinking about it, she was moving. Stealthily. As quietly as she'd got into the alcove, she began to work her way out again.

Jonathan Maddox reached the door of the first occupied cell, at the same moment that Marcie emerged fully from the alcove.

He would have seen her if he'd looked round.

He didn't look round.

Instead, he reached out with his gun hand, and tried to work the door bolt with his free fingers. He was talking to himself, muttering something very low under his breath. When the bolt wouldn't move, she heard discernible swear words.

She took a step towards the table.

Maddox cursed again. He jammed the gun into his waist band, and reached for the bolt again. With his hand now free, he had no trouble pulling it back, and pulling the door open towards him.

Marcie took a final step, snatched up a bottle of Morphine Elixir and hurled it at Maddox's head.

It missed completely, went behind him, and shattered on the wall. Maddox whirled to face the noise, reaching for his gun – swung back again, almost as fast, in time to see another bottle, better aimed, coming straight at him.

Unfortunately, this was a half empty bottle of water, which Marcie had snatched up without looking. Not a formidable weapon, but Maddox instinctively let go of the gun and flung out his good hand in defence.

The bottle bounced harmlessly off his arm.

Maddox was screaming obscenities, hand on his gun trying to pull it free, but it was caught, somehow, snagged on the fabric, and then Marcie herself, following up the bottle attack, collided with him, grabbing desperately at the gun herself, knowing that her only chance was to get it away from him.

She was shouting 'MURDERER MURDERING BASTARD MURDERER!' He fell back under the impact, losing balance, going down hard on the concrete with Marcie on top of him, shrieked in agony as his injured arm hit the floor, and his grip loosened. She wrenched the gun free, holding it by the barrel and he lashed out, flailing at her with his good hand, hitting her arm, her shoulders, her head, as she scrambled frantically backwards. She got a hand on the butt, finger inside the trigger guard, but his hand caught the barrel, knocking it aside as she tried to point it at him.

The shot sounded loud in the confined space, but more frightening was the shrill whine as the bullet ricocheted off walls and ceiling before finally burying itself in something softer. And she was moving, scrambling backwards, out of reach of Maddox's good arm, pointing the gun at him again. Shouting. 'STOP STOP OR I'LL SHOOT I WILL YOU BASTARD STOP!'

Maddox stopped. He had been shuffling towards her on his knees, but now settled back, supporting his weight on his good arm.

Marcie stopped as well. She wanted to get further from him but it was hard to keep the gun aimed while she was scrambling backwards across the floor, and she didn't dare give Maddox a chance. Panting heavily, she got herself up into a sitting position, then kneeling, and finally stood up. Gun still directed at the centre of Maddox's body.

'I won't let you kill them,' she gasped, struggling for breath. 'I won't!'

Maddox was also breathing heavily. His only reply was to raise an eyebrow, as if in surprise.

'I won't let you,' Marcie said again.

Maddox shook his head in disbelief. 'But that's the deal. If anything goes wrong, the children die. Everyone knows that.' He looked her in the eye. 'It's your fault. If you hadn't interfered, this wouldn't be necessary.'

'*My* fault!' Marcie glared at him, mingled surprise and fury robbing her of a better reply.

'Yes, yours. Oh – forgive my manners. I'm assuming that it is Marcie? Marcia Kelshaw? Scenes of Crime Officer? We haven't met, but I've seen you on CCTV, and my brother told me all about you.'

Though rough edged with pain, the voice was still pleasant, almost relaxed. That and the words themselves were completely incongruous, so detached from the situation that Marcie wondered if she was hearing correctly.

'I'm Jonathan. I believe we spoke on the phone once?'

Social convention rears its head at the most unlikely moments. Feeling obscurely under pressure to contribute to the bizarre conversation, Marcie nodded. 'Yes,' she agreed. 'We did.'

'That was over the matter of that camera flash card, which you assured me you'd destroyed. A lie, I take it?'

Marcie nodded again. 'Yes. Sorry.' Now she was apologising to him. Weirder and weirder.

Maddox shook his head. 'That's alright. All's fair, like they say. But my brother didn't trust you.'

'Oh. Why not?' It was easier to talk, Marcie decided, than just to stand and stare at Maddox over the gun.

'Hah! Vince never trusted anyone, except me of course. In your case, it turns out he was right. I should have let him kill you then, as he wanted to.'

'He was going to kill me?' Not surprising news, but not welcome either.

'Indeed. We discussed it in detail. An accident would have been best. Or failing that perhaps something at one of your crime scenes. It wouldn't have been too difficult to set up. After all, you often go into rougher areas of town. A knifing, for example, wouldn't have looked out of place.'

Marcie took a deep breath to steady herself. 'You couldn't have got away with it.'

Maddox tried to shrug, and gasped in pain. 'Perhaps we couldn't. Probably we could have, but I decided against it. Two dead SOCOs in the same city in such a short time would attract attention. And we didn't want that. We'd already had our plans disrupted by the first one.' He nodded towards the empty cell. 'Had to cancel one acquisition altogether, the timing was so put out.'

'So why kill Ben, if it was so disruptive?'

'Ben? Oh, your colleague, of course. That was Vince, I'm afraid. Very impulsive, my brother. Always the same, even when we were kids.'

'He didn't need to shoot him!' Marcie said, shakily. She felt tears trying to force their way out, and struggled to keep them back. She needed her eyes clear.

'It was his own fault!' Maddox sounded annoyed. 'He just wasn't being reasonable. All Vince wanted was the flash card. His own property from his own car! But the stupid man wouldn't co-operate.'

Of course he wouldn't. Not Ben. 'So Vince shot him.'

'We needed that flash card back. All the operational areas were recorded on it. If the police had it, we'd have had to cancel everything. Vince wasn't inclined to stand around talking about it. Not his way. Always a man of action, Vince.'

'So he took all Ben's notes and exhibits. And put that morphine in another car to misdirect the investigation.'

Maddox nodded. 'Rather a neat touch that, I thought. I told Vince so. He doesn't normally think that far ahead, but he did quite well on this occasion.'

'It was pointless.' She had to brush her eyes now. 'Pointless. It was just a burnt out wreck, a TWOC. Ben wouldn't have found the flash card, he wouldn't have bothered looking that thoroughly. I wouldn't have done, if it hadn't been connected with Ben's murder.'

He sighed. 'I do so hate irony. Presumably, the card led you to St Celia's, and then to Andreker?'

Marcie nodded. 'We couldn't get many pictures from it, but enough to identify St Celia's.'

'And so Andreker came here. Forced you to bring him, I suppose, from what I saw of your entrance. I take it you had no idea what sort of man he was?'

She shook her head. 'I hadn't put it together then. Not completely. I knew it was kidnapping, but I hadn't realised that it was one bunch of crooks ripping off another.'

'Crudely put, but essentially accurate, I suppose.' He shifted position slightly, and Marcie raised the gun. She hadn't realised that it had somehow dropped from its original aiming point. She was surprised by the weight of it.

'Please be careful with that,' Maddox said gently. 'I quite understand that you'll shoot me if necessary, but I don't want to be shot by accident. Where were we? Oh, yes, Andreker.'

'A bit dodgy wasn't it? Kidnapping his daughter?' Marcie wished she could sit down again and rest her arms. Couldn't risk it.

'Oh, we knew where we were with him. Naturally, he'd try and find us – so would the others – but we've been planning this for a long time. We know how to drop out of sight!'

'No – not that. I meant – he seemed more concerned with his money than his daughter. How did you know he'd pay up?'

'Oh, you picked up on that, did you?' Maddox tried to move a little, grunted in pain. 'Look – do you mind if I sit up a bit? I can't hold myself like this much longer.' Without waiting for assent, he moved back until he was propped against the plywood wall, his good arm resting in his lap. 'Thanks, that's better. Yes – he's a cold fish, Andreker. But we learnt a lot about his background while we worked for him. More than he realised. He'd married into money, you see. A big crime family in Eastern Europe. He'd probably sacrifice his daughter without hesitation, but explaining it to his wife and her family – that would cost him a lot more than money! I knew he'd pay.'

Maddox grimaced, and shifted position. 'This arm!' He carefully lifted the injured arm with his good one until they were both resting on his lap. Marcie had a clear view of it for the first time: the jacket sleeve was ripped to shreds and blood was dripping slowly from the cuff.

He glanced up at her. 'You do realise that he would have had you killed as soon as he got his daughter back.'

She nodded slowly. 'He's like you. A killer.'

'Ah, no, not like me. I and my brother are killers, yes. Professionals. Andreker is a man who *orders* killings. A subtle difference, but a crucial one when it comes to it.' He laughed, a little hoarsely. 'Just now, Mr Andreker is contemplating the practical nature of the difference while he bleeds to death from the two bullets I put in his stomach.'

Marcie was shocked to find that this was not an unpleasant thought. 'What about his men?' The ache in her arms was growing intolerable. She would have to rest somewhere.

'Oh, my brother dealt with them.'

'Vince? But he – they were shooting him to pieces! I saw him, on the floor!'

Maddox nodded. 'Oh, yes, they thought they'd finish him so easily. But that's what I meant about the difference between a hard man with a gun, and a professional killer. Like Vince. Of course, he was badly shot up, but not as badly as they thought, due to the Kevlar he had under his jacket.'

'He had a bullet proof vest on? He was expecting trouble?' Marcie began to move round the room, towards the stairs, without shifting her gaze or her aim from Maddox. If she could get there she could sit on the stairs to watch Maddox, and be closer to the door.

'He wasn't expecting trouble from you!" Maddox laughed. "He always had a bullet proof vest on. A little paranoid, perhaps, but it goes with the job.'

'So – he shot all Andreker's men?'

'Killed. Not shot.'

Marcie thought about it, as she edged towards the stairs. 'That explosion.'

'Of course. Again, it's about the mindset of a professional. They just had no idea what Vince kept in his pockets!'

'He had a gun in his pocket.'

'Always. But I meant the other pocket. The one he carried a grenade in.'

Marcie reached the stairs, sank down gratefully on the steps. 'He carried a hand grenade around with him?'

Maddox laughed again. 'I know, I know! A little crazy, my brother. But he always said that when they came for him, he'd take the bastards with him. And he did!'

'What about the others? Your people?'

'Micky and Baz? They were upstairs. Andreker's men must have got them, or the grenade did. Otherwise they'd have been down here.'

'You got away, though.'

'Yes.' He shifted position slightly, and eased his good hand under the injured one, giving it some support. 'I wasn't as prepared as Vince. I ran for the office, to get my gun. Andreker followed me. The blast caught him in the doorway, tossed him right over my desk. Some shrapnel caught my arm, but it left me one hand free to deal with *him*! Oh – you should have seen the look on his face!' Maddox shook his head, smiling. 'Priceless.'

He looked up at Marcie. 'You were lucky to be here when it happened. I must admit, I'd forgotten all about you when I came down. But you didn't get away entirely, did you? Your head looks really bad. In fact, you seem all in – how long will you be able to keep that gun on me?'

She straightened up again. Even sitting on the steps and resting her elbows on her legs, it was hard to keep the gun pointed at Maddox. She was aware that her arms were shaking, and the muzzle was wobbling.

'Long enough,' she said, trying to keep a note of desperation out of her voice. 'The police will get here soon. That explosion must have been heard streets away. They'll be coming to investigate.'

'Yes, I know. I made sure of that.'

Marcie stared at him in disbelief. 'You called the police?'

He nodded. 'As soon as I'd shot Andreker, I made a phone call. Reported a gas explosion. Propane bottle. A lot of injuries. The police will be here, of course, but just to cordon off the street, make it safe. The ambulances will get priority. Oh, and I've shut the gates, so that'll give me a few minutes. They may be out there now, looking for the way in. When I'm finished here, I'll stagger out and collapse dramatically in the street. They'll have me on the way to hospital by the time the guns are discovered. And then they'll have to call in Armed Response Officers, but by that time I'll be long gone!' He shrugged. 'It should be easy enough to slip out of the hospital. And I know how to disappear. I've done it often enough.'

'No. You'll be caught.'

'How? I don't have a record. My prints, my DNA, aren't on file. Maddox isn't my real name. In twenty four hours I'll be out of the country, and a different person. No one even knows what I look like.'

'I do,' Marcie said. And her eyes widened as the implications of that struck her.

'Precisely,' Maddox said calmly. 'I'm going to have to kill you, Marcie – and the children as well, of course. But in your case there will be some personal satisfaction for me, since it's your fault that Vince is dead.' The pleasant calm in his voice didn't vary, even then.

'He may have been crazy, but he was my brother, and my only family. Your death will provide some sort of balance.'

'But you – I...'

'What are you trying to say, Marcie?' There was a note of amusement in his voice now. And contempt. 'I can't kill you because you've got the gun? But you can't even point it straight! Look, it's wobbling all over the place! Andreker's gun, incidentally. I thought you might have recognised it. I did mention that I'd gone to get my gun, didn't I? This one, in fact.'

In one smooth, swift motion he pulled a stubby black pistol out from his jacket and shot Marcie. She didn't even manage to pull the trigger herself before a massive blow slammed into her shoulder, smashing her back against the wall. Andreker's silver gun bounced uselessly away across the concrete.

Maddox stood up, taking his time, being careful of the injured arm. Injured, but still useful, as it had concealed the movement of his good hand towards his gun.

He walked across the cellar to Marcie. She lay helplessly watching him approach, unable to move a finger.

'I did tell you about the difference between real killers, professionals, and ordinary people with guns?' He stopped to inspect Andreker's gun, but didn't touch it. 'I'll leave that – if there's any prints on it, yours will overlay mine. Should help to muddy things a bit, don't you think?

'Obviously, you're not a killer, Marcie. Otherwise you'd have shot me as soon as you had the opportunity. Instead of letting me keep you talking until I had *my* gun, and you were too weak to do anything about it.' He tut-tutted, looking down at her. 'So far out of your depth, Marcie. You really shouldn't have got involved in the first place.'

Maddox was bending over her now, looking at the blood pumping out. 'Hmm – right shoulder. Not bad for a snap shot, but not instantly fatal. All the better, because I have something else to tell you, Marcie, before I finish it.'

He bent down and spoke quietly in her ear. 'You remember what Vince promised? About your family? I'm sure you do! I just want you to know that I will see to it that his promises are kept. A sort of memorial to him. Fitting, don't you think?' He straightened up, and pointed the gun at her head.

The door above burst open.

'ARMED POLICE! DROP YOUR WEAPON!'

Through her fading vision, Marcie saw the surprise, and fatal indecision on Jonathan Maddox's face. Drop the gun? Shoot the policeman? Shoot Marcie?

Trapped in uncertainty, he stood with the gun still in his hand, still pointing at her, looking up the stairs.

Then the police bullet struck him between the eyes and slammed him back to the cellar floor.

CHAPTER 15

Marcie had a private room in the hospital. She was never sure if it was something that the police had arranged for security purposes or if John had paid for it, but she was grateful. It wasn't that she didn't want company, she just didn't want curiosity.

John had been with her nearly all the time. In the first few days after the bullet was removed he had slept in the chair next to her. Later on, he brought Rory and Kady, first just for a few minutes but then for increasingly long visits. With the adaptability of children, they got over their initial fear at seeing Mum looking so ill and got used to the situation. Rory wanted to know if he could have the bullet. Kady was impatient for Marcie to come home, because Daddy didn't know how to do things properly.

It broke her heart.

John never asked questions, never spoke about what had happened. He was just there for her. Holding her hand, kissing her forehead, passing her things she needed. Later, when she was ready to talk, he talked about the kids, about the family, about things at home. Passed on messages from the wider family and friends. Made plans with her to go on holiday. A really good one, several weeks somewhere warm, when she was up to it. Discussed arrangements for Christmas and the New Year, when it seemed that she would be able to go home by then.

He never mentioned the police, or Scenes of Crime. There were never any messages from colleagues.

Two detectives had come to see her as soon as the hospital decided she was up to it. They spent a couple of hours getting a lengthy statement. They didn't talk about what had happened since. Reliving the events was unpleasant enough. Marcie didn't want to ask questions.

The story had been all over the news, of course, but by the time she'd recovered enough to take an interest, it was no longer headlines. She was amused by a short TV clip of Sir Brian Reardon. He was expressing best wishes for the swift recovery of his 'very good friend, Marcie Kelshaw.' If nothing else, she'd made it onto Sir Brian's list of 'names to be associated with'.

No one from the media had been to see her. John's doing, she suspected, and she was glad of it. More disturbing was the fact that there had been no communication at all from Faringham Scenes of Crime. Some discreet enquiries with the nurses confirmed that John had indeed put a strict 'no calls, no visitors' rule into place.

She thought she understood that. But as she began to recover emotionally as well as physically, she discovered that there were things she wanted to know. And things that she needed to say.

In between John's visits, she countermanded his 'no visitors' order and made a phone call. Thirty minutes later, Doug turned up, weighed down by enormous bunches of flowers, baskets of fruit and boxes of chocolates.

'I hope you didn't buy all those yourself?' Marcie asked, as he moved round the room, trying to find space for it all.

He grinned and shook his head. 'We've had donations for you from all over the force – I've been hanging on to it, against the day when we were allowed to see you again. This is just a part of it. You can live off grapes for the rest of your life if you like!'

She shook her head. 'No thanks! Do me a favour – any money donated, put it to some sort of charity, OK?'

'Sure, whatever.' He sat down next to the bed. 'Marcie, I told you that I didn't want to be visiting you in hospital!'

'That was about visiting me for injury photographs. No problem, the hospital staff did it while I was under anaesthetic. So you don't have to worry about extra paperwork!'

'Oh, that's alright then.' He smiled at her. 'What can I say? 'I'm glad you're alright' doesn't seem adequate.'

'It'll do. I'm glad that *you're* alright! No one's told me exactly what happened, but I gather you got caught in that explosion?' Information received from a nurse, who'd told her, 'Your colleague's been allowed home today.' She'd pressed for more, but the nurse had been reluctant to talk about it. John's influence again.

'Nothing serious. I got blown over, that's all. Some cuts and bruises. A bit of glass got lodged in my cheek, so they had to get that out.'

She put out her hand and grasped his arm. 'I'm sorry Doug. For putting you in that situation.'

He shrugged, smiling sheepishly. 'No problem. What friends are for?'

'So tell me the rest? How come you were there anyway? I didn't know if you'd even got my text.'

Doug briefly outlined the events of that morning from his point of view. 'After the bang, I picked myself up, a bit dizzy, and tried to report it to Control. But my radio was bust – bit of shrapnel lodged in it. Apparently, Control was going frantic trying to raise *me*.'

He helped himself to a grape. 'The house was a mess – a big smoking hole where the door had been. And bodies everywhere. Bits of bodies.' He looked grim.

'Vince's grenade made more than a loud noise, then?'

Doug nodded. 'They think it had been doctored, somehow. He'd put extra explosive in, made it more powerful.'

'And he carried it around in his pocket? I knew he was crazy, but I'd never have guessed how much.'

'Totally barking,' Doug agreed. 'Anyhow, I was standing there, gaping at the mess and talking into a dead radio, when the gates started to close. I didn't know what to do. I knew that help was on the way, but I didn't know where they were. So I just tried to jam them open. Fortunately there was some sort of safety device that stopped them when I got between the two gates. Must have been a standard fitting – I can't imagine that the Maddoxes would have put it in!'

'Unlikely.' Marcie agreed. 'In fact, they'd probably have disconnected it. Keeping those doors open really wrecked Jonathan's plans. As it was, he nearly got away with it.' She closed her eyes, unwillingly remembering those last few moments in the cellar. 'You do realise you saved my life, Doug?'

He looked her in the eyes. 'And you saved those kids, Marcie. I've read your statement.'

She looked away. 'Get on with the story.'

'Not much more to say. Next thing I knew, ARVs were screaming up the street, and armed cops were all over the place. They were shouting at me to get out, lay down, hands on my head, the lot. I was trying to tell them that the gates were closing, that you were inside somewhere. I was scared stiff that you'd been caught in that explosion.'

'Close, but not quite.'

'So I gathered. When they'd established my identity, they dragged me out of the way, blocked the gates, and went in. Next thing, there was a shot, then they were pulling you out and calling for an ambulance. Ambulances. There was a lot of dead and injured to sort out.'

'Did any of Andreker's men survive?'

'Only Andreker himself.' He saw her surprise. 'Hadn't you heard?'

'I haven't heard much at all. Jonathan Maddox told me he'd shot Andreker.'

Doug nodded. 'So he had. Twice. It was touch and go for a while. As it is, he's only just out of intensive care.' He smiled broadly. 'And he was arrested as soon as he was in a fit condition. So was Barry Tooley. He was at the top of the stairs and missed the worst of the blast, though his legs were so shot up that he'll never be out of a wheelchair.'

'Who's Barry Tooley? Oh – Maddox mentioned someone called Baz.'

'Yes. One of his little gang. Local muscle. Apparently he'd worked for the Maddoxes before, and they brought him in because he knew Faringham. Their other employee...'

'The young lad? Fair haired?'

'Yes. The one you saw at the pizza shop. He didn't make it. Riddled with bullets.'

She thought back, remembered a figure with a rifle coming down the stairs. She thought she remembered fair hair.

'He was so young.'

'Just turned twenty, apparently. But don't waste too much sympathy on him. He had a string of convictions for assault and aggravated burglary. Wanted for a shooting in London as well. Distant relative of the Maddoxes, they think. Nice family.'

'How about the kids? Andreker's daughter and the other two?'

'Better news, there. They all got out OK. Problem is, the morphine Maddoxes used to keep them quiet – well, they'd had enough of that that there might be side effects.' Doug shook his head. 'To be blunt, they may have become addicted! They're hoping to be able to deal with it in the long term, but meanwhile... they were a pair of bastards. No loss to anyone.'

Marcie nodded agreement. 'I can go along with that. Are they back with their parents, then?'

'Ah. Bit of a problem there. Like Andreker, the other kids parents were all past employers of the Maddoxes. Criminals, in other words, although gone up-market and respectable. One was a big contributor to the government, would you believe! But the Maddoxes had done a lot of research on them, *and* on other potential targets. It was all at the house. Information on all the jobs the Maddoxes had ever done, and who'd paid them. More intelligence at Andreker's place as well, when they raided it!'

'Lot of work for CID, then.'

'You kidding? Most of what they found has been handed over to the National Crime Squad or Special Branch, I heard, though of course *they're* not talking about it! But there's been more than a dozen major arrests as a result of this, with more to follow. Overseas stuff, as well – Interpol, FBI – all working late nights on account of you, Marcie!'

She winced. 'Jim did warn me not to open a can of worms. He didn't know the half of it! Neither did I... talking of Jim, how have he and Slippery Mick come out of it?'

'Better than you'd expect. There's been a lot of flak flying over the way the investigation into Ben's murder was botched. We expected to find the corridors full of rolling heads, but you know how Jim can bullshit. Somehow, he managed to talk himself and Mick out of trouble. Last I heard, they've had a rap on the knuckles and been scheduled for 'refreshment training' Which everyone assumes is a polite way of saying 'learning to do their job properly'.

'I'm glad it wasn't worse. I know I had issues with Mick over this, but I wouldn't want to have screwed up his career.'

'Oh, you shouldn't worry on that score – he's perfectly capable of doing that himself! And I doubt if you'll have any more issues with him. You know, Ali came in last week with green and pink striped hair, and he didn't say a word!'

Marcie laughed. 'Green and pink? That's a bit much, even for Ali!'

'So we all told her, and she's toned it down to an acceptable blonde. Same shade as you had, actually. I'm glad to see it came out alright!'

Marcie touched her hair self-consciously. 'So am I. It wasn't me.'

'Oh, I don't know! But the point is, you'll find things a bit more relaxed when you come back.'

She took a deep breath. 'Ah, yes. I'm glad you brought that up, Doug.'

He gave her a wary look. 'What?'

'I'm not coming back.'

Doug looked stunned. 'But – not yet of course, but when you're recovered?"

She shook her head. 'No. I'm going to send in my formal resignation, but I wanted to tell you first. And if you could tell the others, please?'

'Why? Marcie, you're a hero! You solved Ben's murder and saved those kids!'

'What I did,' she interrupted, 'was to nearly get myself killed. I've had a lot of time to think about it, Doug. And you know what? You were right. Mick and Jim were right. I went too far, got out of my depth. Even Vince Maddox and Andreker told me, but I didn't listen. Not to anyone. Just went ahead anyway.'

Doug leant forward, gripped her hand. 'Marcie, you're overlooking the crucial point here! *You* were the one who got it right! If you hadn't stuck at it, followed up on those clues, the Maddoxes would never have been caught!'

'So what if they hadn't?' Marcie shrugged. 'I've got no regrets for them, and I'm glad the kids were rescued, but it was close, Doug. Very close, and in the end it was only sheer dumb luck that I didn't end up like Ben.'

Doug began to protest again, but Marcie shook off his hand, and held hers up.

'Listen. When I was in Andreker's cellar, and when they were taking me to Cyrus Street, all I could think about was John, Rory and Kady. About how much I missed them , and what it was going to be like for them, if I died or disappeared. And John – John hasn't said a word of recrimination to me. He's not once mentioned the fact that I lied to him, deceived him. Not said anything about what I've put him through. And it wasn't just me at risk, either! If Vince or Jonathan had made it out, they'd have taken revenge on my family!'

She took a deep breath, aware of the tears in her eyes.. 'John should be angry with me, really angry, but he can't say anything because I'm the wounded hero. So he's kept it to himself.'

'Here.' Doug passed her a tissue.

'Thanks. I owe it to him, Doug. And the kids, but especially him. So I'm packing it in.'

She wanted to say more, but found it hard to talk. Took refuge in her tissue instead.

Doug sat back, staring at her.

'You do understand? Please?' she choked out.

'Of course I understand. Of course. But we'll miss you.' He forced a smile. 'And they were going to give you a brand new van!'

She matched his smile. 'You take it! And – will you explain to the others?'

He nodded. 'Certainly. Best I can, but they'll be disappointed.' Glanced at his watch. 'I'd better be going. I'm supposed to be on my way to a ram-raid in the city centre!'

'OK. Thanks for coming. Stay in touch, won't you.'

'Count on it.' He stood up, leant over and gave her a gentle hug. 'You get yourself better.'

At the door he turned back. 'Marcie, it wasn't just dumb luck, you know. Keep it in perspective. You had guts and brains, and that's what got you through.'

'My guts and brains were very nearly blown out of me,' she said dryly.

'But they weren't. Give yourself credit. And your instincts were right. From the very beginning, you were right, and you knew it, and you stuck at it! Ben would have been proud of you!'

'No, Ben would have pointed out, in detail, everything I got wrong and would have asked why I didn't get there sooner.'

'Maybe. But he said to me once, 'That Marcie Kelshaw, she's going to be a damn good SOCO one day.'

'What? Really?' Marcie compared his statement with the Ben Drummond she'd known, and shook her head. 'You're making that up!'

Doug laughed. 'OK! But he should have said it! Because you *are* a damn good SOCO, every bit as good as Ben ever was. Without being as obnoxious.'

'Thanks Doug. Truly, thank you. But I won't change my mind. Ben was a sad man who had nothing to live for but the job. I've got a family. I don't need the job, and I don't want to become like Ben.'

'Well, who would? See you, Marcie.' Doug waved from the door, and was gone.

Marcie settled back in the pillows, and began planning what she would say to John when he arrived.

John

Marcie told me today that she was leaving Scenes Of Crime. I can't say how glad I am she's made that decision. And made it for herself, without any prompting from me.

It means I don't have to tell her about the phone call. The one that came in the middle of the night.

It was that same night that she was away. At a friend's, she said. I can't remember when, exactly. I was deeply asleep, and the phone was ringing for some time before I could wake up enough to find it.

'Kelshaw?' I didn't recognize the voice.

'Yeh. John Kelshaw.' I muttered.

'Get your wife.' The voice was harsh, impatient. The tone, as much as the words, began to wake me up.

'Wha... who is this?'

'Get – your – wife! Marcia! I want to talk to her. Now, Kelshaw!'

'But she's not here! Who the hell are you?'

'She knows me!' There was a nasty chuckle. 'Oh, she does! You'd better speak to her, Kelshaw. Tell her Vince rang. Tell her she'd better bring it with her or I'll be coming to see you! And your kids!'

I was fully awake by know. 'What? Are you threatening me? Who...'

'Shut up and listen. You piss around with me, Kelshaw – you or your wife – I'll take it out on the kids first. Boy and a girl, innit?'

'I...'

'And no police. Should be obvious, that, but in case you're as dumb as your wife, I'll spell it out. Call the police, and I will find you. All of you. Got it?'

'Yes – but...'

'See she gets the message. See that she brings it with her.'

'Brings what?'

'She knows.'

Abruptly, the call terminated. I was left holding the phone. And shaking. Shaking all over, in anger – and fear.

Terrible fear. The worst I've ever felt. Worse than I'd known it could be.

Fear that had me paralysed. I don't know how long I sat there, shaking and sweating, trying to get a mental grip.

Finally, I managed to remember the speed-dial key for Marcie's mobile.

'This telephone is switched off. Please try later.'

Too numb to think of anything else to do, I tried again. Several times, before I understood that I couldn't get her, couldn't pass the message, couldn't find out who Vince was and what he wanted.

Which meant that he might come looking for us. For the kids.

When that penetrated, I panicked. Threw on some clothes, dragged Rory and Kady out of bed, half asleep, confused and crying. I felt the same way.

I wrapped them in blankets, told them we were going on holiday, got them out to the car. Kady started to scream that her seat wasn't there. Of course not, it was in Marcie's Focus. I got some cushions, sat them on those, gave them chocolate, and started driving. I found out later that I hadn't even shut the front door.

The kids fell asleep again. I drove and drove. I'm not sure where, exactly, but as it was getting light we were somewhere near Nottingham. I stopped for petrol and the kids woke up. I gave them more chocolate. Tried to ring Marcie again, without success. Drove on a bit further, then found a motel.

With a room service breakfast and a TV, Rory and Kady were settled for a while. I managed to get a grip, enough to assure myself that no one could have followed us, and no one could find us.

I hoped.

Somehow the fear wouldn't go away. I spent most of the morning standing by the window, peering through the drawn curtains, heart racing every time a car stopped nearby. When the kids started to ask where Mum was, and were they going to stay in their pyjamas all day, and what about school? I ignored them, or shouted at them to shut up and let me think what to do.

But I couldn't. I had no idea what to do at all.

I've been able to put it all together since then. Vince Maddox must have phoned me soon after he got the text from Andreker. Supposedly from Marcie, of course. Andreker had switched Marcie's phone off after he'd used it, which was why Maddox tried our home number.

When Doug rang from the office, I was already miles away – probably in the motel by then. So he went off to Cyrus Street.

The gun battle took place while I was looking out of the window of the motel. By the time the kids started getting bored with daytime TV, Marcie was already in hospital, having a bullet taken out of her.

Sometime around mid-morning, someone from work called my mobile, to tell me that the police were trying to get hold of me. Remembering Vince's warning, I nearly panicked all over again, but managed to keep in control long enough to call in and find out what was going on. Well, some of it. The full story didn't emerge until later. But when I heard that Marcie was in hospital with gunshot wounds, I bundled the kids into the car again and headed back for Faringham as fast as I'd left. Dropped Rory and Kady at my parents, and told the police that we'd been there overnight.

Nobody bothered to check up on it, fortunately. I didn't want to have to tell anyone about Vince's phone call, and my panicked flight.

I made light of the whole thing with the kids. Told them not to bother Mummy with too many stories while she wasn't well. Hopefully, they'll have forgotten about it by the time Marcie comes home.

Part of me is still so furious with her, for putting me through all that. But, if I'm honest with myself – and I try to be – part of that anger is from shame. I tell myself it was probably the best thing to have done anyway. If I'd stayed at home, Doug would have reached me, and I would have told him that everything was fine. So he would never have gone to Cyrus Street. And Marcie would be dead.

In spite of that, the picture of me dragging the kids out in the middle of the night and then cowering in a motel room while Marcie was on her way to hospital is not one I care to dwell on.

But I was determined that, whatever else, neither she, nor I, nor the kids would ever be in such a situation again. And that meant that she had to quit Scenes of Crime. I wanted her out of there for good. And if she'd needed convincing, I would have told her what happened that night.

I'm glad I won't have to.

The Author

Paul Trembling started making up stories before he could read or write and has never been able to get out of the habit. His varied career path includes being a seaman, a missionary, a janitor, an administrator and a Scenes of Crime Officer.

To date he has published twelve novels and several short story collections. When not writing, he enjoys walking, photography and, of course, reading. He currently lives in Cheshire with his wife Annie and their two dogs, Edna and Willow.

(For more about his books go to yearningblue.weebly.com)

Local Killer

Within ten minutes of becoming Alison's friend, Judge Ruth Darnel is dead. Alison thinks she knows the killer, but tracking them down isn't going to be easy, Or safe.

Especially when the killer knows who she is...

(Available at most online bookstores)

About Resolute Books

We are an independent press representing a consortium of experienced authors, professional editors and talented designers producing engaging and inspiring books of the highest quality for readers everywhere. We produce books in a number of genres including historical fiction, crime suspense, young adult dystopia, memoir, Cold War thrillers, poetry, and even Jane Austen fan fiction!

Find out more at resolutebooks.co.uk

for the joy of reading

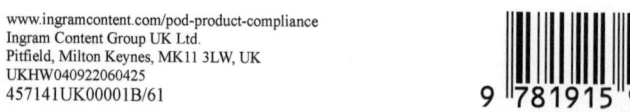